PROSE AND CONS

NEVERMORE BOOKSHOP MYSTERIES, BOOK 5

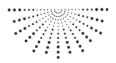

STEFFANIE HOLMES

BACCHANALIA HOUSE

Cover design: Amanda Rose

ISBN: 978-0-9951342-1-8

❀ Created with Vellum

*To all the book boyfriends
who keep me up at night.*

"There are darknesses in life and there are lights, and you are one of the lights, the light of all lights."
— Bram Stoker, *Dracula*

CHAPTER ONE

"*J*'m afraid I'm not here for a book, Mina." Hayes nodded to Wilson, who held up a pair of handcuffs and slapped them gleefully over Morrie's wrists. "We're here to arrest James Moriarty on suspicion of murder."

"What?" *That's... not possible.* "Murder?"

Morrie glanced between the two officers. The corner of his mouth tugged into a smirk that didn't reach his eyes. "I've got handcuffs in my room lined with velvet. They're so much more *sensual* than those old things. I'll wait here while you grab them, and then we—"

Sergeant Wilson shoved him toward the door. "James Moriarty, you do not have to say anything. But, it may harm your defense if you do not mention when questioned something which you later rely on in court—"

"Oooh, is the judge going to bang her gavel and tell me I've been a naughty boy?" Morrie purred. "Kinky."

"Don't say anything," I hissed at Morrie. Heathcliff, Quoth, and I barreled down the stairs and crowded into the hall. Heathcliff blocked the door while I threw my arms around Morrie and glared at Hayes (or the large, broad-shouldered blob I thought was Hayes. We hadn't turned on any lamps downstairs, so now that Heathcliff blocked the only light, all I could make out were shadows). "You have to tell us what's going on. We caught the garroter, so why—"

"This isn't about the garrotings." Hayes' voice was grave. "Mr. Moriarty is our lead suspect in the death of Kate Danvers."

"Who in the blazes is that?" Heathcliff's voice bellowed across the room. Tension rolled off his body – a palpable rage simmering in the room. I knew if we didn't get answers soon he'd go Full Metal Heathcliff and all that would be left of the inspectors would be bits of organs stuck to the ceiling.

"We don't have to explain ourselves to you." Wilson shoved Morrie toward the door. She tried to step around Heathcliff's bulk but ended up pressing Morrie into a shelf. Stacks of books cascaded down on us. "As much as you love to meddle in murders, *we're* the detectives here, and we say Mr. Moriarty's coming with us."

Heathcliff's shoulders tensed, and for a moment I seriously feared for all our lives. With a roar, he flung himself aside, giving Wilson a clear path. "He's innocent, and we'll fight this."

Heathcliff's words dripped with menace, and through my fear, I felt a jolt of hope. Ever since their fraught kiss, Heathcliff had distanced himself from Morrie. I knew Heathcliff felt something for Morrie, but his Heathcliff-ness meant he wouldn't acknowledge or give into it. Instead, he raged and sulked and became a complete shit until he drove Morrie away so then he wouldn't have to deal with it.

But right now, he was ready to fight *for* Morrie. He might not be able to articulate his feelings, but he was a slave to them. Heathcliff didn't know a thing about control, about hiding things that were ugly or scary or uncomfortable. He just *was*. And right now he was ready for a homicidal rampage on Morrie's behalf, and that *said* more than all the sweet nothings he might've whispered in Morrie's ear.

But it wasn't enough. We weren't at *Wuthering Heights*. This was the real world. The police were taking Morrie away, and we couldn't do a thing about it. A shiver ran down my spine. *Why are they taking Morrie? Why are they so certain he killed this Kate woman?*

I watched Morrie's face as Wilson shoved him outside. Flaccid British sunlight poked through the converging storm clouds, illuminating his sharp, chiseled features and the haughty tilt of his chin. Morrie's eyes sought mine, and he flashed me a reassuring grin that was all teeth and bravado.

A grin that I might have believed, if not for the fact it didn't reach his eyes. Morrie's ice-blue eyes were wide, darkened with shadows.

Resigned.

Not surprised.

"I'm sure it's a misunderstanding, gorgeous," Morrie called out as he scuffed the chipped stone steps with his brogues. "Don't worry your pretty head about me."

But that look in Morrie's eyes said otherwise. Whoever this Kate Danvers was, he knew her, and he already knew she was dead.

Why doesn't he look surprised?

My mind whirred with memories from the past couple of months. Morrie frowning at his phone, having his assets frozen, working on an algorithm to track Dracula's movements and making *certain* I knew how to use it. I worried about him, of course, but between figuring out who garroted Danny Sledge, discovering the shop cat Grimalkin was really an ancient Greek nymph named Critheïs *and* my grandmother, and hunting for a blood-crazed vampire intent on enslaving the world, I hadn't had time to get to the bottom of his odd behavior, and now...

... now he's gone and done something stupid.

Wilson pushed Morrie down the steps, tearing his gaze from mine. Heathcliff reached out to hold me back, but I slipped under his fingers and followed the detectives along Butcher Street to the town green, where a squad car waited, door open, ready to whisk Morrie away from me. Hayes placed a hand on Morrie's neck and directed him into the backseat.

"I'm going with him." I dashed around to the other door and slid inside before Wilson could stop me.

Hayes sighed. He was used to me by now. "Fine. We'll see you at the station. If James has his mobile on him, I recommend he contact his lawyer."

The officer behind the wheel nodded at Hayes and pulled away from the curb. He flicked on the radio, and loud violin music pumped through the speakers, so loud it shook the vehicle.

The seats reeked of sweat and urine, a fact I first noticed when the police arrested me on suspicion of murdering my ex-best friend, Ashley. It was hard to believe it was only a few months ago that I'd been sitting in this exact same position, wringing my hands and panicking about what would happen next. it felt like another time, and I was a different person now.

The new Mina – the one sitting across from her boyfriend, the Napoleon of Crime – this Mina wasn't afraid. She was *pissed as fuck*.

"What the bloody hell is going on?" I yelled over the music, leaning over to punch Morrie in the arm. "Who's Kate Danvers, and why do they think you killed her?"

Morrie rubbed his bicep. "Because I did kill her."

"Shhhh." My gaze flicked back to the officer, but he waved his arm about like a conductor, completely oblivious to Morrie's confession. "Don't say things like that. Didn't you listen when they cautioned you?"

"Relax, gorgeous. He can't hear a word over his Vivaldi. I'm more a fan of the Russian composers myself. No sense of melody whatsoever, but they embraced chaos—"

"Stop talking for a second so I can think." I sucked in a deep breath. My hand sought the comfort of Morrie's long fingers. "It's okay. It's going to be okay. Jo's our friend. She'll go over that body fifty times, *a hundred times*, until she finds the evidence to exonerate you. Is your phone in your pocket? I bet you've got some fancy lawyer friend down in London on speed dial. We'll call him and..."

My words trailed off as I noticed Morrie wasn't listening to me. His gaze was glued to his window, where houses and rolling fields whizzed past at top speed. The corner of his mouth tugged upward, but I couldn't tell if it was a smirk or a grimace.

That's odd. We should have reached the police station by now. It was only a few blocks across the village of Argleton. Instead, the oaks of Kings Copse Wood loomed over us as the squad car snaked out of the village, past quaint farm buildings and towering hedgerows, toward the wild peaks of the Barsetshire Fells.

"Morrie..." I poked him in the ribcage. "Why aren't we going to the police station?"

"I haven't the foggiest idea."

"Hey!" I banged on the cage separating us from the uniformed officer. "Where are you taking us? What's going on?"

In response, the officer turned the music up louder. I yelled and shook the cage. Morrie joined in, but neither of us could elicit even a nod of acknowledgment from the officer.

Fear clutched at my stomach. *This doesn't make any sense. Hayes would have told us if we were being taken somewhere else. What's going on?*

"What should we do?" I asked Morrie.

"I don't have my phone on me," Morrie patted his pockets. "I left it beside the bed. I do have a Montblanc pen I might be able to fashion into some sort of weapon—"

"It may come to that." I pulled my own phone from my pocket and dialed Quoth. When I raised it to my head, a weird hissing noise assaulted my eardrum, followed by a series of beeps. "What's that? Quoth? Can you hear me?"

Morrie took the phone from me and tried another call. "It's

not connecting. The cop's got some sort of jamming device in front. We're not getting through to anyone."

I stared at the picture of a litter of guide dog puppies on my phone's lock screen. My vision blurred until the puppies became a blob. "Okay, I'm officially scared now."

Morrie reached over and tried the door and window. Both were locked. He glanced back to me, but didn't say a thing, which only made my chest constrict more. Morrie always had a smartarse comment for every situation.

He laced his fingers in mine and squeezed. That squeeze told me more than words ever could – the indomitable James Moriarty was just as scared as I was.

We drove for what seemed like hours through increasingly barren dales. Limestone outcrops jutted through tufts of heather bent double in the wind. We wound through narrow roads up into what passed for mountains in the UK (an 'arduous hill' in any country with actual wilderness). We passed a small village named Barset Reach – just a collection of stone cottages, a pub, and a petrol station – and turned off the road onto a forest track.

Trees bent over the road, swiping at the sides and roof of the car – the fingers of a forest witch threatening to drag us away to a gingerbread house. Darkness swept my vision as the trees obscured the light, and my temples flared with a migraine as my eyes strained to make out shapes and shadows.

We came to a fork in the road. As the car swung right, Morrie leaned over and read out the sign. "It says, WILD OATS WILDERNESS SURVIVAL SCHOOL,' but it's pointing left." He frowned. "I recognize that name."

"Why are you frowning like that? Did you go there on a company team-building day and they make you eat cockroaches?"

"That's where Kate Danvers' body was found."

Shite. So why has the cop brought us back to the crime scene without telling Hayes? I squeezed Morrie's hand as the sharp stab of my migraine pierced my skull. Fluorescent green and orange lights danced in front of my eyes. Nothing like sheer terror to make vision loss worse.

We drove away from Wild Oats, away from the last sign of civilization, and bumped our way along a deteriorating path until we came to a clearing in the trees. The officer shut off the car and picked up his gun from the seat. The doors made a clicking noise as he released the lock.

"Get out of the car," he growled, tugging his peaked cap low over his face to hide his eyes in shadow.

My fingers trembled so hard it took me three tries to push the handle to open the door. Morrie was already around the side of the car, tugging me into his arms. He steadied me with his possessive grip, and I noticed he angled himself so he was between me and the constable, who I was now certain was not a real officer of the law. "I am a rich man. Whoever is paying you to do this, I'll double it. If you let Mina go, we can talk terms."

"Typical." The officer's voice dripped with derision. "You assume I am as corruptible as you. Girl, hand me your phone."

I thought about pretending I didn't have my phone with me, but I couldn't stop staring at the barrel of that gun. I drew my phone out of my pocket and held it out. The officer leaned forward to grab it from me. His fingers brushed mine and, for a moment, a sickly heat crackled on my skin. I itched to slap him, to scratch his eyes out, *anything* other than standing here like a useless fool.

The officer tossed my phone into a puddle, where it fizzed and sparked. The screen went blank as the puppies disappeared under the brackish water.

We're alone out here with this madman.

Morrie gripped me tighter, and I drew comfort from his presence. It would take a fellow madman to get us out of this mess, but that was exactly what Morrie was. Morrie didn't rage like Heathcliff – instead, he used his considerable intellect to think

7

his way out of every jam. I could already see the cogs moving in his mind, his eyes flicking into the trees and then back at the gun as he considered our options. He tried again. "I can help you. I can give you the money and the means to disappear forever, and no one need know what happened here today."

The officer jabbed his gun in the direction of a narrow path winding up the side of the peak. "Walk. Don't make me ask twice."

CHAPTER TWO

"*W*hy are you doing this?" My fingers clawed at the dirt as I scrambled up a steep bank. "Where are you taking us?"

The officer didn't reply. He jabbed the barrel of his gun into Morrie's back, urging us to keep moving. Morrie gripped my arm, which was a bit awkward given the angle we had to climb, but no way did I want him to let go. Every few feet he gave me a reassuring squeeze.

But there was nothing reassuring about this situation.

The worn tread of my Docs slid in the soft mud as I fought for footing. The rain had eased off now, but fat droplets still toppled from the leaves to splash on my cheeks. I shivered as my wet clothes clung to my skin – if I'd known I'd be hiking around the wilderness with two madmen, I wouldn't have worn a Misfits hoodie and nylon leggings covered with skulls. With every step, I grew more certain that Morrie and I wouldn't make it out of this alive. Before long, our corpses would be buried in this same mud that now caked my favorite leggings.

I never got to meet my new guide dog, or tell Mum how much I loved her, or say goodbye to Quoth and Heathcliff. I won't find out more about my dad. And Dracula...what would he do without us chasing him? I never got to solve the mystery of Nevermore Bookshop or finish writing my novel...

Hell, I never even told the boys I was writing a novel. Being surrounded by books and murder and magic all day had inspired me. I thought maybe... if I could get over my shyness of having others read my work, being a writer might be a great career for me as I lost my eyesight. I wrote a short story about one of our cases and gave it to them over Christmas, but watching them read it made me feel physically ill. I knew it would take me a long time to get the book to a point where I'd be happy sharing it with them. Now... they never would, and someone might find it on my laptop and read it out loud at my funeral—

Argh. I cringed at the thought. *The only good news is that at least I won't be there to hear it.*

As I neared the top of the bank, I snuck a look over my shoulder, trying to recognize the cop. I'd been in and out of the police station so many times with all the murders I'd helped solve I knew nearly all the uniformed officers. Had one of them been paid off by one of Morrie's criminal buddies to kidnap him? If this guy wasn't even an officer... he'd gone to great lengths to whisk us out from right under Hayes' nose.

But the cop had his hat pulled low over his head. All I could tell was that he was middle-aged, with a few wrinkles around his eyes and mouth, tall (almost as tall as Morrie) with a wiry frame but broad, muscular shoulders. Even though I was puffing and drenched in sweat from the walk, he strode on without so much as a single faltering breath. The gun in his hand looked real enough.

My fingers gripped a gnarled root, and I used it to pull me over the top of the slope. An even steeper slope bore down on us, although rough stairs had been hewn into the rock. The officer waved his gun, and Morrie and I trudged our way up.

At the top of the hill stood a small bothy – a tiny hut with a sloped corrugated iron roof, a crooked stone chimney, and a stack of wood in a small lean-to beside the door. Off to the side, I could see a small outhouse, flies buzzing around the door. Morrie threw his arm around my waist and pulled me close as the cop slid a key into the lock and shoved the bothy door open.

"Get inside." The cop waved his gun, beckoning us into the darkness.

My stomach twisted. *This is it. This is where I die.*

My Docs scuffed the stoop as I stumbled inside. I put out a hand to steady myself, and noticed the long-sleeves of my hoodie – the writing along the sleeve read, 'Dig Up Her Bones.' *How appropriate. At least I'll leave a fierce-looking corpse.*

Panicked laughter bubbled up inside me. I stood beside Morrie in front of the cold fire. My fingers sought his, desperate for a last moment of comfort. *I wish I had time for one final searing kiss, for one last chance to tell Morrie what he means to me. I wish...*

The panicked laugher rattled through my body as we faced the officer. Morrie remained perfectly calm, that haughty smirk still playing across his lips. He whistled a tune under his breath.

The constable folded his long body into a sagging wingback chair. Instead of shooting us, he set down the gun and tugged off his hat, revealing a head of dark, curly hair. He reached into a leather pouch on his belt and removed a wooden pipe, which he set between his lips, and tapped a measure of tobacco into the chamber. As he leaned back in the chair, he tugged at the corner of his chin, pulling up a flap of skin until he peeled off a latex mask, revealing a younger, cleaner face underneath.

Beside me, Morrie stiffened. The tune died on his lips. "It can't be."

I glanced at Morrie. His face had turned bone-white. That infamous smirk had left the building.

The Napoleon of Crime looked... *terrified.*

When I glanced back at the officer, his eyes had changed color. At first, I thought it was a trick of my deteriorating retinas.

I leaned forward and squinted harder. No, his eyes definitely changed. Where had a moment ago been plain brown orbs were now a clear and bright grey. His curly hair sat on the table – a wig that hid dark, close-cropped locks beneath.

I was staring at a completely different person.

A seriously *hot* person, all cheekbones and hardness and a cruel, intelligent smile. Firm lips beneath a hawk-like nose curled with disdainful amusement. He reminded me a little of Morrie – intimidating and fascinating in equal measure.

"Who are you?" I whispered.

The constable leaned back in his chair and blew a perfect smoke ring. With sparkling grey eyes watching my face, he thrust out a hand to me, lowering his chin to meet me with an even stare. "Allow me to introduce myself, Mina Wilde. My name is Sherlock Holmes."

CHAPTER THREE

*S*herlock Holmes.

     The Sherlock Holmes.

Hysterical laughter escaped again. My whole body trembled as I clutched my stomach and gasped between giggles. "This is a joke. You're not... you can't be..."

Morrie wasn't laughing. "I assure you, that's him."

Morrie's body remained rigid. He'd regained some of his composure, but he stared at the cop – at *Sherlock* – like a bug he desperately wanted to squash but was afraid he'd end up with smelly guts all over his favorite brogues. "I never forget the face of a betrayer."

"Except that my disguise had you completely fooled." Sherlock tapped his peaked hat and flashed Morrie a smug fucking smile that was painfully familiar to me. "Too much time in this world has made you soft, *Moriarty.*"

"I knew it was you from the moment I got into the car," Morrie shot back. "I was going along with it to see what you had planned."

I choked on my hysterics. That was so clearly a lie, but it

sounded suspiciously like Morrie trying to save face in front of Sherlock, which was so ridiculous I couldn't deal.

"You're lying," Sherlock said. "I can always tell because your left earlobe twitches. You're so predictable."

"*You're* the liar." Morrie's hand flew to his ear. "You said you were popping out for milk and instead you tried to throw me over a waterfall—"

"That's in the past." Sherlock waved a hand. "To answer your question, Mina, what's going on is that I've just pulled off a daring rescue in order to secure Moriarty's liberty, in the hopes I will be able to clear his name, if indeed that feat is theoretically possible."

My head spun. I glared at the gun sitting on the table. "So you're not going to kill us."

"I shan't think so. Unless you plan on becoming a nuisance."

"Then can you unlock Morrie's handcuffs and put the gun away?"

"*Morrie?*" Sherlock's lips curled back in an expression of disgust. "My, but the twenty-first-century penchant for nick-names has not been kind to you, lover."

Lover. The word echoed in my head. *Morrie's old lover is here, right now, in our world.*

Sherlock patted his pockets until he located a key. He stood – his lanky body unfolding like an accordion, his head almost touching the low beams of the cabin ceiling – and crossed to us in two long strides. Sherlock wrapped his fingers around Morrie's wrist, yanking his arm out so Morrie's chest pressed against his. They stood nose to nose, eyes blazing with unspoken words, while tension crackled between them like lightning. I longed to reach out and slap Sherlock away, but the ferocity in Morrie's eyes kept me frozen. I'd never seen him affected like this except...

except by *me*.

And Heathcliff, after their kiss.

Sherlock's fingers lingered on Morrie's wrist as he turned the key and slid off the cuffs. As his fingers grazed Morrie's skin, my boyfriend's lips parted and a tiny sigh escaped.

Well, fuck.

I stared from one to the other as a conversation from a few months ago played over in my head. Morrie and I stood on the balcony of Baddesley Hall Manor during the Jane Austen Experience, and he told me how he'd been in love once before, how that lover had betrayed him, tried to kill him. How that betrayal made it difficult for Morrie to admit his feelings, how it made him afraid of being in love again, of losing himself to another person only to be betrayed.

It was the first time I'd ever seen Morrie vulnerable.

Now, he stood before the same lover who'd affected him so. Morrie appeared in total control of the situation, yet I knew my criminal mastermind well enough to see how shaken he was by Sherlock's sudden appearance.

I wanted to ask how many times Sherlock had removed handcuffs from Morrie's wrists, but I suspected the answer would make me violently ill.

Sherlock Holmes was in the real world. Our world.

Sherlock Holmes had come for *my* boyfriend.

But why? And what does it have to do with this Kate Danvers person?

Weariness crept through my body. I wanted nothing more than to be back at Nevermore Bookshop with Morrie and Heathcliff bickering and Quoth thrashing Nine Inch Nails while he painted something dark and gloomy. I yanked back a tattered armchair and slumped down, glaring at Sherlock. "Step away from Morrie. I don't trust you near him. I want to know everything, and I want to know *now*. Why are you here, and why this elaborate scheme to get us to this remote cabin?"

"I only intended to remove Moriarty to safety. You insisted on coming along for the ride." Sherlock chuckled to himself. "I arrived here the same way Moriarty and Heathcliff Earnshaw and all the others did – through the Classics section in your bookshop. The exact mechanics of it still remain a mystery – I fell asleep in a hansom cab beside my dear friend Watson on the way to investigate a most invigorating stabbing in Dartmoor, and I woke up on the floor of that dusty bookshop."

"When was this?"

"Oh… eight, nine weeks ago."

I glanced at Morrie. "How come we didn't see you then? And how do you know my name?"

"My dear Mina, you didn't see me because I chose not to be seen. When I first appeared on the grotty shop carpet, I went in search of answers but instead found you, Moriarty, and two other men *in flagrante delicto*. I chose not to stick around. I've been watching you ever since I arrived. I know all that goes on in Argleton, and I have eyes on the shop at all times."

I folded my arms. "In the twenty-first century, we call that stalking."

"Indeed. Well, my *stalking*, as you say, may have just saved Moriarty's life. It was I who alerted him to the death of Kate Danvers."

"Who is Kate Danvers?"

"Officially, she's a devoted wife and senior developer at a tech company that makes cloud-based ticketing systems for events. After years of battling with depression and anxiety, Kate committed suicide in November last year. In reality, she's a cunning woman who has been living in the Philippines after faking her own death in November, and has only recently turned up dead with a dagger in her gut."

I glared at Morrie. "Did you by chance have anything to do with this?"

Morrie flashed me one of his signature smirks. "Not the stabbing, but I *may* be tangentially related to her original disappearance."

I folded my arms. "You wouldn't happen to be *tangentially related* via some highly illegal and dangerous scheme?"

Morrie looked sheepish. "I admit, I might not have *entirely* given up on the criminal underworld. I did try to play it straight, but do you have any idea how difficult it is to maintain my standard of living earning money legitimately? So yes, I *might* have been running a small business on the side. It's a public service, really, and totally legit, you understand... Well, *mostly* legit."

I tapped my foot. "A business doing what?"

Morrie's eyes widened in what he obviously thought was an expression worn by a completely innocent person. "I help people fake their deaths."

I tossed back my head and laughed. It was either that or punch Morrie in the face, and even though I was pissed at him, he was quite exquisite and I didn't want to be responsible for ruining his perfect nose.

"Is she okay?" Sherlock jabbed a finger at me. "She's more unstable than that Sebastian Moran fellow you doted on so much."

"I find sociopaths to be the most devoted employees." Morrie tapped his foot. "All you have to do is give them interesting work to do, like assassinating bothersome people or throwing rocks at your *ex*-lovers. If you recall, I briefly toyed with hiring *you*, before your incurable laziness became apparent."

"And yet, it was this layabout working on the side of good who ultimately defeated the most devilishly invigorated spider at the center of London's vast criminal web—"

"Okay, all right, you two." I wiped tears of mirth from my eyes. "You bicker worse than Morrie and Heathcliff. Both of you calm your farm for a second while we figure this out. Morrie, you'd better explain to me how this death-faking business works."

"It's simple." Morrie reached into the pocket of his jacket and removed a business card, which he placed in my hand. It was too dark in the cabin and the words too small for me to read, but the paper felt thick and expensive, with embossed words. "People come to me who want to disappear. I use my resources to help them do it. In most cases, you don't need a body to fake a death – it's all about the paperwork, and I have the necessary contacts and the ability to apply pressure in the right situations to grease the wheels of bureaucracy in my clients' favor."

"So you forge documents." I lifted an eyebrow.

"It's *so* much more than that." Morrie beamed. "I offer consulting services. You wouldn't believe how many people try to fake their deaths and fuck it up. I have years of criminal experience to draw from, and I can stop them making the simplest mistakes. Take Kate, for example. She was going to go fall off her boss' boat and fake a drowning. Ridiculous. People always assume the best way to fake your own death is with drowning, but it's actually the worst idea. A drowned body will usually wash up somewhere, so drownings without a body are instantly suspicious to the authorities. I advised her on a more foolproof plan."

"Which was?"

"She would walk into the woods of Barsetshire Fells and never return." Morrie looked pleased with himself. "Nine out of ten successful fake deaths occur in the wilderness. It's often impossible for rescuers to locate a body, so no one is suspicious when one doesn't show up."

"An excellent plan," Sherlock piped up. "As befitting a brain of the first order."

"Precisely." Was it a trick of my failing eyes, or did Morrie's cheeks deepen with color at Sherlock's praise? "And it all went off without a hitch. In November, Kate attended the Wild Oats Wilderness Survival School with a group of her colleagues. Every year, the company pays for a lavish retreat for the top achievers. This year I had Kate put herself in charge of the bookings, which meant she could control the location and activities, and she sent the group into the heart of Barsetshire countryside to learn how to build fires and drink their own urine. On the final night of the training, all attendees, including Kate, had to spend a night in the forest... alone. When the instructor went to collect her the next morning, all that was left of her camp was the embers of a fire and a suicide note. Search teams were called in, but they never found the body."

"Because there wasn't one," I finished.

"Precisely. I already had Kate on a flight to the Philippines, where I set her up with a job and enough funds to see her comfortably through the next few years."

"You're so beautiful when you talk death fraud," Sherlock purred, his hand reaching up to touch Morrie's cheek.

Morrie slapped it down. "Don't touch me again. This conversation is between me and Mina."

Sherlock glowered at me.

I poked my tongue out at him. Mature? No. Satisfying? Hell yes.

Morrie continued. "I submitted Kate's paperwork, checked in on her funeral and grieving family, and everything seemed to have gone without a hitch. I didn't think anything of it until a few weeks ago, when you were setting up the shop for Danny Sledge's writer's workshop and an anonymous text alerted me that a hiker had discovered Kate's body near Wild Oats. Freshly dead. With a knife sticking out of her chest."

"But..." I had so many questions. "Why would she even be back in the country, if you got her safely to the Philippines? And who would want to kill her? Did it have something to do with the reason she tried to fake her own death in the first place?"

"That's exactly what the authorities have been wondering. Luckily, they found my business card still tucked in her pocket, along with her original passport *and* her boarding pass under the new, fake identity I made for her, so they had a pretty good idea where to start looking."

My head fell into my hands. "Mor-*rie*."

"Don't look at me like that. The card doesn't point directly to me. I'm not a simpleton. It instructs a client to make contact with an untraceable number and jump through a series of hoops to prove their legitimacy and secrecy before I'll even hear their case. Unfortunately, what Detective Hayes lacks in brain cells, he makes up for in connections with top operatives in MI5. They infiltrated my network and discovered me – as Sherlock so eloquently puts it – at the center of a vast death-fraud web. They seized my assets while they investigated me, which is why I couldn't bail out the shop, and I knew it was only a matter of time before they took me in. Of course, that fool Hayes has jumped to completely the wrong conclusion about my involvement, and is coming after an innocent man."

"Innocent?" Sherlock lifted a perfectly sculpted eyebrow, steepling his fingers together. The expression reminded me so much of Morrie it made me sick. "That's not a word I'd use to describe you."

Sherlock was right, but I wasn't about to agree with him. "Okay, then. I know you didn't commit the murder, so we've just got to figure out who did."

Folding himself back into his chair, Sherlock took a deep puff from his pipe. "I've already made some progress on the case. It's the reason I chose this location as a hideout – it's close to the crime scene. It's how I've been able to prove that footprints found near the body exactly match Moriarty's shoes."

"And just how did you prove that?"

Sherlock picked up a pair of familiar-looking brogues from behind his chair and tossed them on the table. "It was elementary. I stole these from the stoop outside your bookshop, and matched them with the casts I took from the crime scene."

"I was wondering where those went." Morrie frowned at the shoes.

"How would you know any were missing?" I groaned, my head in my hands. This was getting worse. "You leave them lying everywhere. As Sherlock has demonstrated, anyone could sneak inside and nick them."

And then use them to frame you.

"I wish never to be far from a decent pair of footwear." Morrie held his chin high. "I get all my brogues custom-made at the same artisan cobbler in London. They made a last – that's a mechanical form shaped exactly like my foot – to obtain the perfect fit."

"Precisely." Sherlock's eyes locked on Morrie's shoes. "The elegant shape and distinctive tread mean that the prints could have been made only by you, or by someone wearing your brogues. My next task is to visit this cobbler and—"

"Excuse me?" I glared at him. "Why are you trying to help Morrie?"

"It's elementary," Sherlock replied. "I intend to win him back. But that would be a fruitless endeavor if he's behind bars."

"You..." A fresh migraine flickered across my temples. *This is not happening.*

"Win me back? *You* planned to push me over a waterfall." Morrie stalked across the room and tore the pipe from Sherlock's lips. I winced as he tossed it against the wall, where it hit with a *CRACK* and broke into several pieces, scattering ash and tobacco into the already stuffy air. "There will never be anything between us again, Sherlock. I'm with Mina now."

"If you say so," Sherlock said in a tone that clearly implied he thought he still had a shot.

No, this is not happening. I'm not going to have a pissing contest with the world's greatest consulting detective over Morrie. Not least because I don't have a dick to piss from. "He does say so. If you're able to accept and respect Morrie's decision, we could still use your expertise in solving the case. Show us what you've uncovered already."

Sherlock reached behind his chair and lifted up a wooden box. He upturned it on the table, and an avalanche of paper ephemera toppled out. Morrie rummaged through some boxes beside the fireplace and came back with candles, which he dotted around the room so I could see what I was doing. I picked up a stack of official-looking forms and squinted at the tiny print. "These are Kate Danvers' medical records? How did you get these?"

"Morrie is not the only one with the skills to deceive your authorities." Sherlock preened. "Kate's records show a history of depression and suicidal thoughts."

"That tells us nothing," Morrie said. "I instructed her to create that paper trail. It established suicide as the most likely cause of her disappearance. If you plant the seed of the idea in everyone's minds, they'll water it until it blooms, and then they won't come looking for her. The last thing we wanted was the authorities investigating it as a suspicious death."

"If she wasn't really suicidal, then why did Kate want to fake her death?"

Morrie shrugged. "You'd have to ask her. I'm not a psychologist. I never asked her, and she never told me."

"You must have some idea."

"There are three reasons people want to fake their death – financial gain, to be with a lover, or to escape violence. Significantly more men fake their deaths for the first two reasons, but that's because they're stupid enough to get caught. All the women I've helped successfully disappear have been fleeing a violent husband, and they've all stayed fake-dead, until Kate." Morrie frowned. "This is really going to tank my Yelp rating."

"I'm so glad your concern isn't at all misplaced. Who's this?" I waved a photograph of a short man with rosy-red cheeks, a ponytail, and a Star Wars t-shirt. He reminded me of Comic Book Guy from the Simpsons except with a beautiful smile and kind eyes.

"That's Dave Danvers, Kate's husband," said Sherlock. "He was the first person I looked into, but by all accounts, he was a loving and devoted husband, and he has no ties to Moriarty's criminal underworld."

"Kate did seem to still like him," Morrie mused. "She got this goofy look in her eyes when she talked about him. I think she said she was doing this *for* him, so maybe they had money troubles. She did ask me to make certain he'd receive her life insurance after she was gone."

"That doesn't mean he's innocent." I turned to Sherlock. "Does he have an alibi for the murder?"

"How should I know?" Sherlock scoffed. "The murder isn't the important part – the fact that this murder was staged to frame Moriarty is the focus of my investigation."

"You mean, *our* investigation. Morrie and I are in this. This is his life and liberty at stake."

Sherlock frowned. Dark curls flopped over his forehead. *He'd be so fucking hot if he wasn't here to steal my boyfriend.* "I work alone."

I snorted. "No, you don't. I've read your books. You bring along Dr. John Watson for every adventure."

"You, my dear, are no Watson. You'll be returning to your world today, leaving Moriarty in the safety of my care."

My blood boiled. "I'm not your *dear* anything. I've successfully solved no less than four murders *and* recovered a stolen Christmas tree. And I'm not leaving Morrie here with you."

"You have to, gorgeous." Morrie's eyes pleaded. "Sherlock's right. If you stay missing, they're going to assume I facilitated this whole thing to kidnap you. That will make things a hundred times worse for me. If you go back with a different story, we can control the narrative and give Sherlock and I time to figure out what's really going on."

I glared at him. "You don't want my help?"

Morrie reached up and slid a piece of my hair between his fingers. "Whoever has done this is trying to topple me from my criminal network. These are brutal people – nothing like the small town hack murderers we usually come up against. I don't want you to get hurt."

I can't believe I'm hearing this. "If you need to go into hiding, that's even more reason why I should be helping. How much sleuthing do you think you're going to get done trapped in a smelly bothy?"

Sherlock crossed the room in two long strides and held the candle up to a wall, illuminating crime scene photographs, newspaper articles, and scribbled Post-it notes, all connected with lengths of string. "Plenty. I've made a thorough study of all the evidence available."

I peered at the wall, noticing two things. First, Sherlock used the exact same methods he employed in Sir Arthur Conan Doyle's stories. His information consisted of drawings from the crime scene, photographs, and studies of bootprints and bark rubbings. Second was that over three-quarters of his wall was not dedicated to the case at all, but to Morrie. There were Polaroids of him leaving the shop, sitting on the tube in London, and shaking hands with a guy in a snappy suit I could only assume was his banker or some kind of crime overlord.

I tried not to let it bother me that in just two months Sherlock had learned more about my boyfriend than he'd ever revealed to me. *Morrie has this whole secret life I'm not a part of. And it might have got him in deep trouble.*

"Who's that?" I pointed to a photograph of Morrie facing off against a sharp-looking man with a handlebar mustache and a white suit. Several pieces of string converged on the man's head.

"Aidan McFarlane. According to my deductions, the current only possible suspect."

"McFarlane's a big name in the criminal underworld. He used to be my right-hand man, but he's been looking to do away with me for years and take over my territory. He's been trying to undermine me for months, accusing me of going soft just because I've been shutting down certain operations," Morrie added. "Plus, he has a sinister-looking mustache. He must be our villain."

Hearing James Moriarty call another man a villain was so absurd, I burst out laughing. I turned to Sherlock. "So what makes you so certain this is the guy?"

He frowned. "My methods are my own."

"You're not going to consider other options? What about the husband, or someone else on this leadership retreat? It could be whoever or whatever she was trying to escape from caught up with her and—"

"I've ruled them all out. No one in her life has any connection to Moriarty. As I have said," Sherlock hissed through gritted teeth, "the victim isn't important here. She was a means to an end. The killer has a grudge against Moriarty – he is the key."

"I think we should at least consider—"

"No offense to your thoughts, Mina, which I'm sure don't seem trifling. You should let the professionals handle this."

"You're not a professional, either," I shot back.

"Fifty-six short stories, four popular novels, and an enduring pop culture legacy would suggest otherwise." Sherlock elbowed me aside as he swept the photographs into his palm and replaced them in the box.

We're going around in circles. "You're a product of the Victorian justice system. Technology *and* society have moved on since then. We should be sharing information and working together."

"I do not work with my intellectual inferiors."

That's it.

I don't care if you are the world's greatest consulting detective, you're going down.

I stepped forward, but Morrie grabbed my shoulder. "You can't kill him, gorgeous. I know he's an annoying wanker, but we need him. His crazy stunt today did buy us some time."

I sucked in a breath, trying to calm the blood boiling in my veins. Sherlock tossed a set of keys to me. "I scrambled the GPS in the car. Right now the police are tracking you up by the Scottish border. All you need to do is drive the car back to Argleton, tell them you were abducted and left in the middle of nowhere with the car, that you don't know where Morrie is, and that you still believe he's innocent."

I shook my head. "There's just one flaw in your plan. Actually, there are a hundred flaws, but I'll point out the biggie. I can't drive."

Morrie winced. "Of course. Your eyes."

I nodded. I had a few driving lessons with Mum during my last year at high school, which mostly consisted of her shrieking in my ear from the passenger seat and insisting we sprinkle sage around the car before we got in to 'clear my negative energy' from the vehicle, because apparently, *that* was the reason I couldn't master parallel parking. But Ashley had her license, so I'd never needed mine. Then I moved to New York City, where no one drives, and I had exactly zero percent incentive to learn once I returned.

"Ah, that complicates matters." Sherlock rubbed his chin. "Clearly, you still retain some vision, so I propose a new plan. Drive the car back to Barset Reach. You're unlikely to pass any other vehicles on this road. At the garage, you'll find an old man. Give him the keys to the vehicle, and leave without speaking a word. Do not look back. He will take care of the rest. There is a bus stop outside the pub, and the schedule is behind the bar. If my memory is correct, the bus should have you back in Argleton before supper."

I thought of the long, slippery walk back to the clearing and the bumpy forest road I'd have to navigate. Morrie must've sensed my unease, for he swept me into his arms, holding me against his chest and staring into my soul with those icy-blues until I forgot Sherlock was in the room.

James Moriarty had the ability to do that, to arrest my attention with nothing more than a lingering look. His fingers splayed across the small of my back, pushing me against him until I felt his cock jerk against his trousers. I tipped my head, enjoying the way he fit so perfectly against me, savoring every inch of his warm body and knowing that I'd miss it like Hades as soon as I walked out that door.

"I wish you were coming with me," I whispered into his shoulder.

Morrie cupped my face in his hands. The ice in his eyes melted into cool blue pools that reflected dappled candlelight. "Me too, gorgeous. You have no idea how much. But that annoying bastard's right – I need to stay. I won't be able to prove my innocence or get rid of the problems in my network from a jail cell."

"Won't running from the law get you in even more trouble?"

"Not if we can figure out who framed me," he whispered. "I know that glint in your eye, Mina Wilde. I know you don't intend to wait for Sherlock to solve this for us. You're going to hunt down whoever murdered Kate and framed me."

"Of course." I rolled my eyes. "I don't take orders from Sherlock Holmes."

Morrie pulled me against him, igniting my body with a searing kiss. "Good," he whispered. "That's my girl. With the two of you working to clear my name, I have every confidence in my eventual return to civilization."

Morrie's lips met mine with all the cocky confidence and bravado that made him who he was. His fingers tightened on my jaw, not enough to hurt but just enough to make me feel possessed, wanted, *needed* by him.

And even as I kissed him back – savoring the touch of his body, the sweep of his tongue, the commanding way he held me – that *need* of his niggled at me. Morrie never admitted to needing anything or anyone. What he said to me through the fire of his kiss and the press of his hardness against my thigh was that he needed *me*. And there was only one possible reason Morrie could need me right now.

He's scared.

When the greatest criminal mastermind of the modern age was afraid, I knew we were in for a world of trouble.

CHAPTER FOUR

*M*orrie walked me back to the police car, knowing that the thick cover of trees meant I'd struggle to see the path. While he walked, he told me a little more about his death-faking business, and all the ways people were caught faking their deaths without his expert assistance. He spoke as though he were performing a public service at great personal sacrifice, but I think he was trying to convince himself.

I listened with half an ear. A hundred thoughts whirled around in my head, but I couldn't find the words to voice any of them aloud. Morrie usually liked to fill the silence with chatter – he always had a million things to say, usually about himself – but he seemed lost in his own thoughts, too.

"Your chariot awaits." Morrie swept his arm dramatically toward the police cruiser as we stepped into the clearing. Sunlight streamed through the gap in the trees, illuminating the twinkle in his eyes and the bobbing of his Adam's apple as he swallowed.

And swallowed.

"Morrie—" I reached out to touch his shoulder. *This might be the last time I see him until this is over.*

If I can't figure out who's framed Morrie, this might be the last time I see him without iron bars separating us. And we need him. We need him to help fight Dracula.

I *need him.*

Morrie shrugged away and raced to the car, throwing open the driver's door. He bent over to adjust the seat. "We'd better make sure you can actually drive this thing. I never did go in for the combustion engine myself, but I have had a play with a few getaway vehicles in my time, and I can show you a thing or two."

I reached the door just as Morrie slammed it shut and backed up the car. In a few swift movements, he'd turned it around in the small clearing so it faced back down the road. He threw open the door and climbed out, indicating I should get behind the wheel.

"I have no idea how to drive this thing," I groaned as I slid into the seat.

"The pedal on the right is the accelerator. That makes the car go faster. This large one in the middle is the brake—"

"I know that much, thank you."

"Just checking." Morrie leaned over me to grab the seatbelt. As he brought it across my chest to snap it into place, his hand grazed my breast. The touch was *everything* – it seared through my soaked hoodie like fire, touching my heart until it ignited into an inferno.

Morrie stiffened, freezing in place. His spoiled, indulgent smile arrested me, but his eyes focused on something behind my head. His chest heaved.

"Morrie, look at me."

He kept staring at that spot as he choked out, "I can't."

"Why not?" I whispered.

"Because if I look at you I'm going to drag you out of that seat and fuck you against a tree, and then you and I are going to go take the fake passports I've got stashed in a locker in London and hop on a plane to start our new lives in Monaco. And none of that is a good idea."

I reached up and wrapped my fingers around his chin. The breeze kissed his skin with coolness. I pressed my fingers into his skin, wrenching his head around to face me, forcing him to look, to face up to the reality he'd created.

The eyes that met mine swam with emotions so complex and dark that my breath hitched. I toppled into those icy depths, and all that was Morrie closed over me, pulling me under into an ocean of pain and lust and hating and wanting and fear and disbelief.

A roar tore from Morrie's lips – an outburst so devoid of his usual mastery over his emotions that he must've been channeling Heathcliff. That raw, aching need clenched around my heart and spread warmth through my limbs.

Morrie lifted me from the seat like I was nothing. I wrapped my legs around his lithe body as his lips met mine in a punishing kiss. Holding me in his arms, he staggered around the front of the car and laid me against the hood.

I gasped a little as the coolness of the metal bit through my clothes. Morrie covered my mouth in his, swallowing my yelp as he bore down on me with the full fury of his need. Morrie's hands were everywhere at once – tangled in my hair, gripping my shoulders, wrapping around my back to press me into him, wrestling with tugging up my shirt and rolling my leggings over my feet.

He wasn't being his usual tease, wasn't trying to drive me to the edge and pull me back again. This wasn't a game. The uncertainty of our future wrapped around us, pushing against my skin, making me want more of him, all of him, right now. I wanted to crawl inside Morrie's skin and kiss away his pain from the inside.

Morrie hiked up my skirt and hooked a finger into my panties. I gasped as he tore away the scrap of fabric and threw it over his shoulder into the bushes. What the fuck? That was my favorite underwear, and it wasn't cheap.

But I didn't have the breath in my lungs to complain, not with

Morrie kissing down my chest, kissing over the ribs, his lips on my clattering heart.

"I need to taste you one last time," Morrie choked, his hands cupping my ass, his shoulders holding my thighs down, spreading me wide as his tongue made contact with my wet folds. My head fell back, and I tried to grip the hood of the car as he lapped at me.

Morrie worked two fingers into me as he kept licking. I could already feel the orgasm building – the thrill of doing this in the middle of a clearing on top of a police car combined with his tongue working its magic and the fear that this might be the last time I felt his skin on mine. The whole thing was just so typically *Morrie*, I almost couldn't stand it.

Shivers ran over my skin as raindrops toppled from the leaves, but the fire shooting through my veins as Morrie's tongue swirled around my clit kept me warm.

Morrie thrust a third finger inside me and sucked my clit into his mouth, driving me right to the edge. I tilted my head forward just enough that our eyes met, and that sent me flying headlong into an orgasm.

My body convulsed, nearly slipping off the slick hood as I shuddered through the wave of pleasure roaring through my veins. Morrie's hand on my arse gripped tighter, holding me upright, claiming me as his.

I lay back against the hood, my chest heaving as I struggled to catch my breath. Morrie leaned over me, that spoiled smirk playing on his lips because he was one smug bastard and he'd never forget that for long. He slid his hand from under my arse to place beside my head, fingers splayed over the hood, while his other hand unclasped his belt and slid his trousers over his hips.

I let my legs fall to the sides, trusting him to hold me. The soles of my Docs skidded against the metal, and I slipped down a little, right onto Morrie's waiting cock. A groan tore from

Morrie's lips as he entered me, that cocky twist of his mouth opening into an O of pleasure.

I lifted my hips as he drove deep, hitting just the right angle to wind me up until I was shaking and desperate again. Morrie's body shuddered against mine as he tore away his need to control and gave over to the chaos that reigned inside him. He pounded into me, relentless, punishing, as a raw sound that was half-groan, half-scream tore from his lips.

I was trapped inside his fury, and I *loved* it. I did my best to thrust my hips up to meet him, but it was impossible to move on the hood without sliding off. Morrie flipped me over, dragging my hips back to plunge into me again. I gripped the wing mirror to hold myself still as he drove into me from behind, spanking my ass a few times. The crack of his palm against me only drove me into him harder, my back arching as another delicious orgasm flared through me.

Morrie's nails dug into my hip as he came undone around me, thrusting one more time as deep and as hard as he dared, his head tossed back, an inhuman sound issuing from somewhere inside him. His cock quivered and unleashed, and the man I loved who tied himself up in knots needing to be the dominant, the master, the one in charge, gave himself over to me completely and utterly.

Morrie lay on top of me, his chest heaving, his sweat slick against my skin. Finally, he drew back, and it was as if he pulled a mask over his face – hiding away his vulnerable side behind the cocky, arrogant Morrie I knew and loved so well.

Morrie tugged off his shirt and handed it to me. "Use that to clean yourself as best you can. I'll take at with me and burn it at the cabin. That will prevent my DNA transferring to the car."

My limbs trembled as I pulled up my leggings, tugged down my sodden hoodie, and climbed back behind the wheel. I had so many things I wanted to say to him, but I knew if I spoke, I'd burst into tears. Morrie's gaze bore into me as I eased my foot onto the accelerator, rolling the car down the path until Morrie was nothing but a tiny shadow in the rearview mirror.

And then, he was gone.

CHAPTER FIVE

I drove back down the dirt road, my heart in my throat every time the tires hit a bump. Not a single car passed me as I crawled into the village. The old man who operated the garage didn't bat an eyelid as I drove the police car onto the lot, got out, dropped the keys into his outstretched palm, and walked away. Just as Sherlock said. I worried about mine and Morrie's DNA all over the backseat – especially the story that it might tell a forensic expert like Jo. But there was nothing I could do now.

I hiked down to the pub, conscious of the fact I had no under-wear on and my leggings were definitely on the old and thin side. I waited for two hours in the drizzle for a bus to arrive. As the bus drove away, I saw a plume of smoke rising from the field – and the shape of a burned-out car behind the garage.

I guess there isn't any reason to worry about DNA after all.

I rested my head against the window, my mind reeling. This day had started off as one of the happiest days of my life – the boys showing me the new room they designed for me in the flat so we could live together. Then, like everything else in my life, it had all gone to shit in the most ridiculous way.

Morrie's in trouble.

He's on the run.

I have to help him.

I hated leaving Morrie behind with Sherlock. *Hated* it. I didn't believe I was a jealous person, especially not while my thighs still ached from what Morrie and I did in that clearing. But knowing my guy was cozied up in a remote cabin with his stalker ex-boyfriend didn't fill me with joy. Judging by the way Sherlock touched Morrie when he unlocked the handcuffs, he wasn't paying much attention to the "ex" part.

Sherlock wanted Morrie back. And he was going to use this case to show off his skills. He wanted Morrie to see what he was missing by choosing me over him.

That meant I had to solve the mystery first.

I'm going up against the greatest detective in the history of literature, and I must *win.*

I spent the rest of the bus journey running over the details in my head, trying to come up with a plan. Sherlock and Morrie were going after this McFarlane character and others in Morrie's criminal network. I knew nothing about that world, and I wouldn't be able to infiltrate it like they could, so that left me with the victim – Kate Danvers. I didn't know the information Sherlock used to eliminate her husband and the other suspects, but I had one key advantage. Namely, I grew up in the modern world. I knew how social media and computers and forensics operated. Sherlock was using nineteenth-century methods to solve a twenty-first-century crime. I could beat him if I worked fast and followed the right clues.

That, and Sherlock worked alone. Whereas I had a posse of clever, beautiful, and dedicated friends who would move heaven and earth to help clear Morrie's name.

As soon as I stepped off the bus at Argleton, a raven flew down from the station rafters and perched on my shoulder.

Where have you been? Quoth's voice inside my head sounded both relieved and terrified. *We were so worried about you.*

"It's a long story." I scratched the raven under his chin. He nuzzled my cheek and made a nyuh-nyuh-nyuh noise. "I'm surprised you didn't follow me."

I had to run back into the shop to transform into my bird. By the time I got back outside, the car had gone. I went to the police station, but when you didn't show up I came back and told Heathcliff. I've been flying everywhere, but we couldn't find you.

"Thank you for trying." I stroked his silky feathers as I cradled him against my chest. "Are the police still at the shop? I know I'll have to talk to them, but right now all I want is a cup of tea."

The SOCO team has finished going through yours and Morrie's things, and Hayes is leading the manhunt for the stolen car. They believe you're heading toward Scotland. I'll take you home.

Home. Hearing Quoth speak that word brought tears to my eyes. For a while back in the woods, I truly believed I'd never see Nevermore or Quoth or Heathcliff or Morrie again. The shop felt more like home to me than anywhere else I'd lived, including the dingy council flat where I grew up. And knowing I got to return, and that Quoth felt the same way about it... I blinked furiously, in case all the emotions flapping about in my head from this wretched day overcame me.

"Yeah, let's go home."

Easier said than done. As soon as I stepped onto the green, villagers mobbed me. A stampede of people raced from the pub and post office to surround Quoth and me, hemming us in with their questions.

"Mina, who kidnapped you?"

"Were they handsome?"

"Did you have to chew your own leg off to escape?"

Bloody hell. At least I knew I wouldn't have to worry about calling Hayes – he'd hear about my return from the village grapevine.

"Make way, make way!" A familiar carpet bag swung in front of my vision. Mrs. Ellis dropped her plump hand around my shoulder, squeezing me against her ample bosom. "You should be ashamed of yourselves. Mina has been through a harrowing experience, and you lot getting up in her face won't help. Why, I bet the poor girl just needs a cup of tea and to be left alone in a hot bath."

"Croak," Quoth agreed.

Mrs. Ellis stared down the villagers until they backed away. I heard Richard the bartender mutter under his breath that my 'bossy feminist' ways were rubbing off on my old school teacher. This only made me lean in to hug her tighter.

"Thank you for rescuing me." I squeezed Mrs. Ellis, squashing Quoth between us.

"Croak!" He managed to pull one wing free, flapping it in defiance.

"There, there. We'll get you fixed up." Mrs. Ellis led me by the arm across the green and up the steps of Nevermore Bookshop. Once a teacher, always a teacher. "Yoohoo, Mr. Heathcliff. I've found something that belongs to you!"

Heathcliff barreled into the hallway, his hands balled into fists and his face twisted in a murderous scowl. "The sign clearly says the shop is closed—Mina?"

He slammed into me, crushing Quoth against my chest as he smushed me in a hug that was both violent and beautiful.

"Do not leave me in this abyss again," he murmured into my hair, the words an echo of something he'd once said to Cathy. "Be with me always. Drive me mad. But don't you ever, ever, scare me like that again—"

"Heathcliff…" As much as I wanted him to keep saying such sad and wonderful things… I managed to extract one of Quoth's feet. He kicked the air violently as he struggled to free himself. "Quoth can't breathe."

"I don't care," Heathcliff growled in my ear. "I—ow, what was that for?"

Heathcliff staggered back, clutching his hand. Blood dripped from a cut on his finger. Quoth burst free and dropped to the ground.

"Croooooooak!" He hopped up and down, shaking with anger as he shook the tip of his wing at Heathcliff. I burst out laughing as tears of relief streamed down my cheeks. Only a few hours ago, I trudged through the forest at gunpoint and believed I'd never see them again. Relief washed over me. I sagged against Heathcliff's wide chest, my legs no longer able to hold up my weight.

Heathcliff glanced over my shoulder. "Where's Morrie? What happened?"

"Don't mind me, dears." Ms. Ellis bustled toward the staircase. "You have your little reunion. I'll go make the tea and draw Mina a bath—"

"Oh, no. You're not getting away with eavesdropping on Mina's ordeal." Heathcliff pointed to the door. "Out."

"But I—"

"*Out.* Or I'll replace the *entire* erotica section with another shelf of knitting books."

"You wouldn't dare." Mrs. Ellis knew that her reading habits were one of the reasons the shop was still hanging on.

"Don't test me, woman," Heathcliff shot back.

"*Fine.*" Mrs. Ellis pursed her lips. She swung her carpet bag over her shoulder and flounced toward the door. "I'm off to the pub. I don't need the truth to spin a good yarn for the village. Mina, I hope you don't mind being kidnapped by handsome pirates, because that's what I plan to tell everyone."

"Only if one of them has a villainous mustache," I grinned. When Ms. Ellis was safely out of the shop, Heathcliff shut the door and rolled a bookcase in front of it, just in case any other nosy villagers decided to barge in. "Tea," he barked at Quoth, who fluttered up the stairs, croaking his protests.

With Heathcliff supporting my weight, I shuffled through to the main room and collapsed in the velvet chair under the window, rubbing my temples where a migraine bloomed with fresh pain. I thought about what Morrie might be doing at this very moment, trapped in that cabin with Sherlock, and my stomach churned.

"What happened to you?" Grimalkin's head popped over the arm of the chair.

I shrieked and clobbered her with a pillow. "What are you doing hiding down there on the floor?"

My grandmother's lips curled back into a sumptuous smile. "I hid a mouse carcass behind the shelves two days ago. I wanted to play with it again."

Gross. Ever since I'd spoken some Ancient Greek words that broke the curse the god Poseidon placed on my grandmother, she struggled with letting go of the feline habits she'd lived with for several centuries. We were letting her continue to live in the shop until she could function well enough as a human to be allowed to roam freely. So far, she preferred to sleep curled up in Heathcliff's armchair during the day, but she did occasionally pop downstairs as either a human or cat to frighten customers.

Grimalkin butted my arm with her head (a very disconcerting thing for your grandmother to do while she was human and naked, let me tell you). Sighing, I stroked her hair, and she rubbed her head into my hand, her whole body trembling with the force of her happiness.

"I appreciate the comfort, Grandma."

Grimalkin shot me a filthy look. "Don't call me that. It makes me sound old." She curled up on the seat beside me, stuck her leg in the air, and tried to lick clean her inner thigh.

"Grimalkin, remember what we talked about. You can't bend the same ways in your human form, and it scares people. The shower is for cleaning."

She set her leg down and frowned. "The rain cupboard? What kind of heathen do you take me for?"

"Sorry. I thought you were a water nymph. As you were."

Grimalkin stuck her foot back in the air, narrowly missing kicking the tea-tray in Quoth's hands as my birdie entered the room in his human form, wearing a pair of black cargo pants and nothing else. *Mmmmm.* My loins (gross word, but accurate in this case) still ached in that satisfying way from what Morrie and I had done on the police car.

Nothing like a beautiful, shirtless boy with a luminous waterfall of black hair bearing hot cups of tea and biscuits. It's every self-respecting British girl's wet dream.

Grimalkin transformed back into a cat to enjoy the saucer of cream Quoth placed on the carpet for her. Next, he set a steaming cup of tea in front of me and curled up beside me. A curtain of black hair draped across his face as he nuzzled into my shoulder. *I'm home, I'm home.*

Heathcliff grabbed his own cup from the tray and slumped into his chair. He nodded at my tea. "Drink first, then you can talk. You'll have to call your mother, and Hayes, too. We can do it for you if you want."

"I'd appreciate that." As much as I knew she'd be out of her mind with worry, the last thing I wanted to do at that moment was converse with my highly-strung mother.

I sipped my tea, feeling the horrors of the day drop away as my stomach filled with warmth. Even impossible things became clear and simple when facing them with a cup of tea.

After a terse conversation where Heathcliff informed Hayes I'd arrived home safe, and that I'd call him a little later when I was able to give a statement, and an even more tense one where Heathcliff held the phone away from his ear while my mother screamed down the line at him, the bookshop fell into blissful silence. That left only my troubled thoughts to scream inside my head. Quoth transformed back into his bird form and preened his feathers. Grimalkin folded her long legs underneath her and regarded me with a regal tilt of her chin. I drained my cup, set it down, and drew a deep breath.

"I need to explain what – and *who* – happened to Morrie. He's been framed for the murder of a hiker named Kate Danvers."

"Of course he fucking has," Heathcliff growled.

"Croak!" Quoth shushed him.

I nodded. "Morrie's innocent of that crime, but someone is trying to pin it on him. His business card was found on the victim's corpse, and footprints matching his brogues found near the body. The police have traced Morrie's involvement to a side-line business he's been operating. A year ago, Morrie helped Kate Danvers fake her own death, only now she's shown up dead for real."

CRACK. I winced as Heathcliff slammed his fist into the desk. "Idiot," he muttered.

"It gets worse. Morrie's known about Kate's death for some time. Guess how? Sherlock Holmes told him."

"Sherlock Holmes?" Heathcliff thumped his fist on the ancient cash register, which pinged in protest.

"Yup. Morrie's ex-boyfriend appeared in the shop a couple of months back and has been creepily stalking Morrie ever since. That's how Sherlock knew about Kate's death before we did. He disguised himself as a police officer, stole a cruiser, and dragged me and Morrie to a cabin in Barsetshire Fells where he and Morrie intend to hide out while they investigate Kate's murder to clear Morrie's name."

"How did we not know Sherlock Holmes was loose in the world?" Heathcliff demanded. "That poxy bastard must've snuck out without us knowing."

"Apparently, it was that night we all..." I placed my hands over Grimalkin's ears. "You know, where Morrie and Quoth and I played with Morrie's handcuffs, and then you and I got primordial in the living room."

"Meow?" Grimalkin shot me a scandalized look. She stood up and stormed from the room, her tail flicking behind her. I sighed. *Life was so much easier when she was just a cat.*

"What's he like?" Heathcliff demanded, drawing me back to the present.

"Sherlock? Tall. Foppish hair. An arrogant prick." I paused. "He's *exactly* Morrie's type."

"Sounds like a twat." Heathcliff's eyes blazed. His shoulders tensed, and a flicker of concern flashed across his features – so quick I blinked and once more stared at the irascible scowl buried beneath wild whiskers. I knew that Morrie had feelings for Heathcliff, but Heathcliff had never given any indication he played for the other team, except for the moment when he'd kissed Morrie back. Before he shoved Morrie across the room and stormed off.

...I froze, my body locked in a rage of lust as Morrie's lips teased Heathcliff with a featherlight touch. Heathcliff's eyes narrowed, and he had raised his fist. I forced myself from my chair, thinking that he was going to punch Morrie...

The memory flickered across my vision. Even when I was completely blind, the image of Heathcliff wrapping his huge hand around the back of Morrie's head and pushing his face hard against his, their mouths smashing together in a hot, violent, punishing kiss, would forever be burned into my memory.

Now Heathcliff leaned forward, his dark eyebrows knitting together, his eyes unreadable. A rough hand reached up to touch his own hair, and I *wondered*.

Why is Heathcliff so interested in the appearance of Sherlock? Usually he's indifferent to anything unless it causes him to miss out on quiet, books, or alcohol.

"Sherlock *is* a twat. I don't trust him," I said. "He's trying to win Morrie back. That's why he chose to stay hidden from us. He's been spying on us all this time. He could have helped during any of the other murders, but he didn't. With Dracula around, we could have used him... yet he shows up now, when it's *Morrie* in trouble."

Heathcliff's dark eyes swept over mine. "You think he's got something to do with this case?"

"I don't know. But I do know I don't want him to be the one to solve it. Sherlock Holmes might be the world's greatest consulting detective, but he doesn't know Morrie like we do." I folded my arms. "We're going to solve this mystery first, clear Morrie's name, and show literature's greatest detective that he can't mess with Mina Wilde's family."

CHAPTER SIX

"*W*ho are our suspects?" Quoth stood in front of a large canvas he'd dragged down from his room and set up on the easel beside the fire. He tapped the board with his pen, the sliver of moonlight from the open window bathing his hair in highlights of coral red and blush pink. "Mina, did you talk to Jo?"

It was odd to see Quoth standing up there, taking charge of our investigation, in the position where Morrie would have stood if he'd been here. From the way the orange fire flared at the edges of his irises, I got the sense Quoth was almost as determined as I was that we'd be the ones to solve this.

After calling my mum and the police to let them know I was okay, I spent the afternoon reading and snuggling with Quoth, trying (and failing) not to think about what Morrie might be getting up to in that cabin with Sherlock. Heathcliff stomped around the shop, slamming books down and swearing at inanimate objects. He called this 'working,' but I got the feeling his agitation had something to do with the absence of a certain annoying master criminal.

Now, we ate a dinner of fish and chips around the fire while we tried to come up with a plan for clearing Morrie's name. I held up my cup, sloshing cheap wine down the front of my Distillers t-shirt.

"I talked to Jo briefly. She's doing the final work on Kate Danvers' autopsy tonight, otherwise she'd be here with us. She said she couldn't tell me anything about the case beyond the fact that Ms. Danvers was stabbed with a long, narrow, double-edged blade, and it definitely wasn't suicide." My best friend, Jo Southcombe, was the Barchester county medical examiner, which meant when we met up for a drink, she always had the craziest work stories. Usually, she couldn't wait to dish the dirt on the corpses that ended up on her table, but now she held Morrie's liberty in her hands, she'd become strangely taciturn. I didn't want to think about what that meant for the case.

Everything will work out okay. Morrie's innocent, and the evidence will show that.

"Long, double-edged blade..." Heathcliff grabbed a handful of chips and stacked them on top of a slice of buttered bread. He folded the bread over and dipped the end of his chip butty into ketchup. "Perhaps a sword?"

"Jo said they found what they think is the weapon in a rubbish bin in Barset Reach, and it was a small decorative blade, probably a letter opener, like that one you have lying around downstairs. Our killer needed access to this weapon. Does it take a strong person to stab someone with a letter opener?"

"Not if the blade is sharp," Heathcliff muttered. "It would slide right in. After all, that's what blades are designed to do. Only when it hits bone do things get tough."

"I'm not sure if I love that you know that, or think it's freaky."

Heathcliff leaned down to kiss my cheek, his scraggly beard grazing my skin. "You love it," he whispered, kissing a trail across my cheek to bite my earlobe.

I nodded. *Mmmmhmmmm.*

Grimalkin made a gagging noise. Quoth cleared his throat. "Do I need to add a note about the blade?"

"Yes." Heathcliff leaned back, although his hand lingered on my shoulders. "Write that the killer had to know what they were doing. What more we can make of it will depend on what Jo says about the depth and ferocity of the cut."

My chest constricted as I took another swig of wine. I felt the loss of Morrie keenly. If he was here, he'd be bossing us all around, throwing around facts about murders, and telling us how brilliant he was. He never would have let Heathcliff open this £6.50 bottle of plonk.

"Agreed. Add another column for the body. We'll fill in the details when I hear from Jo. What about suspects? Sherlock and Morrie are going over Morrie's criminal buddies, looking for grudges, but I think we need to consider Kate's role in all this. I think she's the key. Any thoughts?"

"I think you all should hand me your uneaten fish," Grimalkin purred, crossing her long legs as she peered at me with wide eyes.

I tossed my grandmother my battered haddock. It bounced off the edge of the table and rolled across the rug. She pounced on her prey and held it between her red-painted nails, tearing into the flesh with her teeth. She still hadn't quite got the hang of eating like a human.

Heathcliff grabbed the wine from the table and skulled straight from the bottle. Tension rolled off his body in waves, and I wondered if he too felt Morrie's absence more than he was letting on. "I got nothing. We don't know this girl."

I grabbed Heathcliff's phone and scrolled through the articles I pulled up about Kate Danvers' death. Quoth's art teacher, Marjorie Hansen, was blind – she showed me how to use the text-to-speech function on a phone, which read out the navigation menus and text on the screen so I could find my way around without sight. It was still a bit confusing learning to listen to my phone instead of look at it, but I was getting better at it.

Grimalkin grew bored with rending the flesh of her fish and batted it across the rug, squeaking with delight as she smeared a trail of crumbs into the weave. Heathcliff tossed her a plate, and she shot him a filthy look.

"You have your vices, human, and I'll keep mine."

I cleared my throat just as Heathcliff picked up a fork to throw at her. "Here are the facts I've found from the papers. Kate worked for a big tech company called Ticketrrr. One of the perks of her job was getting to attend a week-long Leadership Summit with twenty leaders from her company. Last year, that summit was a wilderness survival course at Wild Oats, which Morrie said Kate had a hand in organizing. On the last night, her instructor took her out to a predetermined campsite. She was supposed to build a makeshift shelter, make a fire, cook a dinner of cockroaches... all the wilderness skills she'd learned over the week. Instead, when they returned to collect her in the morning, they found her camp abandoned and a note pinned to her shelter. A suicide note."

"Except it wasn't a suicide," Quoth reminded me. "Morrie smuggled her away."

I nodded. "Exactly. Morrie said he whisked her to the airport and sent her to the Philippines. Apparently, that's the best place to go when you want to disappear. She left behind a husband, Dave. Morrie said Dave would have cashed in Kate's life insurance policy by now."

"I thought life insurance didn't pay out on suicides?" Heathcliff lifted his head.

"*I* thought you weren't helping," I teased.

"Maybe I just want this to be over so I can go to bed."

"Mmmm hmmm. I believe you. Anyway, I researched this, too. Health insurance *will* pay out – provided the policy is more than two years old and you haven't recently tried to increase it. Morrie says they'll send investigators for cases where the sum insured is huge, so he advises his clients to keep things modest. He said people got caught by being greedy."

Heathcliff snorted. "Classic Morrie. He runs a secret death-faking business where he fleeces clients for thousands of dollars, then tells them not to be greedy."

"He said he did it as a public service. Maybe he doesn't take payment?"

Heathcliff raised an eyebrow. "Morrie never does anything out of the goodness of his heart."

I thought back to the pain in Morrie's eyes after Heathcliff rejected his kiss, and I wondered if Heathcliff was being deliberately callous. "Anyway, I think the husband might be involved," I declared. "Write that up, Quoth."

"Let me at this suspect," Grimalkin purred, looking up from her fish to inspect her red-painted nails. "A handsome widower mourning his greatest love, so grim and gaunt and vulnerable. I'll get him to tell us his darkest, filthiest secrets."

"You're not going anywhere near him," I said. "He's not your type."

"How do you know?"

"He has two legs and doesn't lick his own arsehole. As far as I know."

Grimalkin hissed. Quoth wrote 'husband' on the board. "Who else?"

"Anyone who was with her during the wilderness weekend might've seen something. Kate didn't just return to England – she went back to the place where she faked her death. That has to mean something. Maybe someone from her job was blackmailing Kate to keep quiet about her fake death, and she came back to finish them off so she could keep her new life. They fought, and she lost."

"Or maybe she told a friend in confidence and that friend decided to blackmail her," Heathcliff growled. "Or she was the floozy of one of Morrie's gang buddies. Or she went walking in the woods and slipped over and fell on her own letter opener. I hate to quote Morrie's ex here, but we're grasping at straws trying to theorize without facts. Morrie's the one who figures these things out, and he did that by hacking into personal records and digging up the dirt. We've got no dirt."

"Exactly. The *point* is that Morrie's not here, and I don't trust Sherlock to do it. So it falls on us. Maybe we don't have Morrie's hacking skills—" I glanced over at his computer station in the alcove beside the kitchen, where the three screens still shone, blinking with lines of code "—but we've got our own methods. I'll distract the husband while Quoth flies in a window and searches his room. Easy as pie."

Grimalkin poked her head up from underneath the table, licking the last morsels of fish from her lips. "There's pie?"

"What about the Wilderness Survival School?" Quoth asked. "As you said, that was where this thing started and ended. Maybe someone who works there is responsible. Or at least, they might have seen something."

"Good idea," I smiled at him. Quoth beamed at my praise. "We need to get on that crime scene."

"You're only saying that because you want an excuse to go back out there and check on Morrie," pointed out Heathcliff.

"Damn right." The thought of what Morrie and Sherlock might be up to cramped in that tiny cabin sent a sickly jolt through my veins. "Even if it means I have to pretend I like the outdoors."

"Count me out." Heathcliff folded his arms.

"Come on, you'll love it. I bet they do all kinds of outdoor activities – rambling, foraging, archery... you're always saying how much you miss the moors. This isn't exactly the same, but at least it's out in nature."

"Hayes and Wilson are already going to be looking closely at us as potential co-conspirators," Heathcliff pointed out. "We shouldn't do anything out of the ordinary, like head off into the countryside to the exact location where Morrie supposedly killed this bint."

"True." I tapped my chin with my finger, not even realizing until after I'd done it that it was a Morrie-ish gesture. "We'll just tell them we're going somewhere else. We can think up a convincing lie. If we make sure we're not seen at Wild Oats, they won't even have to know we were there."

"And who would run the shop while we're gallivanting around the woods communing with nature?"

I raised an eyebrow. "What about Mum? She doesn't have a job at the moment since she blew up Sylvia's shop with one of their soap-making kits, and she's between pyramid schemes, so she wouldn't be compelled to turn the World History room into a recruitment center."

"Are you actually suggesting your *mother* be made responsible for the shop?" Heathcliff scoffed. "What about the time-travel bedroom? What about the occult room or the Classics shelves bringing book characters to life or the fact she's bug-nuts crazy?"

"Simple. We lock the door to the bedroom and pile a bunch of boxes in front of the occult room. That will keep her out of Nevermore's magical corners. She got rid of all the soap kits, so I doubt she can do much damage in a couple of days." *And it would help make her feel more included in my life.*

Mum was doing an admirable job letting me get on with my life and make my own decisions, even though it made her crazy. She was already on her high horse about me moving in with the guys, especially since I refused to officially declare which one of them was my boyfriend. Getting her to help out in the shop would be a great way to make her feel included.

"What about if we gave her a trial run?" Quoth suggested. "You've got your appointment with the guide dog trainer tomorrow. Helen could watch the shop while we're in Crookshollow."

"Oh, yes, the mangy mutt." Grimalkin sighed. "How could you

be so cruel as to introduce such an uncouth creature into this house of learning?"

That's right. In all the madness of the last day, I'd completely forgotten that tomorrow I'd be meeting my new guide dog for the first time. We'd arranged for Morrie to mind the shop while Heathcliff and Quoth went with me to the guide dog training center in the village of Crookshollow, in the next shire over. Heathcliff always had dogs at Wuthering Heights, so it made sense that he come to check out the pup. And we needed to know that any dog we had in the shop could handle the presence of a shapeshifting raven.

A sliver of anger shot through my body – meeting my dog was supposed to be a wonderful experience. I'd always wanted a pet, but we couldn't have one at our flat on the housing estate. Getting a guide dog was the one bright spot of going blind, something I was actually excited about. But Sherlock bloody Holmes had to show up and kidnap Morrie and ruin it all.

And part of me knew it wasn't Sherlock's fault, but the fault of whoever killed Kate Danvers. And Morrie had to take some blame for opening this stupid fake death business in the first place. But the part of me that knew this was across the village at the pub. And the part left behind wanted to smash Sherlock's hawkish nose.

I nodded. "Giving Mum a trial run might work. What do you think, Heathcliff?"

Heathcliff sighed. "You're joint owner of this shop, Mina. If you think it's a good idea, I can't stop you."

"I think it's a great idea." I didn't, but I needed Heathcliff to come with me to Crookshollow. *Mum might be a bit wacky, but she's mostly harmless. I'm sure it'll be fine.*

Totally fine...

～

"Oh, Mina, I'm just so glad you're okay," Mum beamed down the phone. "And yes, I'd be happy to look after the shop. Although, are you sure you want to leave the village again after what that horrid man did to you?"

"I'm sure," I hissed. "If I let this guy get to me, then he's won."

"I'm proud of you, darling. Stick it to that rotten bastard. When the police catch him, I'll be first in line to join the firing squad. How *dare* he touch my daughter." Mum's voice soared an octave. "Have the kidnappers made any demands? That boyfriend of yours is a very rich man. Now, Mina, you're not to allow that inspector to talk you into making the drop. It's too dangerous, and with your eyesight, you're liable to drop a gold bar on your toe—"

"No demands for gold bars yet, although I've prepared some sacks with dollar signs on them just in case," I smiled. We hadn't told Mum the whole story, that Morrie was under suspicion of murder. The less information Mum knew about... anything, the better. "I'm sure Hayes will find the guy and bring them to justice."

"Pfft." Her voice brightened. "Now, while I'm in at Nevermore, I have a few ideas for improvements. I'll bring along my craft kit and—"

"No."

"Oh, but I've seen these crocheted bookmarks—"

"*No.*"

"Well, what about a few nice candles—"

"Candles in a building entirely filled with books? Not happening. Remember, Mum, you're only looking after the place for five hours – just long enough to sell a few books to visiting tourists and gossip with Mrs. Ellis about my kidnapping. Not enough time to make *any* changes."

"Really, Mina. I *have* minded Sylvia's shop before. I know what I'm doing."

That's exactly what I'm afraid of. I pictured the burned-out husk of Sylvia's storefront as I grabbed the keyboard from Heathcliff's hand and mashed the keys until a loud, beeping noise emitted from the monitor. "Oh, bother. I have another call. Got to go, Mum. I bet it's the police with an update on the case."

"But Mina, what about my crochet—"

"Bye, Mum." I jabbed the END CALL BUTTON and tossed my phone down with a sigh.

Heathcliff's fingers closed over my shoulder. *"That's* the woman you've put in charge of our livelihood."

"I don't want to hear it." I rubbed my temple. "It's only for five hours. Everything is going to be fine."

"But—"

"It's *fine.*" I picked up my phone and punched in Hayes' number. How was it that I knew the Inspector's number by heart?

Hayes answered on the first ring. "Mina? Are you all right? Has something else happened?" *He probably has me programmed into his phone by now.*

I tried to make my voice sound weary and upset, which honestly wasn't even a lie. "No. I've had no word from Morrie, or any kidnappers. I just wanted to hear from my favorite detective."

"I wish I had good news for you, Mina. I'm up in Yorkshire now, and we can't find evidence of the car anywhere. We've scoured the countryside and we can't find Morrie. There have been no demands, and I just..." he coughed. "Truthfully, this has me completely stumped."

"Do you still... are you still looking at Morrie as the murderer? If he was kidnapped..."

"I can't rule it out. There's a lot of evidence implicating Mr. Moriarty, and this kidnapper might be an accomplice. I know he's your boyfriend, but he hasn't exactly been truthful with you about his business ventures."

No. No, he has not. "If there's anything I can do to help, let me

54

know. I also wanted to ask if it was okay for Heathcliff, Allan and I to go to Crookshollow tomorrow? It's only for a few hours, to meet my new guide dog. And we might have to go again – I've got a couple of weeks of intense training coming up. We might have to sleep over."

"Yes, yes, that's fine." In the background, someone yelled at Hayes, and a siren blared. "Just give me the address of the kennels in Crookshollow. And whatever you do, don't go sticking your nose into Morrie's case. We've got a team of experts on this, Mina. We'll bring the lad home."

So you can lock him up, I thought, but didn't say.

Hayes rang off. That chore done, I went to find the guys in their usual evening locations. Heathcliff slumped in his chair, and Grimalkin sprawled across his lap. I thought Heathcliff would have revoked Grimalkin's lap privileges now that she revealed herself to be my grandmother, but they'd been companions for a long time before I came along, and that kind of insouciant friendship endured even though Grimalkin could now shift into a human at will.

Kind of like how raven Quoth defecates on anyone who quotes Poe and it's hilarious, instead of disgusting.

Heathcliff closed his book as I crossed the room and planted a kiss on his cheek. As I pulled away, his arm shot out to grip my wrist, holding me in place. He turned his face slowly up to meet me, and the firelight danced across his features, capturing the blaze in his eyes.

"Are you okay?" His gruff voice rumbled through my body, shooting a wave of lust. Everything about Heathcliff was just so... primal.

"I—" I didn't really know how to answer that. "I miss Morrie."

"What do you need?" He choked the words out, his finger tightening their grip.

I need to forget. Just for a moment.

I opened my mouth to speak, but I should have known Heathcliff and I were beyond words. He yanked my arm down and stood up, tossing me over his shoulder. I made to fight but he cupped his enormous, rough hand over my arse and I... I didn't want to fight.

Heathcliff grunted as he flung open the door to my room – the room the three of them made for me, filling it with beautiful textures and kind touches only they could think of. As Heathcliff tossed me down on the bed and crawled up beside me, I noticed Morrie had kept the hook he used for bondage play in the ceiling.

And then I ceased to think. I challenge any hot-blooded woman (or man) to initiate cohesive thought while literature's most infamous gothic hero has his tongue down your throat or his hands tangled in your hair.

Except not, because no bloody way am I sharing Heathcliff Earnshaw with anyone.

Except maybe Morrie, if we ever got him back.

I lost myself in the kiss, and before I knew it my shirt flew across the room and hit the wall. Heathcliff crushed my mouth with his kiss as he flung away my skirt and tore the replacement pair of panties in his haste to get inside them.

"Bloody hell, lingerie doesn't grow on trees..." my protests turned into moans as he sucked a nipple into his mouth, his hand plunging between my legs to send me spinning into a near-instant orgasm. His body crushed me into the sheets, and I was lost in the scent of him, the... Heathcliffness of him, all rage and feral need.

"Your skin smells like Morrie," he rasped against my neck as he parted my legs with his knee.

"Yes... well, we *might* have had sex on top of the police car before I drove it to the village."

Heathcliff dragged my hips back against his as he impaled me on his dick, swallowing my gasp. His size knocked the breath out of me, but in the best possible way. He pushed his arm between us so he could reach my clit, rubbing the nub until I writhed beneath him. Heathcliff wasn't being gentle tonight. He pounded out his fear and rage and powerlessness into me with every thrust, and I rose up to meet him, matching his rage with my own.

And I caught a whiff of it – Morrie's grapefruit and vanilla clinging to the sheets, to the walls, to every part of us. Because he was part of us.

The groan that escaped Heathcliff's throat tore me apart. His finger battered my clit as he broke into pieces for me. Morrie's scent twined between us, larger-than-life and in our faces, just like the man himself. Heathcliff slammed into me until our legs trembled together, until we collapsed onto the sheets in a tangle of body parts, not knowing where one of us ended and the other began.

I am Heathcliff.

Another orgasm broke over me like a wave, and the clench of me around his cock sent Heathcliff over the edge. His head rolled back. I bit his throat, tasting the salt on his skin as he shuddered inside me.

Heathcliff rolled off me and collected me in his arms, and a black bird fluttered down out of the darkness, hopping along the side of the bed. My eyes fluttered shut as weariness overcame me, and when I opened them again I looked at a beautiful boy with a curtain of shimmering black hair and eyes rimmed with fire. Quoth crawled under the covers and clicked off the light, and the two of them held me. I breathed in the mingled scents. Heathcliff's earthy peat. Quoth's fresh spring air and wildflowers. And the tiniest hint of Morrie's zesty grapefruit-and-vanilla still wafting in the air – the ghost of my third boyfriend.

Morrie, wherever you are tonight, know that I love you. That... I'm going to fight for you. And that I'd never, ever, push you over a waterfall.

CHAPTER SEVEN

*C*RASH. BANG. SMASH.

"Fuck!"

I bolted upright, my heart pounding. Rain pattered against the window, and a shaft of grey light from the open curtains illuminated a square of unfamiliar room. It took me a few moments to remember where I was – in the bedroom at Nevermore Bookshop the guys made for me – *my bedroom.*

"Pox-ridden bastard! Dishonorable cur!"

And someone was downstairs destroying the shop.

A warm arm stretched around my waist, tugging me back into bed. I brushed my fingers through Quoth's hair as it fanned across the sheets. He lifted his face to mine and met my lips with a languid kiss. I sank back into the bed, forgetting what it was that had startled me in the first place as Quoth's fingers drew patterns across my skin.

SMASH.

That sounds like glass shattering...

Sighing, I threw the covers aside. Quoth transformed into his bird form and hopped onto my shoulder as I pulled on my dressing gown, shoved my feet into my fluffy skull slippers, and padded downstairs. As I neared the bottom, I discovered the cause of all the chaos.

Heathcliff stood on a rickety ladder, his arms loaded with tiny taxidermy. At his feet were scattered picture frames and other oddities we used to decorate the shop. He held up a hand when he saw me.

"Don't come any closer. I knocked over the sodding lamp. There's glass everywhere."

I flicked on the lamp I'd positioned at the bottom of the stairs, and noticed shards of glass glittering on the rug. "It's okay. In a few months, I won't even need it. What are you doing?"

"Isn't it obvious? I'm Helen-proofing the shop." Heathcliff jumped down from the ladder and grabbed an armload of stuff. "Anything she could sell, decorate, or that could spark one of her dangerous ideas is going into the storage room."

"That's not necessary. She's hardly going to touch our taxidermy…"

Heathcliff looked at me like I'd gone mad. "If you recall, last time she was here she brought sequins to 'bling them up'."

"Right. Silly me. Of course, it's necessary. You should remove all the books from the Business section, too."

"Already done." Heathcliff pointed to the empty shelves at the end of the hallway. "I thought I'd tackle the occult and self-help sections next."

"Give me a minute to make our booking with Wild Oats and then I'll help."

Heathcliff came back to pick up the rug and shake the glass into the bin. I sat down under the window, pulling open the thick drapes to let in the natural light. The sun streaming in gave me visibility over a good third of the room, but even so, my temples throbbed from the strain of squinting at my phone screen as I searched for the Wild Oats website.

You're supposed to be using the voice software.

My ophthalmologist Dr. Clements said this adjustment phase would be hard because I still had some sight and I'd fall back on it out of habit, even when it was a strain. "Sometimes, people find it's easier to wait until they're completely blind before they consider learning braille or adaptive technology. You'll always be trying to use your limited vision, and it may make you more frustrated."

Frustration be damned. I need to learn this stuff. It's the only way I can stop myself from going crazy.

I turned on the screen reader and navigated to the Wild Oats website. According to their homepage, the Wild Oats Wilderness Survival School offered a range of different courses throughout the year. The next course was scheduled over the weekend and focused on foraging for edible foods. It involved an overnight stay. *That will do nicely. We'll investigate the center, then sneak off to see Morrie when everyone's asleep.*

"Hey, Heathcliff," I yelled out. "How do you feel about learning how to forage for food?"

"Indifferent," he yelled back. "Hurry up and make the booking. Your mother will be here any minute and we've still got to put OUT OF ORDER signs on all the bathrooms. The last thing I want is to come home to find she's turned our loo into a turtle-breeding facility."

Urgh, I never should have told him about when I was seven and Mum tried breeding turtles in our bathtub to sell around the estate as pets, and ended up flooding the flat beneath ours.

I pressed the phone to my ear. A gravelly male voice picked up on the second ring. He introduced himself as Sam and seemed overjoyed to hear from me. I imagined Sam as a grizzled old hippie with a long beard, and then immediately felt guilty for stereotyping him.

"Sure, we can accept three more intrepid foragers on the weekend course. Would you like to pay by credit card now or—"

"There's just one thing..." I paused, collecting myself. "I'm actually going blind. I have a rare condition called retinitis pigmentosa, and most of my peripheral vision is gone. I also find it hard to see in darkness. Do you think I can still take the course?"

I held my breath, surprised by just how much I wanted him to agree I could come, and preparing to fight if he said no. I knew that part of my future meant being locked out of things other people took for granted, but I wasn't going to take that lying down.

"I've never been asked that before." I imagined Sam stroking his long, hippie beard. "I don't see any problem. You may not be able to see everything, but so much of foraging is about feel and scent, I think you could even have an advantage. As long as your tastebuds work, I think you'll enjoy the experience."

"Thanks, Sam." I glanced down at the photograph on the website, where a smiling instructor held up some kind of wriggling grub, and wondered what exactly we'd got ourselves into. "We're looking forward to it."

"Me, too, Mina," Sam laughed. "I'm excited to meet you. Having a blind student is new for me, but I can't wait to introduce you to the joys of cooking from the forest floor. It's going to be an interesting weekend for us all."

Yes, but probably not for the reasons you think. I wasn't sure how to take this Sam character, but I appreciated his enthusiasm. I already found myself hoping he wasn't Kate's murderer.

I hung up the phone and made a second call, this time to Dave Danvers, whose details I'd hunted down last night. I was quite proud that I'd managed to find him without Morrie's help. The newspapers said Kate Danvers lived in Crookshollow, and that her husband was a plumber. It only took a quick search online to find Danvers Plumbing with a phone number. From there, I found Dave Danvers' Facebook page, got a sense of who he was and his unusual hobbies, and formulated a plan.

I called Dave with my prepared plan, and he agreed to meet us after the guide dog center, which meant we'd be making our first steps towards helping Morrie.

That done, I rose to help Heathcliff when someone banged on the window.

"Argh!" I jumped up, tipping Quoth off my shoulder.

"Croak." He glared at the window, then fluttered into the hallway to head upstairs.

I spun around and came face-to-face with Detective Hayes through the glass. I yelled for Heathcliff to move the bookshelf from the front door so he could come inside.

"I didn't know you were back already. I was just about to head down to the station to make my official statement before my appointment in Crookshollow." *And then go meet my guide dog and interview Dave Danvers, but you don't have to know that.* I managed a wobbly smile. "I'm still a bit shaken up."

"Of course you are. This case... I've been sent back to work from here, while Yorkshire police continue the hunt." Hayes pulled up a chair to the opposite side of the desk. "I think this is better, if you'd like to make your statement here. We can talk where you're comfortable."

"So you haven't found the kidnapper yet?" I knew he hadn't because Sherlock ensured they were looking in completely the wrong place, but I needed Hayes to believe I was ignorant.

Hayes shook his head. I reached across the desk and flicked on the two lamps I kept there, lighting up his face so I could see the dark circles under his eyes and the slump of his shoulders. "We've got nothing. Even the GPS in the squad car the kidnapper stole has stopped working. It's as though the vehicle vanished into thin air. The working theory is that they dropped you where they did deliberately to throw us off the scent. While we're fooling around on a wild goose chase, Morrie and his accomplice have already skipped the country."

Panic shot through me. "I don't think this guy is his accomplice. Morrie seemed pretty scared."

Hayes gave me a sympathetic look that made my blood boil. "You're not the first girl to be taken in by a charming con artist. Men like Morrie can be excellent actors. But we're keeping our minds and options open, for now."

Quoth came downstairs with a tray of tea and scones for all of us. He slid out of the room and a moment later, a black raven fluttered in and settled above the chamber door.

I'm here if you need me, his voice appeared inside my head.

I appreciate it, I thought back.

As Hayes directed a tape recorder at me and made notes, I explained the story we came up with – I was blindfolded and driven to some large building, possibly a barn, judging by the smell. Morrie and I were tied up alone for hours before our kidnappers decided to release me. They threw a bag over my head and tossed me into the trunk of a car and drove me into the middle of nowhere. They rolled me out and left me on a country lane. I trudged toward civilization and found myself in York, where I took the bus back to Argleton.

Hayes asked a hundred questions, each more difficult than the last. *What time was my bus? What did the lane look like? Did I remember anything about the sound of the car or the trunk? Did Morrie say anything to the kidnappers? Why hadn't I gone to the police in York?* I piled lies on top of lies, doing everything I could to make Morrie sound as innocent as I believed him to be.

"We'd like to place a trace on your phone line." Hayes showed me the equipment he brought along with him. "If Morrie or the person who took him try to contact you at the shop, we'll be able to figure out where they are. We'll do the same with your mobile."

"That's fine, although the kidnappers destroyed my phone. I'll let you know when I replace it." I knew Morrie wouldn't be stupid enough to call the shop, so I shoved the old-fashioned landline phone toward Hayes. "Do you have any idea how the kidnapper managed to infiltrate the police station?"

"Rest assured, we're investigating every angle." After a few more questions, Hayes left us, grabbing one of Quoth's scones for the road. He met my mother at the door.

She backed him against the shelves and launched into a tirade. "How *dare* you let my daughter be kidnapped on your watch. It's disgraceful. You must have the lout in custody now. Let me at him. I'll give him a right thumping. No one messes with my Mina. He'll know the fury of a mother's wrath—"

Hayes tried to duck around Mum. "I can assure you, Ms. Wilde, we're doing everything we—"

Mum knocked the scone out of his hand. "Oh really, then why are you getting crumbs all over my shop when you should be out there hunting down my daughter's kidnapper?"

Heathcliff made a choking noise. "*Your* shop?"

Mum advanced on Hayes, her arm drawing back her tote bag as though she intended to whomp him with it. Hayes, sensibly, abandoned his scone and backed out of the door. "I'd better get back to the station. Lots of bad guys to bring to justice. Mina, thank you for your time. I'll keep you updated."

"Thanks, Detective Hayes," I called as his figure dashed past the window, safe from my mother for another day.

Mum leaned out the door and waved her fist in the air. "You'd better run!"

Above the door, Quoth's body trembled. He made the *hyuh-hyuh-hyuh* noise that meant he was laughing.

Heathcliff stormed in and fixed my mother with one of his terrifying glares. "You're early."

"I thought I'd be a responsible employee and arrive in plenty of time." Mum peered into his hands. "What are you doing with the armadillo?"

"Oh, he's... got fleas." Heathcliff whipped the stuffed

armadillo behind his back. "I'm putting him in a cupboard so he doesn't infect the customers."

"That's a shame." Mum rummaged around in her bag. "I brought some new eyes to put on him. Those glass ones are a little scary. They terrify the children, so I got these instead. They're much more fun."

She plonked down a bag of plastic googly eyes. Heathcliff's own eyes bugged out of his head so much they matched perfectly.

I stifled a laugh. "I think Heathcliff would prefer if you left the shop the way it was, Mum."

Googly eyes forgotten, Mum flew around the table and wrapped me in her arms. "Mina, I'm so glad you're okay. Those rotten men didn't hurt you, did they?"

"No, no, like I said yesterday, I'm fine." I tried to wriggle out of her grasp, but she only held me tighter. "I'm a little shaken up, but it'll take more than a kidnapping to break me. I'm worried about Morrie, though. The kidnappers still have him, and the police think he's conspiring with them to get away with murder!"

"Are you talking about that body found up in the Barsetshire Fells?" Mum's voice rose in horror. "I heard they were looking for a suspect. They can't imagine a respectable professional like Morrie would have anything to do with such a heinous crime?"

"It's on their minds." I shuddered. "I just want to know he's safe. But I'm going crazy sitting here waiting for the phone to ring. I need the distraction, so thank you so much for minding the shop. You don't know what it means to me, to us."

"I'm always willing to lend a hand, you know that." Mum pecked me on the cheek, finally releasing me. "Have fun, Mina. I'm proud of you."

Have fun. At first, I couldn't figure out why she was suggesting I have fun interviewing a potential murderer, but then I remembered. In all the excitement of Morrie's case, I'd almost forgotten the real reason I was heading out – I was going to meet my new guide dog for the first time.

My stomach gave a nervous flip as I pulled on clothes, ran a brush through my hair, and zipped up my leather jacket. This dog was going to be my eyes once mine didn't work anymore. I'd pinned so much hope on being able to continue my work at the bookshop and live a normal life, and today I'd find out if that was true.

CHAPTER EIGHT

*T*he kennel was in Crookshollow, which was one of the larger villages in Loamshire, the next county over. We hopped off the train and walked down the high street, taking in the Halloween kitsch. Crookshollow was known as one of the most haunted villages in England, so there was a witch statue in the middle of the green and every shop played with the theme. We passed a bakery called *Bewitching Bites*, which judging by the skull-shaped cupcakes in the window we would definitely be visiting for lunch, and a whole bunch of crystal shops and occult booksellers. I stopped in front of a display of tarot cards.

"Mum would love these," I breathed. There was even a set featuring brightly-painted cats dancing all over the cards.

Heathcliff nudged me along. "We don't have time for—"

Too late. The shop bell tinkled as I headed inside, my eyes wide as I took everything in. Crystals hung from every inch of the ceiling, reflecting dancing prisms of rainbow light around the dark room. Dragon statues, crystal pyramids, and skull incense-burners crowded every surface, and the air reeked of patchouli and wax candles. A young woman with funky short hair dyed with pink bangs stood behind the counter, reading a thick tome.

"Your shop is wonderful." I beamed at the girl as I took it all in. The shop – which was called *Astarte* – reminded me of the magic store in one of my favorite movies, *The Craft*. It was far more colorful and less intimidating than the room of occult books at Nevermore.

"Oh, it's not my shop." The girl turned the book around to show me the title. *The Dynamics of an Asteroid*. "The woman who owns it, Clara, is visiting her son up at Raynard Hall, so I'm minding the shop as a favor. My name's Maeve."

"Nice to meet you, Maeve. I'm Mina, and I'd like to get this tarot deck, please. Also..." I leaned over to inspect boxes of colored crystals lining the edge of the counter. "Which crystals are good for attracting wealth?"

"Um..." Maeve raked her fingers through her short hair. "Here's the thing. I don't believe in this stuff. It's all a bunch of nonsense. Real magic isn't about carrying rocks around in your pockets. It's all up here." She tapped her head, then touched her chest. "In your brain. Or in your heart."

"Agreed. It's a present for my mum, and she believes in this stuff. Okay, so..." I fumbled through the box and pulled out a couple with swirling colors. "These ones are pretty. I'll tell her they're for finding your fortune."

"That's the spirit, no pun intended." Maeve glanced over my shoulder as she rang up my purchase. I turned to see what she was looking at. Quoth hovered in the doorway, his fire-ringed eyes mesmerized by the swirling colors of the crystals, while Heathcliff paced and glowered outside. Maeve leaned across the counter, arching a perfect eyebrow. "Tell me, which one of those beautiful men is yours?"

"Oh... um..." I fumbled with my bat purse.

"Or are they *both* your boyfriends?"

Heat flared in my cheeks, which gave Maeve all the answer she needed.

Maeve's eyes twinkled. "No judgment here. I'll tell you a

secret. I live in a big castle overlooking the village with my *five* boyfriends. They like to joke that they're my harem."

"Five boyfriends?" I grinned. "You have my sympathies. I can barely deal with the bickering with my three."

"Three, huh?" Maeve tore a page from a moon cycle notepad and scribbled something down. "This is my number. I'm studying at Oxford, but I'm around Crookshollow on weekends. Call me if you ever want to talk about our... reverse harems."

"Mina," Quoth called from the door. "Heathcliff is yelling."

"Coming." I paid for my purchases, waved goodbye to Maeve, and bolted outside. Quoth slipped his hand in mine and dragged me up the street. Of course, with his avian instincts for direction, he knew exactly where we were going without even glancing at his phone's map.

The guide dog kennels were housed in a small cottage on the corner off the main road, opposite a tattoo parlor called *Resurrection Ink*. Heathcliff and Quoth flanked me as we walked up the path, doubt piercing my heart. *What if this doesn't work?*

I clung to Heathcliff's arm as a flare of bright green lightning zigzagged across my vision. The light flashes were more frequent than ever now, and with my peripheral vision practically nonexistent, when they hit they blinded me completely.

As I strode into the unknown, the noise of excited yips and barks reached my ears, and the arrow of doubt and pain that had pierced my heart withdrew, replaced by excitement fluttering in my stomach.

I'm about to meet the creature who's going to be my eyes and my new friend.

We entered a small waiting area lined with plastic chairs, water bowls, and dog toys scattered everywhere. I stepped close to the wall to admire the large, bold posters of bright-eyed dogs standing, walking, and sitting wearing their distinctive coats and harnesses.

"Mina?" A new voice called from behind me.

"Edie." I spun around and identified the shape of the guide dog trainer on the other side of the room. We embraced warmly. Edie had visited me at Nevermore Bookshop a few weeks ago, when I first applied for a guide dog, to assess my vision needs and independent mobility and the environment my dog would be working in. I hadn't expected to be matched with a dog so soon, but when she called last week to say she had the perfect guy for me, I did a Snoopy dance right there in the middle of the shop.

"It's lovely to see you again. I'm Edie." She held out her hand to Quoth, who'd been in his bird form when she came by. He shook her hand, and I noticed the stiffness in his body as he focused on staying in his human form. I knew all the doggie smells would be freaking him out – I made a quick prayer to Isis and Hathor and all the goddesses he'd be able to get used to it, or I wouldn't be able to have a dog in the shop. "We're so happy to match you with a guide dog."

Up closer, I could tell Edie was smiling – one of those smiles that lit up her whole face. *She probably has the best job in the world.*

"I'm thrilled to meet him." The butterflies did an excited flip. "It's amazing what you're able to do at the center. I read how much it costs to train a guide dog, and I thought I'd have to pay for it myself."

"Nope," Edie grinned. "We believe that independence is a right everyone should be entitled to. We rely on sponsorship and charitable donations to cover the cost of raising and training each dog, which is around thirty thousand quid per animal. Around two million people in the UK alone live with sight loss, and around a hundred and eighty thousand of those people rarely leave their homes alone because they can't do so independently. These pups are a way to give people back their freedom."

Freedom.

A lump rose in my throat that I hadn't expected. It was the way Edie used that word. Freedom. It meant more to me than she could ever know.

Beside me, Quoth squeezed my hand. He knew exactly how precious freedom was.

"Your boy is outside with his brothers and sisters, waiting to meet you." Edie offered her elbow. "Would you like me to guide you?"

"I'm okay." But I clung to Quoth's arm as we made our way down a wide ramp and through two sets of sliding glass doors into an outdoor penned area. The barks increased as a line of excited golden retrievers met us at the fence.

Edie unchained a gate and led us through. Five golden bodies bounded over, jumping and pawing and swamping us with sloppy kisses.

"Hey, hey, calm down, you lot. Mina, this is Oscar." Edie bent down and clipped a lead onto the collar of the smallest retriever. Oscar was no longer a puppy, because he'd just completed two full years of training, but there was a flicker of mischief in his intelligent brown eyes that reminded me of Morrie, and my heart melted.

"Hey, little dude." I bent down to his level, offering a hand. Oscar's ears flapped, and he bounded over to lick my face, his tail wagging with excitement as he sniffed me all over.

I wrapped my arms around his neck, and I didn't want to ever let go.

"As you can see, he's excitable," Edie said. "We've matched you with Oscar because you're young and active, and you'll be spending your time in the bookshop. Oscar's a sociable boy – he loves being around other people and animals, but when he's working, he's got excellent focus. He also loves dark spaces and tunnels."

"He sounds perfect." I choked on the words as I struggled to hold back tears. Reluctantly, I slid my arms out from around Oscar's neck and stood up.

"This is his harness." Edie showed me how to hold out the harness. As soon as Oscar saw the harness, he stepped into it, and

Edie helped me find the buckles to do it up. "Oscar's been trained to know that when his harness goes on, he's working and he has to be a good boy. You hold your arm out like this, with your pointer finger looped through the harness and lead. This gives you the best control, but means that you can let go easily in an emergency. Now, we'll go over the gestures and commands for walking, sitting, turning, etc."

Oscar and I walked around the obstacle course – he located steps, a ramp, and then brought me to a chair so I could sit. Edie stayed with me, repeating the commands and helping me to refine the gestures I'd use to let Oscar know what I wanted. After a couple of hours, my head was spinning with all the new information, but I didn't want to hand the lead back to Edie.

"I love him so much." I fumbled with Oscar's harness as he slipped it over his head. Once he was free, I wrapped my arms around him again and gathered him to my body. Oscar leaned his body against me, and his wagging tail whomped against my thigh. My heart fluttered as an instant connection flared between us – an unspoken promise that we'd always look out for each other. "When can I take him home?"

Edie laughed. "I'm so happy – he's smitten with you, too. The two of you will need to complete training before we can release him to you, but it won't be much longer. We'd like you to come in every day for two weeks of training with Oscar. We'll do some training here at the center, but also out in the community and in situations you might normally find yourself in. Will you be able to get the time off work?"

"Yes," Heathcliff said before I could answer.

I looked at him in alarm. What about solving Morrie's case? But I couldn't say that in front of Edie, so I forced a smile. "Yes, I'll be here. I wouldn't miss it."

Oscar nudged my leg, his tail beating against my shin. Anxiousness tugged at me as I handed the lead back to Edie. Oscar should be coming with me. He was mine, and I was his.

Oscar peered up at me with those feisty brown eyes, and I knew he felt it, too.

As we left the guide dog center, Quoth squeezed my hand. "You're smiling."

"He's adorable, don't you think?" I beamed, even as I blinked back tears.

Heathcliff walked ahead of us. I expected him to shrug or grunt some non-committal response. When he turned around to face me, a wide grin spread across his face. "It'll be nice to have that wee fella around the shop."

I widened my eyes. "Is that Heathcliff Earnshaw expressing desire for the company of an animal?"

Heathcliff shrugged. "I like dogs. Much better than customers."

"You really are excited about this." Quoth nuzzled his head onto my shoulder. "Six months ago you would've been freaking out right now."

"I'm not the same person I was six months ago," I said.

It was true. I returned to Argleton from New York City shrouded with shame. I thought my life was over. Famous last words. Rediscovering Nevermore Bookshop – and being with the guys – had rekindled something inside me I thought had been lost forever. Sure, there might have been a few more murders than I preferred, but I knew now that I was going to continue to have an amazing life.

I still had moments when I was afraid of losing my sight completely, where I mourned for the things I would lose, but I didn't carry that fear around like a funeral shroud. *My eyes don't make me the person I am, and losing my sight is not the end – it's just another beginning.*

"Do you want us to come with you to training every day?" Heathcliff asked. I might've been imagining it, but he sounded hopeful.

"I think that depends on what Mum's done to the shop." I

linked arms with Heathcliff. "But we've got a couple of hours before we have to worry about that. Come on, let's go lie to a widower to save our friend."

CHAPTER NINE

"*R*emind me how your crazy scheme is going to work?" Heathcliff muttered as we sat on a park bench opposite Dave Danvers' pokey flat, in the worst area of Crookshollow. He definitely wasn't living large with his insurance money.

"It's not a crazy scheme." I rummaged around in my bag and removed the costume I brought along. "It's brilliant and foolproof. Kate's social media accounts have all been deleted, and apart from a notice about the funeral, Dave hasn't updated his for months. But a scroll through his old photographs revealed he and Kate were uber-geeks. They attended fan conventions up and down the country dressed in cosplay."

"Cosplay?" Heathcliff wrinkled his nose. "Is that some kind of venereal disease?"

I laughed as I pushed my bra straps down and pulled it out through the sleeve of my Joy Division t-shirt. "No, although it can definitely ensure you'll never have sex again. It's short for 'costume play' and it's where people dress up as their favorite characters from books, TV, movies, or comics. Here, hold this up."

Heathcliff held up a towel while I tugged off my t-shirt and skinny jeans and pulled on the costume. I couldn't believe I managed to find all the components of a halfway decent Princess Leia outfit in my wardrobe. Once I'd pulled on the dress, I slipped Heathcliff's phone from his pocket and loaded up a video tutorial I found on Kate Danvers' website on recreating her iconic side-buns. Quoth helped me shove pins in my hair as Heathcliff stared at us like we were both aliens.

"And you're joining their ranks because... you never want to have sex again?"

"Hey, for some people, this outfit is a wet dream come to life. But no, *I'm* here to talk to Dave about giving a workshop at the first annual Nevermore Bookshop Science Fiction and Fantasy Convention." I winked at him. Heathcliff shuddered. "And while I'm at it, Quoth is going to search his house, while you wait out here in case either of us gets in trouble."

Heathcliff sighed. "This is exactly the kind of harebrained scheme Moriarty would've come up with."

I shrugged. "What can I say – the Napoleon of Crime has rubbed off on me."

I smoothed down the front of my costume and walked across the street. Quoth soared ahead of me and disappeared into the overgrown front garden of the small townhouse. I stared at the silver number on the door, mulling over what I was about to do. Dave Danvers had just lost his wife for the second time, and I didn't want to compound his pain by lying to him.

But I needed answers, and he had them.

And besides, a science fiction convention at Nevermore Bookshop could be fun. It'll make Heathcliff blow smoke out his ears, which is almost worth all the hassle. I wonder if I can get him into a Han Solo costume...

By Isis, I really do sound like Morrie.

I knocked.

For the longest time, I heard nothing. Just as I raised my fist to knock again, footsteps shuffled across tile and the door swung back to reveal a short man in his thirties wearing a Spider-Man t-shirt. I recognized him instantly from the picture Sherlock had back at the cabin. He wiped a beefy hand across his face, sweeping a greasy lock of hair behind his ear and staring up at me with the biggest, kindest brown eyes I'd ever seen.

"Hi, are you Dave?"

"Mina?" Dave held his hand out, and I shook it. I expected it to be clammy because I was a terrible person with no respect for geeks, but it was warm and firm. Dave threw the door open and gestured for me to come inside. "Come on in. Love the costume. I'm sorry the place is a bit of a mess."

Every surface in the short hallway was crowded with nerdy memorabilia. As I toed off my boots, I got a close look at a couple of the photographs on the wall, and saw they were of Dave and Kate in various costumes, standing on stages or engaged in mock battles. One of them was of the pair of them wearing Hogwarts robes and blazers fighting a Death Eater outside one of the Oxford colleges. *They look like they had a lot of fun together.*

Dave led me through to a living room piled with things. Plastic figurines of orcs and robots crowded the shelves on either side of the fireplace. More shelves behind the sofa overflowed with books, boxes of comics, and DVD boxsets. A tangle of video console cords waited under the TV to ensnare an unwary visitor. Dave cleared a stack of horror novels off the sofa so I could sit down.

"Would you like a cup of tea?"

"Sure. Thanks." As Dave pottered in the kitchen, I caught sight of a black shadow hopping down the hallway. *Quoth is in the house.*

Dave returned, carrying a steaming mug shaped like a cauldron. "I thought you'd appreciate the cup," he smiled, and my heart broke for him. I couldn't even imagine going through what he'd experienced, and yet, here he was being a gracious host.

"I do." The mug was actually awesome. I'd have to ask him

where to get one. "Thanks so much for seeing me. I know this can't be an easy time for you, I heard on the convention grapevine about your wife—"

"I *want* to do it. Kate loved cosplay. She said it made her feel powerful to pretend to be someone else for a day." Dave turned away for a moment, his shoulders sagging. I noticed a giant bald patch on the back of his head. "I think she'd be happy knowing I was helping other people to come out of their shell with cosplay. I keep thinking that maybe if she got into the scene earlier, she might not have done what she did."

"What do you mean? I thought someone killed her."

"I don't really want to talk about it," Dave said.

Damn. "I'm sorry for prying. Let's talk about the convention instead. It's going to be smaller than the kind of conventions you're used to, but I've got a couple of amazing science fiction authors I can invite along, and we'll make a big book display. Maybe you could show some slides of the costumes you and Kate have done, and then talk about how people can create their own costumes, and then maybe you could judge the costume competition."

Dave beamed. "I'd love that. Sometimes people think creating elaborate costumes requires lots of money, but it doesn't have to. Kate was great at hunting out bargains at the charity shops and crafting details and realistic weapons from cheap materials. But if you really love a character you might want to spend a bit more. There's this old castle up the road called Briarwood – a young Irish fella who lives there is an artist with a blacksmithing forge. He makes these incredible sculptures, and he's done fantasy armor for a few members of our community."

Hmmm. I wonder if the artist is one of Maeve's boyfriends.

We hammered out some details, then Dave offered to show me some of the costumes he and Kate worked on together. I followed him into the hallway. Dave paused in front of the photographs. I recognized Kate from the pictures in the paper. In this one, she was dressed as some popular anime character in a short pleated skirt, white knee-high socks, and clutching an intricate magical staff. "There's Kate on the happiest day of her life. She won the cup for the best cosplay at the London FanCon. This was six months before she…" he trailed off.

"Dave, are you okay?" I could hear rustling upstairs as Quoth searched the rooms, but Dave didn't seem to register it. His eyes had glassed over, and he stared at Kate's picture as if it alone could give him the answers he needed.

"It just doesn't make any sense," he muttered.

"What doesn't?"

"Last year, when the police found that note…" Dave's Adam's apple bobbed up and down as he swallowed several times. "It hurt so much, but at least it made a kind of sense. Kate had been withdrawing from life, from me. Ever since she started working at that company, Ticketrrr, she'd been struggling with her mental health. I tried everything I could to make her happy. We even took all our savings to start our own fan event company – something she dreamed about doing her whole life – but it wasn't going as well as we hoped. The money stressed Kate out, but I could tell that wasn't the only thing bothering her. I tried to get her to talk to me, to a therapist, to anyone, but she closed herself off. And then I got the phone call…" Dave shuddered, bowing his head, lost in the memories.

I stepped up to him, placing my hand on his back, wondering if he'd appreciate a hug. Dave continued in a shaking voice. "I was devastated, but at least I could understand. Only, now I find out she's been alive all this time – the police think she deliberately faked her death, which is *insane*. It's like something from a movie. And as if that wasn't enough, someone *murdered* her. She was the most precious person in the world to me, and someone hated her enough to…" he shook his head. "I didn't know Kate at all. I can't believe she would do this. We were in such dire straits with our finances, and it even crossed my mind she might have done it so

I'd get the insurance money, but then we didn't get a payout, so..."

My head snapped up. "No life insurance? But they pay out in the case of suicides if—"

Dave shook his head. "I thought so, too. But the insurance company refused to pay out because we didn't have a body. They said that after the Canoe Man case a few years back, they were being more strict about suicides where the family was in financial trouble. I guess they were right to be cautious since it turns out she wasn't dead at all."

Shite. Morrie didn't know that. He thought he was helping Kate get that money for Dave, but really her death just caused more pain.

"The irony is, now that she's been murdered, I get paid out the insurance." Dave's lower lip trembled. "I'd much rather have my wife back. But I still can't understand who would want to do that to Kate. The police think it's the guy she paid to help her fake her death, but It's just too unbelievable."

"Surely the police must have asked you if Kate had any enemies? Anyone who would have wanted her dead?"

"They did, but they seemed convinced they already had their man. Apparently, he's on the run now, which I guess means he must be guilty, but..." Dave jabbed the picture of Kate with her trophy so hard it rattled against the wall. I leaned forward, my nose touching the glass as I squinted where his finger was pointing. Behind Kate was a crowd of people in costumes, all of them grinning and applauding except for one girl wearing an identical costume to Kate. She scowled at the camera, her arms folded across an ample chest. "That's Tara Delphine. She runs a popular cosplay Youtube channel, and she was a guest of honor at FanCon. She always has a line of adoring fans waiting to get her autograph, and you'd think that would be enough, but no. Tara couldn't stand it that Kate's cosplay won the grand prize. A few minutes after this photo was taken, Tara jumped on stage and tried to wrestle the trophy out of Kate's hands. She threatened Kate right in front of everyone – you can see it on YouTube. Tara's had it out for Kate for years, but of course, the police didn't seem to think she was a suspect. There were some shoeprints at the crime scene, but they're too large for Tara's feet."

The footprints Sherlock found, the ones that exactly matched Morrie's brogues. But if someone wanted to frame Morrie, they could have just worn different shoes, especially if they were someone used to creating costumes...

My mind whirred with possibilities. "Anyone else?"

Dave tapped his chin. "Yeah. Kate wouldn't talk to me about her job. After a while, she just shut down. But it was definitely a big source of her anxiety, and the main reason she desperately wanted our company to succeed. A few months ago she let slip that her boss, Grant Hosking, found a picture of her on the internet in one of her cosplay outfits and pinned it beside his desk."

"That's gross."

"You're telling me. I told Kate to make a formal complaint. She did, but nothing came of it. She worked for a tech company. It's a boy's club." Dave's face darkened, and his hands formed into fists. "Hosking told my wife it was *her* fault for having the photographs on the internet in the first place. She became known as a troublemaker, so she stopped being asked for Friday night drinks or given roles on important projects. I think she was only invited to the leadership summits because Grant wanted to sleep with her."

"So this Grant was on the wilderness adventure with her?"

Dave nodded. "She went to two, including the one where she... Grant was at both. I didn't want her to go. We had a big row about it, but Kate insisted she had to stand up to him. When Kate strode out the door that day, I thought she was determined that she wasn't going to let Grant intimidate her anymore." Dave turned away, his shoulders heaving. "I had no idea she meant to—"

As Dave broke into sobs, a small, dark shape appeared at the top of the stairs. With one hand making soothing circles on Dave's back, I pulled open the front door. Quoth hopped down the stairs. His feathers brushed my ankle as he escaped out the door and dived into the rosebushes.

"I'm so sorry, Dave. I didn't mean to bring all this up."

"No, I'm sorry." Dave swiped at his eyes. "I didn't mean to lay all this on your shoulders. I don't have many people to talk to these days. Kate and I convinced all our friends to invest in our events company, and when that went under... Anyway, I have to stay strong, and it's hard sometimes. You seem so nice, Mina, and I—"

I'm not as nice as you think. I wrapped my arms around Dave, squeezing him tight. I didn't normally hug strangers, but in this case, it felt right. "Thank you for opening up to me. I'm happy I could be here when you needed someone, even though we don't know each other very well. Sometimes it's easier to open up to strangers, you know?"

He sniffed. "Yeah. You're right."

"You've got my number. If you need anything, let me know. I'll call you next week with details about the event."

I waited for Dave to close the door before I headed back across the road. Heathcliff glowered at me as I sat down opposite him and started to pull the pins from my hair.

Quoth stepped out from behind a shrubbery in his human form, tugging down his t-shirt. My mouth watered, and I almost begged him to leave it off. That boy was too beautiful to exist.

"Did Mina's feather-brained scheme turn up anything?" Heathcliff growled at Quoth.

"Dave's closet is a strange and remarkable place. He has two drawers full of what I'd call normal clothing and the rest is skintight catsuits and superhero capes." Quoth plucked a black feather from his hair, then bent down to tie the laces on his New Rock boots. Since he started art school he'd been dabbling in gothic fashion – floaty poet shirts and leather pants – and I had to say I approved. "He's still got Kate's costumes, too, unless he likes to wear school-girl uniforms."

"Having Kate's costumes nearby probably helps him grieve," I said.

"That's not all I found." Quoth straightened up. "University transcripts and job applications in the office drawer – Dave has a Master's in computer science, but it looks like he couldn't find a job, so he'd been working for his dad's plumbing company. I also found bills. Lots and lots of bills. Kate was top of her class, as well, but that couldn't keep them out of financial strife. Kate and Dave sank a ton of money into putting on a fan convention in Crookshollow, and it tanked, big time. They lost all their investors' money along with their own, and they still have debts to pay. Even with the two of them working they couldn't stay above water, and now that it's just Dave things are a hundred times worse."

"Didn't he get the insurance money?" Heathcliff asked.

I shook my head as I tore off the Leia outfit and replaced it with my Joy Division shirt. "Nope. The insurance company wouldn't pay without a body. It sounds like a new policy – Morrie couldn't have known that. Although now that Kate's shown up dead Dave will get the money after all."

"You realize that gives Dave motive to murder his wife."

I snapped my head up. "I don't think so. You had to meet him. He cried when he was talking about Kate. There's no way Dave's the murderer. But I do have a couple of leads." I told them about cosplaying rival Tara and Grant, Kate's boss at Ticketrrr.

"Neither of those people has any connection to Morrie," Heathcliff pointed out.

"We don't know that for sure, and besides – they don't have to be connected with Morrie to want to frame him. That's what

Sherlock doesn't understand. This doesn't seem like it came from the criminal underground to me – I think someone saw Morrie as a convenient scapegoat, nothing more."

"They do seem like solid possibilities," Quoth said. "Although those footprints at the scene... whoever framed Morrie took the time to steal his shoes. This was carefully planned, and that means that at the very least the murderer had to be close enough to Kate to know she faked her death."

"If Morrie were here, he'd volunteer to interrogate the scantily-clad one," Heathcliff said.

"Not strictly true," I grinned at the memory as I linked arms with Heathcliff and Quoth, and the three of us meandered toward the train station. "Remember when he made you have dinner with Amanda Letterman to find out if she knew who garroted Danny Sledge?"

Heathcliff shuddered. "My body still bears the scars."

From the train station, we took the long way back to Nevermore, circling through the back streets on the edge of the village to avoid the town green and any nosy villagers. We walked down beside the abandoned station where the local homeless population congregated. I waved at Earl Larson, who hung out the window of a rusting train car, smoking a cigarette with his kitten curled on top of his head.

"At least we get a few days of peace and quiet," Heathcliff muttered, pushing open the door to the shop. "Without Morrie around—"

He stopped dead, his body stiffening as his head swooped in all directions, taking in the damage my mother had wrought.

I squinted, trying to see what he saw, but the place looked almost... normal. If a little bare without all the weird taxidermy and Quoth's art on the walls.

Heathcliff clearly saw something I didn't, because he stomped through to the main room, practically bowling over two customers who scrambled to get out of his way. I raced after him, grabbing his shoulders as he loomed over the desk. My mother yelped as she looked up from behind a stack of envelopes in fright.

Heathcliff slammed his fist on the ancient till. "Ms. Wilde, what have you done to my shop?"

CHAPTER TEN

*M*um's eyes widened as she set down the envelope she'd been addressing, peering at Heathcliff over the top of her reading glasses. "Whatever do you mean?"

What is it? What's happened?

In a panic, I raced around the room, flicking on all the lights and lamps so I could peer into every corner. I *still* couldn't see anything wrong. The shop was neat – tidier than when we left it, actually. A few of the shelves seemed a little out-of-order, but that was typical after customers came in and messed them up.

Heathcliff glared at me, and I realized what he was getting at.

The shop appeared *normal*.

Too normal.

Mum hadn't changed a thing. She hadn't put up a display of financial planning guides or offered energy healing sessions or started a smoothie bar. I sniffed. There was a slightly fishy smell in the air, but we kept a bowl of wet food for Grimalkin behind the poetry shelves and it was probably that. I pulled one of the envelopes off the stack and noticed she'd carefully lettered a customer's name and filled out the customs slip.

"These are books?" Heathcliff leafed through the stack. "Our books? You sold them all?"

"I certainly did! I sold them all online. You have a lot of engaged customers on the shop's Facebook page, desperate for a little personal service. And look, I've kept track of all my sales in the ledger." Mum shoved the page under my face.

"That's... that's amazing, Mum." And I meant it. She'd sold more books in a few hours than Heathcliff usually did in a *week*.

"And you both doubted me," she sounded a little hurt. "You thought I wasn't responsible enough to look after the shop."

I scanned the titles in the ledger. *The Pearl*, John Steinbeck. *Girl with a Pearl Earring*, Tracy Chevalier. *Pearl Harbor: the Hidden History*, *Pearl Jam: The Unauthorized Biography...*

Hmmmm. I'm sensing a pattern.

My mother-senses tingling, I set down the book and sniffed the air. That fishy smell was quite pronounced near the desk, more so than I'd expect from Grimalkin's food. "Does it smell faintly of fish in here?"

"That's just my lunch."

I whipped around. My grandmother sat on the couch, clothed (praise the goddesses), long legs tucked beneath her, that sensuous cat-ate-the-cream smile playing on her lips. "Helen and I had fish and chips. Divine. I declare fish and chips covered in vinegar to be the food of the gods."

Shit. I glared at her. *You were supposed to stay upstairs. Who does Mum think you are?*

Mum beamed over at Grimalkin. "Mina, meet me new friend, Cat."

"We've met." I folded my arms.

"I'm often slinking in and out of the shop," Grimalkin purred. "I love all the dark corners in here, just perfect for hiding secrets."

I know. I've stood on one too many of your secrets in the middle of the night and ended up with mouse guts between my toes.

"Cat came in to find a book on spinning yarn, and we got to

talking. She's been helping me around the shop. We've had quite an eventful day. A mouse ran across the Children's room and Cat chased it right outside." Mum held her hand over her heart. "It gave me such a fright, I had to buy her lunch. Did you know that new bloke who owns the bakery is doing fish and chips now? They're *divine*. Cat agrees they're the best in Argleton, and the handsome man serving them is a definite bonus."

"Me-*ow*." Grimalkin raked her nails through the air like claws and shot me a look that clearly said now that Mum was supplying her with fish, she'd forgiven Helen Wilde for that whole seducing her son and causing him to be trapped in time thing.

"Right, well, if there's nothing else, I'll be going." Mum leaned across and kissed my cheek. The fishy smell was quite strong around her, but I guessed she just hadn't washed her hands after lunch.

As she swung herself toward the hallway, her bag bumped my side, and the corner of something large and sharp jabbed into my leg.

"What have you got in there, Mum?" I had a vision of her removing one of the occult books from the shop and unwittingly summoning the demon hordes of hell for tea.

Heathcliff must've had the same idea, because I'd never seen him move so fast. In a flash, he crossed the room, dug his giant hand into Mum's tote bag, and pulled out a shiny rectangular object.

I leaned closer, my stomach clenching as I searched the object for occult symbols. *By Isis, that's not a book at all. It almost looks like...*

A laptop?

My mother didn't own a laptop. She could barely change the channels on the telly. She didn't understand technology, and judging by the way our microwave cowered in fear every time she approached, technology wasn't fond of her, either.

So why did she have a laptop? And quite a fancy one, by the looks of it.

Mum grabbed the laptop from Heathcliff's hands. "That's mine. I bought it from the proceeds I got from selling off my Flourish business to an aspiring young entrepreneur. I'm using it to set up a website for my tarot business. I want to do readings over the internet. And I play solitaire, okay? I'll thank you not to dig around in a lady's purse, young man. If this is the way I'm treated just for doing you a favor, I have half a mind not to offer my services in future."

"We're sorry. We didn't mean anything by it." *We just thought you were trying to sneak off with a dangerous book.* I hugged her again. "Thank you so much for your help today. We appreciate it; really, we do. We were actually going to ask if you'd be able to come in regularly over the next two weeks. I have to go back to Crookshollow for more guide dog training, and this weekend, Heathcliff, Allan and I have a… um, team building event to attend."

"Should you really be leaving the village so much, after what happened to you?" Mum's mouth twisted with worry. "I don't want those nasty kidnappers to come back for you."

"I'll be fine. I've cleared it with Detective Hayes. I know it seems strange, but honestly, the only way I'm coping right now is by distracting myself with work and training." *And hunting for the person who killed Kate and framed Morrie, but I'll keep that to myself.*

I told Mum all about Oscar and how much I loved him. She kissed me again and left us alone. As I watched her stroll off toward the green, Grimalkin leaped across the room in her cat form and practically plastered herself to the window. "Meow?" She scraped her claws along the glass, as if despairing that Mum would ever return.

I narrowed my eyes at the former cat. "Care to explain yourself? Last month my mother was public enemy number one."

Grimalkin's whiskers twitched, as if she was saying, "that was before I got to know her. I believe we're going to be good friends."

Something strange is going on. The two of them are up to something.

But I already had a more important mystery to focus on. Heathcliff flipped the shop sign to CLOSED and locked up downstairs. I dragged my weary body up to the flat and headed to the kitchen. Tea was essential. I flipped the kettle on to boil and pulled out four clean mugs before staring at Morrie's and shoving it back on the shelf.

Tears pricked in my eyes. *Don't fall apart, Mina. Just shove the mug where you won't stare at it.* I bent down to hide it at the back of the cupboard under the sink. As I did, my hand brushed the edge of an unopened cat food box.

Weird. I could have sworn I'd finished a packet of food yesterday. Why hadn't Mum opened another one for Grimalkin? She was supposed to feed her breakfast.

But Mum was unpredictable. I'd left her specific instructions on what and how much to feed Grimalkin. And that didn't include fish from the bakery. Come to think of it, Mum's handbag had smelled a little fishy, too. Probably she had some kind of organic, vitamin-infused cat food from one of her get-rich-quick schemes in there. I'd feel sorry for Grimalkin, but she seemed to enjoy it.

I unlocked the door to our room and slumped on the bed, arranging the pillows under the brightest lamp. I sipped my tea as I slipped Heathcliff's phone from his discarded jacket pocket (it wasn't like he'd miss it), downloaded my favorite apps, and scrolled around on the hunt for Tara Delphine.

I didn't have to look for long. The first search result brought me to her Instagram profile. She had over fifty thousand followers – judging by their comments, mostly grotty old men fishing for the slip of a nipple. Most of her images showed her posing coquettishly in skintight superhero outfits.

No slut-shaming from me. Truthfully, Tara's outfits looked

fierce. She had this Harley Quinn ensemble I would *kill* for. But I could see that Kate's cosplays showed a higher quality. Many of the characters Kate cosplayed were already heavily sexualized – she didn't feel the need to exaggerate that further. I liked how in her pictures Kate showed the characters at their most confident and powerful, and tried to bring across something of her own personality as well.

Tara's website had her listed as doing a fan meet-and-greet as the cosplay guest of honor at FanCon down in London. The event was on this week for five days, but since we were already going to Wild Oats over the weekend, we'd have to fit in a visit on Friday.

But I have to go to guide dog training. And Inspector Hayes will want to know why I'm so interested in going to London—

Hang on. Edie said she wanted to take me and Oscar to a more populated and unfamiliar area so we could practice the commands I learned. I dialed Edie. When I told her I wanted to make a trip to London because Heathcliff was totally obsessed with Tara Delphine and he had tickets to meet her but I'd forgotten about it in my excitement, she thought it would be the perfect training outing for us. "Oscar and I will meet you at the Argleton station at 10AM tomorrow."

Perfect. That gave me just enough time to meet Jo for breakfast. I needed to get the skinny on Kate's autopsy results and figure out just how deep in the shite Morrie was.

～

*E*ven though Heathcliff and Quoth wrapped themselves around me, I barely slept. I stared at the ceiling while the guys made adorable squeaking sounds, thinking about Morrie stuck in that cabin with only his ex-boyfriend for company. I ran over the details of the case over and over, but I couldn't see a clear suspect. So much didn't make sense.

If Kate successfully faked her death and escaped to the Philippines, what made her come back? Why was she in Barsetshire Fells? She must have been meeting someone...

And the question no one else seemed to want to ask, but that niggled at me more than anything. Why did Kate decide to fake her own death in the first place? I was certain the answer to that question was the key to solving the mystery and clearing Morrie's name.

Eventually, I fell into a fitful sleep, waking to an angry alarm and Heathcliff snoring beside me. Quoth was already at the stove filling a bowl with nuts and berries when I padded into the kitchen. He handed me a mug of tea because he was amazing. I drank it as I swiped on some makeup, pulled on a long-sleeve skater dress covered in tiny bones I'd screen-printed myself, added my cherry Docs and my favorite bat purse, slipped Heathcliff's phone (now my phone) into my pocket, and headed outside to meet Jo.

It was a surprisingly beautiful day for February in England. With sunlight pouring down, drying the rain, I could see. A rogue lime-green squiggle of light flashed across my vision, but I was too distracted by a weird noise emitting from Heathcliff's phone.

It's never made that noise before.

I pulled the phone from my pocket and held it up to my face to peer at the screen. An alert flashed across the screen.

WARNING: POSSIBLE DRACULA EVENT

Morrie's algorithm. In all the chaos of being kidnapped and Morrie going into hiding and trying to clear his name, I'd almost forgotten the looming shadow that threatened not just Nevermore Bookshop, but the entire world. Count Dracula was here in England, and he was enacting the plan he tried to carry out in Bram Stoker's book before Van Helsing and his crew stopped him.

I clicked on the link. A news headline buzzed on the screen. Beneath numerous links to stories about Morrie's disappearance and pleas from the police to help if the public catch sight of him, was a piece about a robbery in the nearby village of Lower Loxham. A garden center specializing in collectible plants had two rare Romanian orchids stolen last night.

My heart pattered. Lower Loxham was only a forty-mile drive from Argleton. If Dracula was this close—

SMACK.

I slammed into something hard, sending me sprawling to the cobbles. I winced as my tailbone bounced on hard stone and Heathcliff's phone clattered from my hand.

"Mina, I'm so sorry." The wobbly shape standing above me resolved into my best friend. Jo held out her hand. I took it, and she hauled me to my feet. "I was just coming to see you at the shop. I called out to you and I thought you saw me, but by the time I realized you hadn't I was in your way and—"

"It's okay." I rubbed my tailbone. "I shouldn't have been staring at a screen while I walked. And there's no need to be my seeing-eye friend. I've walked the path to the bakery so many times, I can do it sleepwalking or blindfolded or in the middle of a zombie apocalypse."

"Noted. I probably would've been more help saving us a table. Apparently, the new fish and chips are a big hit, and the place is already packed. But speaking of seeing-eye friends, how's the guide dog training?" Jo grabbed the phone off the ground and peered at the screen. "I know you have pictures."

I swiped the phone from her, heart pounding. *If she sees Morrie's app, she'll demand to know what's going on.*

Jo frowned, her hand still hanging in the air. "Are you okay? I know this Morrie thing must have you worried, but Mina, if you're in communication with him, you need to tell the police—"

"No! I mean, yes! I mean... I'm sorry." I laughed, but it came out sounding forced. "I didn't mean to snatch the phone. I *am* worried as hell, but I haven't heard from Morrie. I guess... I'm still jumpy after that guy kidnapped us. It's so surreal – I'm still processing, you know. It feels like it happened to someone else."

"I know. That's a classic reaction to trauma." Jo wrapped her arm around me as we headed to the bakery. "But don't you think you should be at home, giving yourself a break for once?"

"Nope. I need to stay busy or I'll go crazy. Besides, training with my new guide dog is keeping my mind off Morrie. I did meet him yesterday. His name is Oscar, and he's the absolute cutest. And yes, I do have pictures."

I scrolled through Heathcliff's feed, my heart warming at just how many photographs he'd taken of Oscar and I navigating the obstacle course. He even had a video of me giving Oscar the commands to walk straight and turn left or right. My heart rate returned to normal as we got in line for our treats. Jo must not have seen anything about Dracula on the phone, because she was the type of person to have called me on it immediately.

Ever since I discovered the baker, Greta, was guilty of murdering Gladys Scarlett – town matriarch and head of the Banned Book Club – the bakery on the corner of Butcher Street had stood empty, much to the town's chagrin. It was a testament to how much the British love our pies and slices that the village petitioned the court to have Greta's sentence shortened so she could get back to her shop sooner. Fortunately, common sense prevailed and the poisoner was still safely behind bars.

Luckily, just after Christmas a new baker moved in. Not only was Oliver Swinbourne a great chef with a flair for the best coffee in Argleton, but he was tall and broad-shouldered and easy on the eye. (Not that I could be relied upon any longer in that department, but my mother, Mrs. Ellis, and Grimalkin were smitten, and Jo confirmed he was a damn fine specimen).

Visiting the Daily Bread bakery with my morning coffee orders became a much more enjoyable chore, let me tell you.

"Hey, ladies," Oliver beamed as we stepped up to the counter. "What's your pleasure?"

"Heathcliff got your fish and chips for dinner the other night, and they were *amazing*," I grinned. "Is there anything you can't do? You're going to give all the men of this village an inferiority complex."

Oliver tapped the blackboard behind him, which I couldn't read but I presumed listed the fish and chip options. "I've already had three offers of marriage since putting my shingle out. What'll it be, ladies? I'm afraid I don't start serving my marriage-wrecking fish-and-chips until eleven."

"Two flat whites," Jo said. "And we'll try two of your steak and kidney pies."

"Oh, and treacle tarts," I exclaimed, peering into the counter. Someone behind me in line made a comment about me putting my nose on the glass (it wasn't) but I ignored them.

"You're lucky," Oliver said as he handed over our tarts. "If that developer chap has anything to say about it, these will be the last pies I ever bake."

"What do you mean?" A thought occurred to me. "Not Grey Lachlan?"

Oliver pointed behind us shoulder to a man retreating across the green toward the pub. From this distance, he was just a blur to me. "The one and same. He's been in here every day trying to buy the building out from under me. He keeps upping his offer, but I'm not budging. I came into an inheritance, see? I own the entire building right up to your bookshop, including two flats and the butchery and the flower shop next door. I love this town and I don't want to sell up – Lachlan won't move me unless it's in a body bag."

"That's the spirit." Jo bit into the treacle tart Oliver handed her. "This village needs you."

Interesting. After striking out with Heathcliff, Grey's trying to buy up the buildings around the bookshop. That can't be a coincidence.

"So…" I slid into the table across from Jo. She sorted through the mug of sugar packets and handed me the coconut one I liked. It was amazing how quickly we'd fallen into this pattern – Jo saw that I had difficulty with something and so she just did it. It was weird, because I usually felt frustrated about the things I couldn't do myself anymore, but Jo handing me that sugar without making a big thing of it made a happy lump rise in my throat. *She's a great friend.* "What did you learn from the autopsy?"

"You know I'm not supposed to be sharing details of an active case with you, *especially* since you're the girlfriend of our chief suspect."

"So Morrie's still a suspect? Jo, you know he wouldn't murder someone. And I don't care what Hayes believes – he's not in cahoots with his kidnappers. I was with Morrie when they took us – he was just as confused and scared as I was."

I hate hate hate lying to my friend. But if it keeps Morrie safe while we find the killer…

"I only know what the evidence shows." Jo bit into her pie. "As for Morrie… how well can we ever truly know a person, anyway? Think about all the murders you've helped solve. Not one of those people seemed like the textbook definition of a brutal killer, and yet they were stabbing and poisoning and garroting up the village. I didn't know Morrie was operating a death-faking business, and from your face I'm guessing you didn't either. We can always be surprised by the people you thought you knew."

I nodded, toying with the sugar packet. "Is his business against the law?"

"It's a legal grey area." Jo sipped her coffee. "Technically, faking your death isn't a crime – it's all the things you need to do after you've faked your death, like insurance fraud, forgery, identity theft – that can land you in trouble."

Legal grey area – that's Morrie's favorite type of area.

I wrapped my arms around myself. "You *have* to let me know

what the police have on him. *Please.* I'm going crazy not knowing what's going on. I *was* kidnapped, if you recall."

"Yes, you were." Jo reached across the table and squeezed my hand. "Are you sure you're okay? That must've been scary."

I nodded. I hated lying to my best friend, but Jo was a scientist. She liked everything to have a logical explanation. 'My boyfriends are fictional heroes brought to life by a magical bookshop and my father is the poet Homer who fancies himself a vampire slayer' was not going to fly with her. "I'm better when I'm not thinking about it. Which is why I was hoping you'd distract me with grisly autopsy details."

"Fine." Jo leaned forward. "You know I can't resist talking about work, anyway. So here's the lowdown. Kate disappeared last year. She was seen talking with a guy who fits Morrie's description at a village pub a few hours before she got on a bus to the wilderness center. She was with a big group of blokes on a survival course as part of a company retreat, and the pub staff recall she seemed withdrawn, and the men didn't talk to her unless it was to make lewd comments. She was the only woman in the group. On the last night of the retreat, she left her camp and was never seen again. A note pinned to her shelter – written in her own hand – let police to believe her death was a suicide. But then she showed up a week ago, murdered."

Jo swallowed. "On her body was a business card that led the police and MI5 back to Morrie's death faking business. There was some contamination of the crime scene, but shoe prints have been identified near the body that match Morrie's signature brogues *exactly*, and I found dried mud on a pair of his beside Nevermore's front door. In the lab I was able to match pollen in the mud with the unique flora of the wood – Morrie was at the crime scene."

"Or someone wore his shoes there, to frame him."

Jo shifted in her chair. "This is why I didn't want to tell you this. I knew it would be upsetting to you. Look, according to your statement, Morrie doesn't have an alibi for the day of the murder. You and Heathcliff were in the shop, and you said Morrie was down in London. We have CCTV footage of him arriving at Charing Cross, but we can't confirm when he returned. It's possible he went to London, then doubled back to Barsetshire Fells."

"I'm sure as soon as the police find Morrie, he'll be able to explain what he was doing in London and provide an alibi. He's often there for business—"

"Mmmhmmm, an alibi for his not-totally-legal fake death business. That won't be at all suspicious." Jo pushed her mince pie away from her, even though she'd hardly eaten a bite. "There's one more thing you should know. The blade that stabbed Kate was a letter opener, quite a distinctive one, shaped like a sword. We found it in a bin in Barset Reach the day after Kate's body was discovered, covered in her blood. I lifted Morrie's print from the handle. And look at this."

Jo dug out her phone and flipped through to a picture taken at one of our many Friday night drinks. Jo, Morrie, and I stood in front of the blazing fire, dressed in ridiculous costumes. Jo pretended to faint while Morrie held a jewel-encrusted letter opener to my throat. "That's the *exact* weapon we found. It didn't just look like the letter opener you have at the shop. It *was* the letter opener from the shop."

I swallowed. Once. Twice. Three times.

Morrie's print on the murder weapon.

Morrie doesn't have an alibi for Kate's murder.

Morrie's shoes are covered with mud.

This doesn't look good. In fact, if I didn't know better, I'd say Morrie did it.

Jo studied my face as I digested the information. Was that the look of a concerned friend, or was she seeing how I reacted, gauging if I was in on the crime? I shoved the thought away. Jo would tell me if I was in trouble here.

"Um…" I struggled to form words. "Is there… is there any evidence that supports my conviction that Morrie is innocent?"

"Actually, yes." Relief crossed Jo's face. "So, the face was pretty scraped up and decomposed, which doesn't help with ID, but DNA came back positive – the body is definitely Kate Danvers, although she's put on weight since she was last seen alive. The strangest thing is that she wasn't killed by the stabbing. She died by ingesting poisonous mushrooms."

"What?"

Jo nodded. "I know. Weird, right? You'd have thought the first thing she learned on that wilderness survival course was how to distinguish edible spores from the deadly ones. And there was something else weird, too. She lost a lot of blood – more than I'd expect from a knife wound inflicted post-mortem. I found two small puncture marks on her body, but I can't tell if they're related to the blood loss.

Puncture marks? My mind immediately went to Dracula, who was out there, getting stronger and closing in on me with every passing day. But that was crazy – the whole world didn't revolve around me and my enemy. To think otherwise was pure selfishness. No, Kate Danvers was murdered by a person, not a vampire.

I tuned back into Jo "—the stabbing took place a few hours after death, probably even more. None of this exonerates Morrie, but it does show that this murder is more complex than it first appeared."

"Any other physical evidence?"

"Yes. She'd been banged up pretty badly, but all the bruises had been administered post-mortem. The working theory is that the killer stabbed her at a remote site near the top of the ridge and then dragged her through the forest to the fallen log, but I can't see that tracking with the pattern of bruising right now."

Take that, Sherlock. I bet you couldn't tell all that with your nineteenth-century methods. Modern science will prove you wrong yet.

Even though my mind was reeling, I squeezed my friend's hand. "Thank you so much for telling me the truth, even though it was ugly. I can see how bad things look for Morrie, but I still believe he's innocent."

"I know, me too." We held each other's gaze, and I could sense Jo searching my features for some clue, some sign that I knew more than I revealed.

She knows something's up.

That suspicion could come from anywhere. I was keeping several secrets from Jo. I wished I could break down and tell her the truth about who the guys really were and the strange things that happened in Nevermore Bookshop, and the ultimate danger of Dracula. But I knew that was a Pandora's Box that once opened, couldn't be closed. I'd never had a girlfriend like Jo before, and I wanted her to stay my friend. I was afraid that if I told her about the magical bookshop, she'd decide I was bonkers and never talk to me again.

I couldn't handle her looking at me with pity. So I held my secrets tighter, and distance stretched between us.

Jo walked me back to the shop, where Heathcliff was handing over the keys to Mum. Because we were going to London, where there were people everywhere, Quoth decided he would be joining us in his raven form, which meant Heathcliff was swinging a giant black birdcage under one arm.

"Are we sure this is a good idea?" I peered at Quoth. "Will they even let him into FanCon?"

"Sure they will." Heathcliff stepped into the street. He was dressed in a crisp white poet shirt. My jaw hit the ground.

"What... are you?"

"All the weirdos wear costumes to this event, so I'm Edgar Allen Poe. Quoth is my stuffed raven, part of my costume. He's been practicing perching still." Heathcliff tapped Quoth's foot, and he froze in place, his eyes wide. It was pretty impressive – I really couldn't tell he was alive.

A giggle burst from my throat. "You said you weren't going to be a part of any crazy schemes, and here you are with the wackiest scheme of all."

"You're not the only one who's learned a few tricks from the criminal genius. Let's go." Heathcliff yanked me around the corner, only instead of heading toward the train station, he pulled my face to his for a searing kiss.

"What was that for?"

"It was for me," he growled. "You're making me travel to that cesspool of humanity and I need fortitude."

I tangled my fingers in his hair, drawing his head down to devour him. "I'll fortitude you any time you like."

We managed to untangle ourselves just in time to dash across town. We arrived at the station just as Edie stepped off the train with Oscar in tow. He wasn't wearing his harness yet, so I bent down to pet him and scratch his ears. Oscar nuzzled up to me, his tail wagging with glee. I fancied he remembered me, and that made me so happy a lump rose in my throat.

Oscar stared up at frozen Quoth with wide eyes. But my beautiful birdie didn't move a muscle. Not a single feather twitched. To everyone else, he appeared stuffed, but I knew Oscar could smell him and was desperate to leap up and investigate. Luckily, Edie handed me the harness and we got down to business. As soon as I clipped his harness, Oscar focused on me, although his eyes followed Quoth as Heathcliff stood at the machines to purchase our tickets.

Edie handed me Oscar's leash. "He's wearing his red coat, so he's officially on the job. That means you can't allow anyone to pet him, even if they ask really nicely. And they will ask, because he's such a gorgeous boy."

"Got it."

"Good. Do you remember the command to find the escalators?"

We practiced getting on and off the escalators while a line

built behind me. Normally, I'd be mortified at making all those people wait, but no one seemed annoyed. They wanted to watch Oscar at work. One girl even had her phone out recording him.

I waited on the platform as the train pulled in. When it came to a stop, I gave Oscar the command to find the door. He took me directly to the nearest set of doors and guided me to the edge, where I could use the rail to locate the steps with my feet. We were on the train in seconds.

"Do you remember the command and gesture to ask him for a seat?" Edie asked.

I did. Oscar took me to the first empty seat he saw, which happened to be a collection of three in the disabled section nearest the doors. I told Oscar to lie down, and he draped himself over my feet like he'd been doing it his whole life, his ears pricked up. He was still working, aware of his surroundings and waiting for my next command.

I glanced across at Heathcliff, startled by the expression on his face as he watched me. Instead of his usual darkness, he features had softened into an expression that might have looked angelic on another person, but just made him appear slightly less deranged.

My heart raced a mile a minute as the train sped into London. *This is really happening. I'm really taking my guide dog into the city.* I bombarded Edie with questions about Oscar, his training, his life, the family that had socialized him before he was matched with me. Meanwhile, Oscar's eyes focused on Quoth's body, but he didn't move from his spot at my feet.

The train pulled in, and people stood back to give Oscar space to lead me off the train. He found a path through the crowds like a pro, and after a few tries practicing crossing the street, we walked to the convention center. Edie and I milled around while Heathcliff got in line for tickets, watching the strange and marvelous costumes as fans streamed past. I noticed a Ticketrrr sign by the entrance, and saw fans scanning electronic tickets on a booth and downloading a convention app. *That's the company Kate worked for – they must run the ticketing for this event. I wonder if Grant Hosking is here.*

As Edie was telling me about the mischief Oscar got up to during training, a teen girl in a Sailor Moon costume came up to us. "What a beautiful dog. Can I pat him?"

"I'm sorry, he's working," I said, firmly. Edie beamed.

Heathcliff came back and handed me and Edie each a ticket. "They won't let Quoth inside, even though I said he was part of my costume. The woman behind the desk saw through my stuffed-raven routine immediately, but she's going to watch him and feed him his berries."

We joined the throng pushing to get through the main doors. Yennefer of Vengerberg jabbed me in the side. Two Stormtroopers compared lightsaber lengths in a delightfully earnest way. Heathcliff kept close to me, his beard tickling my ear as he whispered, "These people are unsettling."

Once inside, I scanned the crowd for Tara's signing, but the place was so enormous, it was impossible to orient myself. I staggered beneath an animatronic Ent as lime-green lights danced in front of my eyes. I almost didn't notice it amongst the swirling, multi-colored crowds pouring into aisles to buy figurines, anime DVDs, and Harry Potter wands.

"Look, there's an app to help you navigate." Edie pointed to the Konnekt stall. "That company have a good reputation for accessibility—"

"No apps. They've given us a map." Heathcliff frowned at the pamphlet in his hands, turning it every which way. "But I can't comprehend it. Muggles? Rivendell? Witchers? They must've given us one in a foreign language."

"The language of Geek." I noticed a couple of girls in skintight Catwoman costumes, with hair an identical shade of pink to Tara Delphine's famous fuchsia locks. One of them had a Tara-branded tote bag slung over her shoulder. They stopped in the middle of the aisle to squeeze their heads together for a selfie, then headed toward the back of the room.

"Oscar, follow those girls!" My four-legged eyes trotted off after them, weaving through the crowd like an expert. Many people stepped out of the way as they saw me, and more than a few exclaimed over how cute he was. I saw a stall selling superhero bandanas, and made a note to stop there on our way out to pick up one for Oscar, because he was totally my hero.

Oscar reached the end of the row and stopped, his head bobbing left, then right. "Sometimes even a smart dog like Oscar can get confused, disoriented, distracted, or tired," Edie said. "He's your eyes, but he's also a living animal, and he has good days and bad days. He probably can't tell if—"

"There they are!" Heathcliff pointed to the girls, who'd joined the end of a long line, snaking through the next aisle before ending at a booth set up like a French salon. I couldn't make out the figure from this far away, but judging by the scant-amount of fabric worn by her fans, I guessed it was Tara.

We shuffled in behind the girls. "Good to see even geeks enjoy indulging in the great British pastime of queuing." Edie shuffled her feet. "Do you think you'd be okay here for a bit? I'd like to find a bathroom."

"Sure. Oscar and I have this under control."

As soon as Edie was out of earshot, Heathcliff leaned down to whisper to me. "I feel like a pervert."

I glanced down the line. He was right – every single person in the queue was a young girl in a skimpy outfit. He towered over them all. Several curious faces turned, and girls jabbed each other to get a glimpse of the brawny mass of muscle and fury that was Heathcliff Earnshaw.

"Not a pervert. You're in serious danger of stealing Tara's spotlight. Morrie would be over there right now, flirting with the staff to try and get us to the front of the queue."

"I'll save my flirting skills for Tara." Heathcliff waggled his bushy eyebrows and did his best attempt at a lovesick expression. It was the exact scowl he used when Morrie pissed him off. I burst out laughing.

The line moved quickly, and before I knew it we were standing in front of Tara. Before I could say anything, she grabbed me, holding my arms out to get a look at my outfit. "Hey, love your costume. Oh, what a cute doggie!"

She bent down to pet him. Oscar turned his head to me, his eyes wide as if to ask if this was okay.

It was not. I wrenched the leash away, annoyed. "You can't pet him, I'm sorry. He's a guide dog and he's working."

"That's silly. He wants me to pet him, look." Tara had her arms around Oscar's neck. "Look at those big, brown eyes—"

"Hi, sorry, Tara." A woman with black hair and a FanCon Staff t-shirt rushed over. She flashed me a sympathetic look. "Your fan here is blind, and this is her guide dog. You can't touch a dog like that when he's working. But why don't you sign her merch and pose for a selfie?"

"With the puppy?" Tara shrieked. "Omg, yes. This would be amazing on my Instastories. Come stand here, doggie!"

I didn't want Oscar anywhere near her. I stepped aside and shoved Heathcliff forward. "We didn't actually come for me. Heathcliff here is your biggest fan. He was wondering if you'd sign his bicep. He's going to get it tattooed."

"Oooooh." Tina ran her fingers over Heathcliff's arm, her face lighting up with glee as she took in all of his rugged, wild, Heath-cliffness. "Step right this way. I looooove meeting my male fans. Are you a member of my exclusive fan club? Because I'm offering private meet-and-greets in my hotel room after the con—"

Heathcliff shot me a 'get-me-the-fuck-out-of-here' look.

"Keep her drawing on you as long as possible," I whispered. "Get her talking about Kate."

"How the fuck do I do that?"

"Use your Heathcliff wiles."

"I don't have any of those."

"Sure you do. You're the greatest romantic hero of all time for a reason. Now get over there and romance her ass into a confession."

Heathcliff made a face like he'd rather suck an arsenic lollipop, but he allowed Tara to drag him over to a Baroque-style dressing table she'd set up with glittery pens and stickers, along with stacks of photographs of herself to sign.

"Now, Heathcliff..." his name rolled off Tara's tongue. She licked her lips as she curled her fingers into his collar. "In order to get at those bulging biceps of yours, I need you to remove your shirt."

"I'll do it." Heathcliff tore his shirt over his head. Buttons flew in all directions. A collective gasp echoed from the girls in line behind me.

I must admit, my chest fluttered, too. To see Heathcliff standing there in all his wild glory made a deep ache rumble in my core. His chest was a thing of beauty – poets should write sonnets about him. A white scar from some long-ago brawl stretched across his pecs, giving him that sinister edge that made him so completely irresistible.

Tara made no secret of her lust, flicking her tongue over her lips as she fucked him with her eyes. She held up two glitter pens. "Do you want pink or blue sparkles?"

Heathcliff collapsed into a white chair that was far too small for him. Tara bent over him, her hands trailing all over his body as she giggled. As she leaned in to start drawing, she licked his skin. Actually *licked* it.

My hands curled into fists. Oscar peered up at me, as if to ask, "Was this part of the plan?"

I have to let her do it. It's the only way to get the information we need to save Morrie.

I slunk back to stand in the line, trying to look like I didn't give a fuck that Tara was now straddling my boyfriend, grinding against his crotch as she decorated his arm with swirls and love hearts. I couldn't go back behind the velvet rope, so I ended up standing beside the two staff members.

"Typical Tina," the assistant leaned toward her friend. "She's fawning all over that guy because she knows she can get away with it, since his girlfriend's blind."

"She's disgusting. And *so* desperate. Did you see her have an argument with that Ticketrrr CEO backstage? What's his name, Grant?"

My ears perked up. *Grant and Tara are together?*

"No. Spill the deets!"

"Grant and Tara have been an item, and her latest photoshoot was sponsored by his company. She's been telling everyone she got Ticketrrr the gig here at FanCon, but in reality that was Kate's pet project. Tara seemed to believe Grant was giving her a permanent job as a Ticketrrr brand ambassador, but I heard him say he was looking for someone more 'young and fresh.' He's been over at the Ticketrrr booth all day, handing out his business card to every pretty girl who walks past and telling them to apply for jobs at his company. If he's trying to break the gender barrier in the tech industry, he's going about it the wrong way."

"I wish it was Kate here today instead of Tara," the second assistant lowered her voice. "Did you hear they found Kate's body out in those woods where she disappeared, and it wasn't suicide?"

My ears pricked up. *They know about Kate.* I shuffled closer until I was standing right beside them. I expected them to withdraw or stop their conversation, but they kept on talking as if I wasn't there. I remembered something Marjorie told me about being a blind person. "Sometimes people will treat you as if you're invisible." I knew there would be times when that would hurt like a motherfucker, but right now it was a blessing. I could spy in plain sight.

"...my friend has an in with the police, and apparently, Kate faked her suicide last year. Isn't that crazy? I bet she did it for the insurance money after that weird events company of hers folded. Only now someone's killed her for real. My money is on Tara. She wouldn't be able to bear the idea of Kate coming back and stealing her spotlight, especially since it seems like she's also trying to take Kate's old job—"

"Can I pat him?" Someone tugged on my dress.

"Oh, sure," I muttered as I strained to hear the conversation.

"—although it could've been that Grant character. I was working the bar at the FanCon VIP event last night, and he was telling everyone who'd listen that he and Kate had a sordid office affair. He said she faked her death so they could run away together, but then she just disappeared—"

No way. I can't believe that. Someone's lying, and I bet it's sleazeball Grant. I have to find a way to get a meeting with him—

"Mina!" Edie appeared in front of me, her hands on her hips. "What are you doing?"

I glanced down in horror. While I'd been focusing on eavesdropping, ten girls had broken free of the line to crowd around Oscar, stroking and patting him all over. One had even tied a giant pink bow on his collar.

"Oops. Shite." I tried to shoo them away.

Heathcliff appeared at my side, his torso covered in dripping glitter and his face and neck smeared with lipstick kisses. "I feel violated. Get me out of here."

CHAPTER ELEVEN

"*W*ell, that was… interesting." I looked pointedly at Heathcliff as we pushed our way outside. I wanted to try to get to the Ticketrrr booth, but it was packed with people and Edie was already annoyed with me about letting those girls fuss over Oscar. We'd have to figure out how to get to Grant another way.

"My nipples hurt," Heathcliff muttered as he tugged his shirt back over his head. "She pressed the pen *hard*. I need a drink."

"You have your flask in your pocket." I bent down to tie the Superman bandana to Oscar's lead.

"Yes, but I should make an effort to appear normal in company." He pointed to a small cafe on the corner of the convention center. "I'll go pick up our bird friend while you grab drinks? You know what I like."

"Coffee that's as black as your soul. I'm on it." Heathcliff shoved his way toward the box office while Edie, Oscar and I headed toward the cafe. My head buzzed with everything I'd learned. Tara and Grant an item? That couldn't be a coincidence. But I couldn't see how it related to Kate's murder…

Oscar tugged on his lead, and I felt a new confidence as I gave him his command and we headed for the door to the cafe. *Everything is going to be okay. We've got a new lead in Morrie's case, and with this little dude by my side—*

"Excuse me, ma'am, you can't come in."

I kept walking, not realizing the person was talking to me. A disgruntled server stepped in front of me, blocking our way. Oscar reeled, stopping in his tracks so I didn't crash into him.

"What did you say?" My fingers gripped Oscar's harness.

"We don't allow dogs inside for hygiene reasons."

Edie glanced at me. I realized she wasn't going to say anything. *You'll come up against people all the time who don't understand the rules about service animals,* she told me during training. *You'll have to learn to stand up for yourself.*

I swallowed the lump forming in my throat. "This is a service animal. You're required by law to allow us inside."

"I don't think so. You can sit outside, if you *must*, but my customers won't be happy. I'm sorry." He didn't sound sorry at all.

"You will be. I'll complain to your manager. This dog isn't a choice. He's my *eyes*." I meant the words to sound foreboding, like I had the power to crush him under the soles of my Docs. But my voice wavered.

The server put his arms against the doorframe, blocking us with his body. He narrowed his eyes at Oscar. "You can't come in."

I stepped back, feeling the sting of his words against my cheeks as if he'd slapped me. All around us, people looked up from their tables, watching but not saying anything. I gave Oscar the command to turn and spun around to get to fuck out of there—

And ran straight into the wall of Heathcliff.

I slumped against him, and the tears flowed down my cheeks. I railed against myself inside my head – *this is stupid. He's just a dumb man, and it doesn't matter. You were in the right* – but the tears wouldn't stop. My whole body shook as the shock of being denied entry hit me full force.

"Mina, hey." Heathcliff used the tip of his finger to blot away my tear. "You want me to go crush him like the dung beetle he is?"

I shook my head, sniffling. On his shoulder, Quoth peered down at me with those eyes ringed in fire.

Just say the word, and I'll fly over there and defecate on him.

Heathcliff crushed me against his chest. "I know you're upset, but you handled that well. The Mina I knew five months ago never would have stood up for herself like that."

"I didn't... hic... stand up for... hic... myself." Great, I'd dissolved into the kind of soul-wrenching sobs that absolutely no one could pull off with their dignity intact.

"You did. You stated your case calmly and firmly. You tried to talk to someone in authority. You didn't punch him in his stupid nose, which is more than I might say for myself."

I nodded, leaning against Heathcliff as the four of us shuffled toward the train station. And even though I knew Heathcliff spoke the truth, I couldn't help the dark thoughts that spiraled in my mind.

If I can't even walk into a cafe with Oscar, if people are going to stare, how will I ever be able to have a normal life?

CHAPTER TWELVE

*W*e arrived home to find, once again, the shop was in perfect condition, a stack of books sold, packaged, and ready to ship out, a fishy scent in the air, and a very smug Grimalkin luxuriating on the couch under the window. As soon as Mum left, I went up to my grandmother and shook her awake.

"Human form, now."

Grimalkin shot me a filthy look, but she obliged. Her whiskers retracted into her face, her ears moved down her head and became round and dainty, and her limbs cracked and buckled into new shapes. A few moments later, my very naked and very attractive nymph grandmother stood in front of me.

I glared at her. "What's going on with my mother?"

"Whatever do you mean?" Grimalkin was all wide-eyed innocence, which only made me more suspicious.

"I *mean*, the shop is immaculate, and how has she sold all these books?"

"Your mother is an exceptional saleswoman, and there have been many visitors to the shop. Your friend Mrs. Ellis has called in no less than three times."

"Yes, because she wants the gossip on Morrie's disappearance! And why are you so friendly with Mum all of a sudden?"

"She gave me an extra piece of fish for lunch." Grimalkin rubbed her stomach.

"Right. Well..." I didn't know what to say to that. "Just keep an eye on her. Let me know if she does anything strange or scares away customers."

Grimalkin's lips curled back into a smile. "I assure you, if your mother does something I disapprove of, you'll be the first to know."

Wild Oats emailed over a packing list for the weekend – according to Sam, we were to dress for 'typical British weather' – aka, cold and wet and miserable – and the only non-clothing items we were supposed to bring were a small, personal first aid kit, water purification tablets, a drink bottle, a lighter or water-proof matches, a small coil of wire, a pocketknife, a selection of fishhooks, and a solar blanket.

"Solar blanket? Water purification tablets? What is this crap? I thought we were supposed to pack the bare essentials." Heathcliff opened his rucksack on his desk and shoved a bottle of whisky inside, then dropped a battered copy of Jack London's *Call of the Wild* on top.

"Is that whisky essential?" I raised an eyebrow.

"If we manage to find Morrie, it will be." Heathcliff added a second bottle. "Haven't you noticed how much more peaceful things are around here without him?"

"Can't argue with that," Quoth added.

I glared at them both. "Morrie is our friend, and we'll do everything we can to save him."

"If you say so." Heathcliff dropped a third bottle into his ruck-sack. "What's a pocketknife?"

"It's like a small portable knife that flicks out of a handle – but it usually has other tools as well, like a can opener, toothpick, or screwdriver. Something small that will fit in a pocket—"

"Like this?" Heathcliff pulled a curved hunting blade.

"That doesn't fit in your pocket."

"It does if I cut the bottom seam out." Heathcliff dropped the knife in his bag, then bent to peer under the desk. "Now, where's my sword?"

"Victoria Bainbridge kept it, remember?" Victoria was an occult book dealer who owned the building Nevermore Bookshop occupied during the late 1800s. We met her when we decided to spend the night in the time-traveling room – it turned out we were getting carnal in her bed, and she kept Heathcliff's sword as recompense. He borrowed a rapier for his Jane Austen costume, but he'd had to hand that in to the police after it had been used in the fight that had unmasked Christina Hathaway as the killer. Personally, I wasn't sure I wanted my hulking, often-drunk, grumpy boyfriend to be swinging a sword around, but he'd saved my arse too many times to discourage him. I just had to hope he wouldn't discover some late-night medieval combat shop that could sate his last-minute stabbing needs.

"It's time she gave it back. Want to come with me?"

"Hell no." I shuddered. As we'd left her home in the past, Victoria said that the next time I saw her, I'd be covered in blood. I didn't want to risk stepping through that door and hurting Heathcliff.

Heathcliff nodded, then stormed off.

Quoth handed me a steaming cup of tea. "Do you think he's going to get Victoria's room when he opens the door?"

"I don't need Morrie's brilliant mathematical mind to tell me that with all the possible periods in history, the odds of him opening that door to find Victoria Bainbridge with his sword in her possession and in a mood to return it to him are infinitesimal."

There was a glint in Quoth's eye. "Fancy a wager? Say, for the last wagon wheel in the packet. My money's on the dinosaurs."

I laughed. "I hope he terrifies some poor medieval scribe."

Quoth held out his hand, and we shook. My cheeks warmed at the touch of his skin on mine. "You're on."

As I raised the cup to my lips, the entire flat rumbled with a deep roar that reverberated in my chest. Quoth's eyes met mine, and the corner of his mouth tugged up.

SLAM.

A moment later, Heathcliff stumbled into the kitchen, his eyes round as saucers.

"Sooooo…" I struggled to keep a straight face. "Did you get the sword back?"

"Is Victoria well?" Quoth chirped.

Heathcliff slumped into his favorite chair and pressed a hand to his brow. "I need whisky."

"You packed all the whisky."

"Then I need to bleach my eyeballs." He grunted again.

Quoth and I exchanged a glance, and without a word I slid the biscuit package toward him.

I turned to Quoth. "We should bring some things for Morrie, too. We've only got Sherlock's word that he's properly stocked that cabin."

"What kind of things?" Heathcliff hugged his rucksack to my chest. "He's not getting my whisky."

"I don't know… what things would you want if you were trapped in a mountain cabin indefinitely—"

With only Sherlock Holmes for company.

Quoth glanced over at Morrie's desk. "We can't bring his computer, but he'd probably like some books. Maybe that reverse harem one you were reading the other day, with the ghost haunting the elite music academy."

"*Ghosted* by Steffanie Holmes? He's not getting that. I'm still reading it. It's giving me all sorts of ideas about what to do with the three of you." I grinned wickedly.

"Right." Quoth swallowed. "Um, Morrie probably wants his

toothbrush. Also, that expensive aftershave he likes, perhaps some underwear—"

Heathcliff glanced at Quoth. 'Don't forget the stash."

"What stash?"

"Morrie built up a stash of emergency supplies in case he ever had to go into hiding." Heathcliff swung himself from the chair and headed into my bedroom. In the place above Morrie's old bed, Heathcliff lifted a section of paneling from the wall. I couldn't see a thing in the dark space, but as Heathcliff pulled objects out into the light I recognized the essentials of Morrie's trade. Burner phones. A laptop and some other electronic devices. A small package of dehydrated food. A lock-picking kit. An envelope stuffed with fake passports and driving licenses. Heathcliff tossed it all into his rucksack.

"I have no idea what half of this is," Heathcliff held up a long, silver object. "But he must've thought it important."

"Heathcliff…" I'd just figured out what the silver thing was. "I'm… I'm not sure I'd touch that if I were you."

"Why the devil not? It's just some weird long shaft with a knob on the end and—Ah!" Heathcliff tossed the vibrator at the wall. "You do the rest. I need to go chop off my hands."

He raced off to the bathroom, and I heard the water running.

I tossed the last of the items into the bag. As I did, my fingers brushed something wedged into the back corner of the compartment. I wiggled it free and inspected it under the light. It was a velvet drawstring bag with small, hard objects inside.

Quoth held out his hands, and I tugged the drawstring open, spilling the contents into his fingers. What fell out surprised me.

Jewels.

Glittering precious stones in beautiful colors tumbled across Quoth's fingers. The light captured their exquisite facets, dancing a rainbow of light across my vision.

I turned the jewels in my fingers, mesmerized by their beauty. *Why does Morrie have a stash of precious jewels hidden in his room?*

An ugly thought twisted in my head, a thought I didn't want to consider but had to. *Are these... dirty? Are they connected to a crime in some way?*

I dropped the jewels into Quoth's hand and stepped away. His eyes met mine, and I saw my own concerns reflected there. Wordlessly, Quoth tipped the jewels into the pouch and placed it back into its hiding place.

"Are you sure you want to go on this course?" he asked. "We could solve this mystery just as well from the shop."

"I'm sure." I plastered a smile on my face. "Let's learn how to eat bugs."

CHAPTER THIRTEEN

*H*ayes gave us the all-clear to leave the village again, as long as we agreed to check in with him when we got to our destination. We couldn't actually tell him where we were going, so I invented a rare manuscript convention in Leeds. Predictably, as soon as he heard that, Hayes' eyes glazed over from boredom and he didn't ask any further questions. I was getting far too good at being a criminal mastermind.

Edie was so impressed with my progress, she agreed to let me take Oscar for the weekend. We took the train to Crookshollow to arrive at the guide dog kennels as she opened up. Oscar leaped into my arms as soon as he saw me, nuzzling my face and smudging my makeup.

"I'd go with you, but I have a mountain of paperwork to do." Edie gestured to her desk. "Have fun sleeping in the rain and eating tree bark."

I had a feeling Edie's 'paperwork' was really a convenient excuse not to have to spend a night in the wilderness. Personally, I'd prefer a bed over a pile of leaves, given the option, but if it helped us solve Morrie's case and got us to see him again, it was worth the sacrifice.

We returned to the station and purchased tickets to Leeds, because I knew Hayes would check up on us. We got off at the second stop and transferred to a bus that would take us to Barset Reach, the tiny village at the base of the mountains. With every mile we covered, my chest tightened. I wanted to see Morrie again, to know that he was all right. (I also wanted to kick Sherlock's arse, but I wasn't prepared to admit that).

But Morrie would have to wait. We had investigating to do. If Kate had been killed with poison mushrooms, the most obvious suspects were anyone connected with Wild Oats.

As we climbed off the bus, a white minivan with mud splattered along the sides pulled up, looking every bit like the kind of car a creepy stalker would cruise around in. As we got closer I was able to make out the words 'Wild Oats Wilderness Survival School' stenciled along the side. A tall guy in his thirties with a scraggly beard and frizzy ginger hair pulled back in a ponytail practically bounced out of the cab.

"Hi," he greeted me with an enormous bear hug. He smelled of dirt and moss and possibly badger urine. Oscar peered at him with curiosity, but he didn't try to pet him, which I appreciated. "I'm Sam. I'll be your instructor this weekend. We're going to have the best time gorging ourselves on the delights of nature. You must be Mina. Hop on in. Do you need help?"

"I'm good, thanks." I couldn't help it, I liked Sam already. He had one of those earnest, open faces, and I could tell he was passionate to the point of evangelical about wilderness survival. Weird, yes, but he didn't scream 'crazed, stabby killer' to me.

I climbed into the bench seat and settled Oscar at my feet. Heathcliff and Quoth squeezed in next to me. The van smelled of rotten cheese. I fumbled for my seatbelt, only to find two lengths of worn rope. Heathcliff tied his rope together.

Sam laughed. "Sorry, things are a bit tight around here, not much money for repairs, but I figure my clients appreciate the rustic touches. Do you three spend much time in the great outdoors?"

"The three of us work in a bookshop." Oscar nudged my leg. "I should say, I guess Oscar works there now, too. We're more into reading about nature than exploring it."

"Ah, pencil-pushers wanting to get a taste of the wilderness? You read a Bear Grylls book and thought it sounded easy?" Sam grinned as he floored the gas. The van rumbled away from the curb and bounced over the rough gravel road. "We get a lot of your types around here. Don't worry, I'll mold you into true wild people."

I grabbed for the handle as the van hit a particularly large pothole and my head slammed into the roof. "Heathcliff's wild enough already. He grew up on the moors in Yorkshire. He's got a bit of experience in the great outdoors."

"Ah, but he has ever had to fend for himself during the harshest nights of winter, with nothing but his wits and a bowie knife to keep him alive?"

"Yes," Heathcliff answered.

"Oh, really?" Sam sounded taken aback.

"Well, it was a broadsword I stole from Hindley's study, but it did the trick in a pinch," Heathcliff growled. "It makes short work of ferrets. You should add it to your packing list."

"Um… yeah…" Sam nodded, not sure what to make of Heathcliff. "Ferret-killing broadsword, sure. I'll look into that."

We drove past a large, mono-pitch cabin, made of rough-hewn logs. Brightly-colored hammocks dotted a wraparound verandah, and carved signs decorated with loopy handwriting pointed toward accommodation, toilets, and 'forest hot tub.' Police tape stretched across the gravel parking lot, blocking the building from the road.

"You'll have to forgive the disorganization." Sam's fingers drummed against the steering wheel. "That's our visitor center and Airbnb – off-limits now, so we've set up a temporary base a few miles up the road. The police have closed off my usual stomping ground because of an ongoing investigation. Completely unconnected to Wild Oats, of course."

That has yet to be established, especially if they've included your visitor center as part of the crime scene. Suddenly, I didn't feel so confident about Sam's innocence. I decided to test him. "We heard some girl killed herself, but I thought it was months ago."

Sam's jaw set in a line. "She didn't kill herself."

"Do you mean it was an accident?" I held my hand to my mouth. "It wasn't on this course, was it? What if she was allergic to something she ate?"

"No, it was nothing to do with us," Sam said quickly. "She came on one of our courses last year, as part of a workplace teambuilding weekend. She ran away from her camp and left a message behind that originally read as a suicide note. We searched every inch of the mountains but didn't find the body. By the time they called off the search, my Yelp reviews were so terrible that no one wanted to take our courses. All my bookings canceled and I had to lay off all my staff. Then, I had this brainwave – I'll play off the bad publicity and reinvent this place as a wellness center, with Kate's story at its heart. We were going to offer yoga, mindfulness, foraging and wild cooking classes – the idea being to offer a place where people who felt like Kate could come and learn to get back to nature, so that maybe a horrible tragedy could be prevented. Two weeks ago, I was scouting the ideal site for our moonlit ritual space when I stumbled upon the body buried in a fallen log. So now, I'm dealing with more bad press – no one wants to go to a murder retreat to get away from their problems, and I'm not even allowed back to the visitor center to lead hikes." He forced a smile on his face. "But never mind that. We're going to have a great weekend learning about the culinary wonders offered up by Mother Nature in her rawest state! Tell me, Mina, have you ever drunk tea made from fresh nettles, or made your own *ceviche* from fish you caught and gutted yourself? Why, I can't tell you—"

Sam chatted all the way into the forest, extolling the virtues of a menu of increasingly disgusting-sounding dishes. My stomach growled – if all that was offered was nettle tea and raw fish, I doubted it would be getting much sustenance this weekend.

We pulled into a small clearing where a temporary shed had been set up. Beside it was a small pup tent, and a clothesline of hemp t-shirts and harem pants stretching between two trees. *Sam's sleeping here. Wild Oats must really be struggling.*

And it's all Kate Danvers' fault.

But would he kill her over it? It didn't make much sense – Sam might have had reason to be angry with Kate, he might even have wanted to kill her. He had the access and knowledge of poisonous mushrooms necessary to do the deed. But why do it so near his own business and then report the body? All he'd achieved was bringing Wild Oats even closer to ruin.

No, Sam's innocent. I'm sure of it. Which means we're back where we started. I tried to keep the disappointment off my face as we stepped out of the van. I glanced around at the empty lot. "We're the only ones on the course?"

That wasn't what I wanted. It would be much more difficult to sneak away to see Morrie if Sam was focused on us.

Sam beamed. "You are my sole charges, which means even more personal learning time for you. Ever since Kate Danvers... *you know...* we haven't had many bookings. People think this place is haunted or something. But enough about that, it's time to turn our attention to the fruits of the forest. I want you all to line up and show me your rucksacks."

We filed out of the car and placed our rucksacks in front of us. Oscar sniffed at the pocket where I'd stashed my emergency Snickers bar, and I backed him away. Heathcliff's rucksack made a loud CLANG as his whisky bottles clinked together, but at least they hid all the supplies we brought along for

Morrie. Sam unlocked the door to the shed and pulled out some plastic bins loaded with compasses and whistles and other random things. "People always forget something essential."

"Not me." Heathcliff yanked open the drawstring on his ruck-sack, drew out his whisky, and took a deep swig.

"You can't pack those bottles in here." Sam frowned into his sack. "Or this knife. Or these paperbacks. Did you bring *anything* on the list?"

"Only the essentials." Heathcliff shoved the whisky bottle into his belt. Sam opened his mouth to argue but one glare from Heathcliff and he snapped his mouth shut.

"Right, well... I can give you the supplies you need." Sam dumped an armload of gear in front of him. "I'll tell you how the weekend is going to work. First, you'll need to pay attention during my safety demonstration, as I teach you how to use all the items in your rucksack, and what to do if you find yourself separated from the group."

"Jump for joy?" Heathcliff muttered so only I could hear.

"Then, we're going to hike about five miles into the forest. It will take several hours, because we'll be stopping along the way to collect different types of plants, insects, and edible roots, and hopefully lay some traps—"

Traps? *Insects?* My stomach churned. *Why couldn't we have signed up for one of the yoga and wellness courses? I like the sound of a sacred skyclad circle...*

"—at the end of the hike, we'll make camp and then you will cook dinner for the group using what we've foraged and caught." Sam grinned. "The more you listen and learn, the more delicious supper will be."

Sam launched into a long lecture about the proper way to tie a fishing line and the best place to make camp if you want to be found by the rescue helicopter. He was so earnest and enthusiastic I half expected him to break into a singalong about having to eat your friend's foot to survive. Sam looked like the kind of guy who'd eaten a foot.

"—the second rule of foraging is to only collect from plentiful sources, and only what you plan to consume—"

Oscar panted, his tail thumping against my leg as he held on to Sam's every word. Beside me, Quoth's fingers laced in mine, and he kept glancing at the trees nervously, as if the scents of nearby birds might make him shift. On the other side of me, Heathcliff leaned forward, rapt by Sam's story of how he had to hide up a tree to escape a bear in the Canadian Rockies.

"Tell me, are these bears available, and do you think they'd consider working in a bookshop scaring off customers?"

Finally, Sam declared the safety lecture over, handed us all hi-vis vests to wear over our jackets, and directed us to follow a path twisting through the trees. I hoisted my rucksack onto my shoulders, picked up Oscar's harness and lead, and fell in line behind Heathcliff.

About a half-mile up the track, Sam stopped in front of some bushes. He crouched down and broke off a handful of leaves, which he passed around.

"We're just coming out of January, so there aren't many leafy foods around at the moment. Mostly, we're hunting winter fruits and nuts, and we're just coming into mushroom season, but we'll deal with those later. First of all, this little guy is—"

"Horse parsley," Heathcliff answered.

"Correct. It's also known as Alexanders, and it was introduced to Britain by the Romans. It's biennial, so you'll only see these every second year. You can eat all of the plant, but the stalk is the best bit. Here." Sam picked a bunch of the scraggly plant and handed me a stalk. Tentatively, I held it up and sniffed. It smelled a little like parsley. I tried a nibble off the end of the stem.

"Oh. It's quite sweet!"

"Yes, it is. I love it in salads, but you can also boil the leaves and stems or add them to a stew. Or just eat them raw—"

Beside me, Heathcliff shoved the entire handful in his mouth and chewed vigorously.

We walked further, munching on our stems of horse parsley, while Sam kept up a steady stream of chatter. We stopped to pick wild garlic, harvest the tender tips of nettles, and dig for the spindly casings of chestnuts on the forest floor. We even found a few wild blackberries still clinging to a bush. It was actually kind of cool. My pockets burst with random things, and everything in the forest smelled fresh and bright.

Oscar was having a ball of a time, too. His nose twitched as new smells crossed his path every few minutes, but he never wavered from his job. After a while, I removed his collar and harness so he knew he was 'off-duty.' He bounced after butterflies and barked at a fox stalking through the undergrowth.

"Ah, now here's something special." Sam turned over a rotting log to reveal a line of orange-brown caps growing in overlapping tiers. "These little beauties are *Flammulina velutipes*, or—

"—Velvet shank," finished Heathcliff.

"Very good, Heathcliff. You seem to know your shrooms. You'll find these little fellas on dead and decaying trees, especially ash, oak, and beech, from November to March. You need to be careful as they look similar to deadly funeral bell – mixing them up could be a fatal mistake."

"As the resident blind person, I don't think I want to be in charge of fungi." I shuddered. Death seemed to find me everywhere these days; no way did I want to dice with mushrooms, especially not after what happened to Kate.

"Don't worry, Mina. Identifying mushrooms is an advanced foraging skill. Only *ex-spore-ienced* outdoorsmen like Heathcliff and myself should locate and cook fungi." Sam held up one of the velvet shanks. "Trust me, these babies will be delicious in tonight's feast. While we hunt out some others, I think you and Allan should be in charge of finding our protein."

"Protein?"

Sam lifted another rotting log, revealing a couple of cockroaches scuttling back toward the darkness. I jerked away.

"They're perfectly safe. Unlike the cockroaches around your house, which have probably been snacking on toxic materials and sprayed with insecticides that have failed to kill them, these little blighters have had a healthy free-range diet and they're packed with protein. It makes them an excellent choice for wilderness survival, if you know where to look for them."

"I'm not sure why I'd ever want to *look* for cockroaches," I shuddered.

"Cockroaches are actually incredibly fascinating," Sam continued as if I hadn't spoken. "They touch each other and use a pheromone in their body to recommend the best nearby food sources. That's why you often find them eating in a group, like they are here. We're going to feast tonight."

"Nothing you said makes me any more interested in eating one."

"I think you'll be pleasantly surprised." Sam scooped the disgusting insects into his billy and screwed the lid on. "When sautéed in a little butter and garlic, they're actually quite tasty."

"You're right. I will be surprised... if you can get me to eat one of those." The billy emitted pinging noises as the roaches fought for freedom. Sam clipped the pot back onto his rucksack and continued up the path.

After another couple of hours, my feet ached and my shoulders protested from lifting the rucksack on and off my back constantly. Heathcliff leaped off the path to hunt for mushrooms, and Sam added another handful of cockroaches to his stash. Quoth found a hawthorn bush with a few berries. "We could use these to make a sauce for our stew."

"Our cockroach stew? Sure, you can add whatever you like, because I won't be eating it."

"I'm sure it will be delicious."

"You regularly eat bugs and gross things as a bird. I don't trust your judgment." As Quoth picked berries and Oscar sniffed something foul under a tree, my mind whirred with the issue of how to escape Sam to get to Morrie – preferably before he tried to make me cook and eat cockroaches. I snuck up beside Heathcliff as he plucked more mushrooms from the center of a decaying tree stump, cupping my hand over his ear. "Psst, Teacher's Pet."

"Don't call me that."

"It's true," I grinned. "Sam is so happy to have someone to talk to about mushrooms. I think he might ask you to marry him."

"Keep joking about it, and I'll make you eat the biggest cockroach," he growled.

I shuddered. "How are we going to get away from Sam the Mushroom Man? He's going to notice if we all disappear before dinner. And it *will* be before dinner, because if I have to eat a cockroach, I will die, and then I'll be no good to anyone."

"Don't worry." Heathcliff waggled an eyebrow. "I have a plan."

"All you have is mushrooms, Mr. Teacher's Pet. What good are they?"

"You'll see." There was an evil glint in Heathcliff's eye that reminded me too much of Morrie.

We stopped again so Sam could show us how to make simple snares and set animal traps. By now, my feet were falling off. I was certain my left toe was more blister than human. Even Oscar seemed to be dragging his feet. Just as I was about to throw down my rucksack in protest and declare I wouldn't walk another step, Sam stopped in a clearing and declared it the perfect spot to make camp for the night.

I thought that meant it was time to relax, but no, we had to set more snares, gather wood for a fire and to make a lean-to for shelter. Oscar was amazing the whole time, leading me where I needed to go and not dashing off after the squirrel that ran overhead. Although I doubted we'd catch anything in the traps with a dog around.

Next, Sam forced me and Quoth to sit through a fire-starting lecture while Heathcliff lined up his spore-ific finds and started to divide them between two pots.

"I'm cooking," he declared, picking off wild garlic leaves with deft fingers.

I narrowed my eyes. "But you burn toast. Remember when you tried to bake me a chocolate cake and it turned out like a hockey puck?"

"Baking is not a skill required on the moors." Heathcliff stirred the pot. "Prepare to be amazed."

"I'll take care of the protein. Get these in the pan while I chop the wild garlic." Sam placed a frying pan on the flames and handed Heathcliff the cockroaches.

As Heathcliff pried the lid off, Oscar leaped at him, pawing at his chest to find out what he was doing. "Arf, arf."

"Aw, shite." Heathcliff dropped the container. I jumped out of the way as cockroaches scattered across the dirt and skittered away. Only one cockroach landed in the pan, where it rolled over, its legs curling up as it succumbed to death.

I wrapped my arms around Oscar's neck. "You're the best, boy. I knew I could count on you."

"Arf!"

Sam pouted. "Damn. I was really hoping to win you all over with my garlic roaches. Most people say they taste a bit like chicken."

I bet you a million quid they don't. "Another time."

"You've still got one left. I'll try it," Quoth piped up, staring at the lone roach sizzling in the pan.

"You, sir, are my hero." Sam tossed in some garlic and a few herbs he collected and happily stirred. A few minutes later he presented Quoth with a blackened roach in the middle of a pile of wilted greens. The garlic smell was delicious, but I couldn't watch what came next. I turned away just as Quoth crunched down on the insect.

Ew. Eewwwwwww. Ew.

"Mmmm." Quoth swallowed, and I threw up a little in my mouth. "Very garlicky. Definitely tastes a bit like chicken."

Heathcliff lifted two steaming billies off the fire. Even as my stomach churned from Quoth's appetizer, I had to admit the stew smelled delicious. He divided the contents of the larger between three bowls and set the smaller one down in front of Sam. "This one is just for you, our fearless leader."

"Thanks, Heath, old chum." Sam took a deep whiff of the pot. "This looks grand."

Heathcliff watched as we all tucked into our food. I had this vision of him wearing a chef's hat and nothing else, glowering at Morrie while my criminal mastermind tried to smack his arse with a spatula. It was the kind of image that made my heart patter and a deep ache pool between my legs.

I wish Morrie was here. He'd love this.

I finished the stew and scraped my plate clean. The flavors were incredible. I was quite impressed we'd found every ingredient ourselves. The mushrooms, in particular, were divine, and Heathcliff cooked them to perfection.

Sam tossed his plate aside, smacking his lips. In the firelight, his eyes were wide as saucers. He leaped to his feet.

"We should make shelters. Shelter from the cold. Yes, yes, we need shelter sticks." He darted around the clearing, picking up sticks and waving them in the air, laughing gleefully at jokes the rest of us didn't understand.

I glanced at Quoth, but he shrugged. Heathcliff had taken Oscar for a walk to a nearby stream to wash the pans. I stood up and held out a hand to our instructor. "Uh, Sam? I'm not sure you should be dancing like that so close to the fire—"

"Sssssssssssh." Sam dived behind me, his fingers gripping my wrist so tight my fingers tingled. He peered into the trees with his saucer eyes, his body rigid with fear. "Is that a bear?"

"I don't see anything—"

"I said, be quiet!" Sam shook my arm. "It is. I can see it. It's an enormous brown bear! Quick, everyone, get back. I'll beat it off."

Sam elbowed me in the gut as he shoved me toward the trees. I stumbled over a log and fell back. Warm hands caught me under the arms, and Quoth pulled me to his chest, holding me tight. Sam grabbed a log from the fire and waved it in front of him like a sword.

A dark shape emerged from the trees. My stomach twisted as the shape towered over Sam. *It can't be a bear. We don't have bears in England. That's impossible—*

"The bear has a cub! You have to run. Mother bears are fiercely protective of their cubs." Sam swiped the stick through the air. The bear cub leaped behind its mother and let out a frightened whimper.

A *familiar* whimper.

"Oscar!"

"Watch what you're doing with that thing," the bear growled. Heathcliff stepped into the firelight and closed his hand over Sam's, twisting his wrist so he dropped the log. "You'll put someone's eye out."

"The bear speaks!" Sam dropped to his knees, touching his forehead to the dirt in a gesture of reverence. "It is a spirit of the forest. Oh, spirit guide, tell me what I must do to earn your gifts."

"What are you doing?" I shook Sam's shoulder. *Why's he acting so odd all of a sudden?* "That's not a bear. It's Heathcliff and Oscar, my guide dog."

"I know you're blind, Mina, so you're going to have to trust me. I know the difference between a dog and a spirit bear. You must bow in reverence—"

"Sam..." Heathcliff growled. "The forest spirits have chosen you as our representative on earth. I've come to test your worthiness. You must dance the dance of the forest."

"Yes, spirit bear. I will dance the dance of the forest!" Sam ran off into the woods, skipping like a schoolgirl as he sang about fairies.

I yanked Oscar's lead from Heathcliff's hand and glared at him. "Our instructor is dancing around like a maniac, and you don't seem surprised. What did you do to him?"

"Nothing." Heathcliff grinned. "He should have paid more attention to the mushrooms I added to his pot."

"I aaaaaaaam the forest," Sam warbled as he pirouetted through the trees.

It took a moment for Heathcliff's confession to sink in. Weariness overcame me, and I sank to the ground, unable to hold myself upright any longer. "Please tell me you didn't feed our wilderness survival instructor psychedelic mushrooms."

The corner of Heathcliff's mouth tugged up. "Okay, I won't tell you."

I buried my face in my hands. "That's such a Morrie response. Is this your plan for getting us away from Sam?"

"It worked, didn't it? With the number of shrooms he consumed, he's not going to remember his middle name, let alone whether or not you were here for the night." Heathcliff shoved several objects into my hands. "Take this. It's a map of the mountains and the trails, with a few cabins and bothies marked. I swiped it from Sam's shed while he was giving his stupid safety lecture. And here's Morrie's junk." He grabbed his whisky bottles from his rucksack and looped the strap over my shoulder.

"How do you know about psychedelic mushrooms?"

"I spent days at a time on the moors. How do you think I entertained myself?" Heathcliff held out the pot. "Want to give it try? Sam's left half the stew behind."

"Tempting, but I think I'll pass."

"Moan all you like, but I got the annoying tree-hugger out of your way." Heathcliff tossed the flaming log back into the fire. "I'll stay here and make sure he doesn't dance his way over a cliff. You and the birdie get to Morrie."

I groaned. While his plan sounded good in theory, the last thing I wanted to do was stand up and do more walking.

Quoth tugged on my arm. "We have to go."

My feet refused to budge. "I'm not moving. I'm going to sit here until erosion brings the bothy to me."

"Don't you want to see Morrie?"

"Morrie who?" I yawned. "The only thing I care about right now is never using my feet again."

"Okay…" Quoth looked confused.

"I'm kidding. Give me a second to get up, and then we'll get going. All I can say is, Morrie better appreciate the sacrifices we've made for him." I hauled myself to my feet. "I don't think we should take Oscar with us. Can you look after him, too?"

Heathcliff took the lead from my hands and stroked Oscar behind the ears. He leaned forward to kiss my forehead. "Stay safe."

"I aaaaaaammmm the trees," Sam warbled. He leaped into the clearing, only his foot slipped over a log and he went down, sprawling in a heap. He twitched, muttering into the dirt.

"Sure, Sam. You're the trees." Quoth and I stepped over our prone instructor and headed into the forest. Quoth leaned his head against my shoulder, but I shrunk back.

"You're not getting near me with that cockroach breath. Besides, I need you to guide me."

I gripped the crook of Quoth's arm – this was how I'd been taught to allow a person to guide me. His skin felt warm and reassuring beneath my fingers. In the dark, Quoth's eyes glowed with a rim of orange light. He retained much of his bird vision in human form, so he'd do the work of navigating for the two of us. Even with the beam of his flashlight shining on the trees, I couldn't see a thing. Each step plunged into the unknown, but with Quoth's steady pace guiding me, I didn't feel afraid.

Is this what it will be like when I'm blind? I imagined it to be like closing my eyes in the middle of a room – a constant and fearful disorientation. But this was different. I trusted Quoth, and so it didn't feel scary. It was just… experiencing a world in a new way. I listened hard, discerning nocturnal creatures, the rustle of wind through the trees. Our boots crunching on dead branches. All the sounds of nature that I'd never bothered to experience before, revealed once I stripped back the layers of sight. Beautiful.

"I can see the cabin," Quoth said after a time.

My heart leaped in my throat. I surged forward, catching my foot on a root. Quoth swept me into his arms before I face-planted in the dirt. *Urgh, yup. Blindness still sucks.*

"Easy." His lips brushed mine as he set me upright again. "You won't be able to see Morrie if you fall and break your neck."

Blackberry bushes tore at my leggings as we pushed our way through a thick patch, stepping into a clear space. I could sense the air moving around me, the bulk of the trees not as oppressive. "We're on a path now," Quoth said. "It slopes up the mountain, and there are steps cut into the rock. Do you want me to carry you or—"

"No, we'll get there. Slow and steady." I fell behind Quoth, changing my grip and sliding my feet along the ground so I could feel the way. After a time, I removed my hands from his and used them to feel the steps as I climbed. I remembered the last time I climbed these steps with Sherlock's gun pointed at the back of my head.

Morrie, Morrie, Morrie…

Quoth's fingers wrapped around my wrist, tugging me over the final step so I could stand. The cabin stood in front of us – a gloomy, oppressive shadow. Lamps burned at the windows – fiery eyes leering at me from the gloom. Sinister as fuck, like the cover of a Norwegian black metal album.

And inside is my Napoleon of Crime.

I hope.

I banged my fist on the door. "Morrie, are you there? Open up."

The door creaked open. My heart soared as the flickering lanterns dotted around the cabin offered me a glimpse inside. There in the doorway, his skin luminous in the moonlight, was Sherlock Holmes.

Stark fucking naked.

CHAPTER FOURTEEN

*S*herlock's fucking enormous cock waggled at me in greeting. The lamplight within the room gave me a perfect view of... everything.

"What are you doing here?" he rasped. "I'm busy."

He moved to shut the door, but I barred it with my foot, debating whether I should give him the grab-twist-pull treatment to get him out of my face. *Why is he naked?* A hundred terrible thoughts whirled around in my head, but the only way I'd get answers was to get inside.

Sherlock slammed the door against my boot, but he underestimated the toughness of Docs. I wriggled my shoulders into the gap and shoved past him, swinging out my knee to catch him in the groin.

"Ooof." Sherlock wheezed, his back slamming against the wall. The door flew back as I burst into the cabin.

"Morrie? Where are you?"

The bright lights overwhelmed me, and bursts of neon green and pink danced across my vision. I stumbled toward the back of the room, where I remembered the bed. *Please don't let me see—*

"Shhh, gorgeous. I'm here." A figure emerged from the gloom.

Warm arms wrapped around me, and my heart soared as I breathed in the grapefruit and vanilla scent that could only belong to my favorite criminal mastermind.

Morrie.

He's here.

He's alive.

"I missed you." I burrowed my face into Morrie's neck, savoring the scent of him, the weight of his arm around me, the hard planes and muscles of his body.

"Not as much as I missed you." Fingers clasped my jaw, tipping my head back as Morrie seared my lips with a scorching kiss.

Mmmmmm. I don't know what I was so afraid of. Morrie kissed like a man possessed, relinquishing the games he loved to play with me to give in to desperation. He kissed like he needed me to breathe.

Quoth fluttered into the room as his raven and rested on Morrie's shoulder, head-butting his cheek. Morrie broke our kiss to pet Quoth's head. "I missed you, too, little birdie."

I collapsed against Morrie, relief, fear and desire swirling inside me. I didn't know whether I wanted to throw him on the bed and molest him in the best possible way, or if I wanted to shake the smile off his face and rage at him for getting us into this mess.

A shape loomed behind us. Literature's greatest consulting detective collapsed into the chair by the fire, peering at me through a veil of wild curls sticking out at all angles from sleep. "What dark specters have disturbed our slumber?"

"It's Mina." Morrie tightened his grip around me. "And Quoth. You have no idea how happy I am to see you. I've been three days in this room with him and already I'm contemplating Sherlockicide."

"Morrie, why is Sherlock naked?"

"That's how he sleeps." Morrie rolled his eyes, but I couldn't help but notice he wore only a pair of silk boxer shorts himself. Droplets of sweat clung to his naked chest. "And he hogs all the blankets."

I stared in horror as the room came into view, and I took in the tangled sheets and pillows thrown everywhere, the crime scene photographs and reports rumpled beneath them. I imagined Morrie and Sherlock lying together, their feet touching as they pored over the details of his case, Sherlock's arm grazing Morrie's as he reached for Sherlock's shoe imprint cast, Morrie's mouth cocking into that self-satisfied smirk before their mouths met in hot need. "You're sharing a bed?"

Morrie shrugged as if it was no big deal, but I noticed he kept his eyes on Sherlock. "Mr. Smug Git over there called dibs. It was either share with him or take the armchair, and I found a cockroach nesting in it yesterday, so that wasn't happening."

I shuddered. "Don't mention cockroaches. Why is it so warm in here?"

"We're burning open flames in a small, poorly insulated box. The temperature will rise," said Sherlock haughtily.

Morrie glared at his ex-boyfriend, and an unspoken conversation passed between them. My fingers tightened around Morrie's arm, and I knew I was being possessive and jealous and stupid. Just because they had a history, and they were locked together in this tiny room doing what they did best, using their big stupid brains to solve a puzzle, didn't mean Morrie would cheat on me—

"Ignore him, gorgeous. He hates that." Morrie cradled Quoth in his arms and led me over to the bed. He shoved a pile of crime scene material onto the floor and patted the mattress for me to sit down. I heard the flick of a lighter, and a row of candles along the headboard burst to life, tiny fireflies in the gloom. "Tell me what you two doing are here."

"I needed to know you were okay."

"I'm fine. Going a little crazy in here with nothing to stimulate my substantial intellect, but nothing a kiss from you won't fix. How'd you get out here without Hayes following you? He must be watching you like a hawk. Or at least like a pigeon with mild dementia." Morrie narrowed his eyes. "You did make sure you weren't followed, didn't you?"

"Of course. Hayes thinks we're at a rare manuscript fair in Leeds. He has no idea we're here. Heathcliff, Quoth and I are following a lead. We signed up for the Wild Oats wilderness survival course."

"You got Old Sourpuss out of the shop?" Morrie glanced around. "*For me?* I'm impressed, and a little terrified. Where is he?"

Morrie's voice caught on the last syllable. My mind flicked back to the kiss he shared with Heathcliff in the shop and the tension that remained unresolved between the two of them ever since. Morrie wanted Heathcliff, and I think Heathcliff wanted Morrie, too, but he didn't want to admit that. Heathcliff saw being with Morrie as cheating on me, and nothing I said would convince him otherwise.

"He's back at our camp, looking after our instructor Sam while he experiences a magic mushroom trip."

"You're going to have to explain." Morrie's voice hitched, like he couldn't quite decide if he was supposed to be laughing or crying. His grip tightened around me again, like he was ready to crawl inside my skin.

"You wouldn't believe me if I told you." I rolled my eyes, but then I remembered who I was talking to. "Okay, maybe you would. It turns out Heathcliff has a hidden knowledge of edible plants from all those days he spent roaming like a wild beast upon the moors. He's the teacher's pet on our foraging course, which is hilarious. Sam entrusted him to forage for mushrooms. Heathcliff put some, uh, *special* mushrooms into Sam's dinner so he'd be out of it and Quoth and I could make our escape to see you. When we left, Sam thought he was a forest fairy and Heathcliff was petting Oscar and about to polish off the last of the stew, so by now they're probably both as high as kites."

Morrie burst out laughing. "You're telling me that right now, somewhere in the forest, Heathcliff Earnshaw is tripping on psychedelic mushrooms?"

"Croak," Quoth nodded vigorously.

Morrie doubled over, his whole body trembling from laughter. "Oh, what I wouldn't give to be able to see it. And who's Oscar?"

"My guide dog." A hard lump formed in my throat. "I've had a few days of training with him, and his trainer agreed to let me bring him over the weekend. He's... amazing. He's so bright and intelligent and mischievous and I wish you could meet him and I—"

I collapsed against Morrie, bringing my lips to his. I couldn't find the words to say what I needed to say, but I didn't need words around Morrie. His fingers tightened on my neck, holding me just so as he deepened the kiss, sending a shiver of need coursing through me.

Behind us, Sherlock coughed, slumping further into the armchair. The candles scattered across the table gave me a clear view of... all of him. I went to turn away, but then stopped myself. He was the one sitting around naked. He should be embarrassed, not me.

Quoth perched on the other side of the bed, and in a flutter of wings and limbs, another naked man sat beside me. Only this one was beautiful. A curtain of black hair fell over Quoth's chest as he leaned forward, nudging the rucksack across the floor. *Scraaape.*

"We brought you some supplies." Quoth dropped his head as Sherlock glared at him. *I could cut the tension in this cabin with a knife.* "If you don't mind, I'll just step outside for a bit. I... I saw a mouse, and I'm starving. Call me when you've... when you need me."

He transformed again and fluttered out the window into the

night, leaving me with Morrie and Sherlock and an aching need inside me.

"You raided my stash. I don't think I've ever loved you more than I love you at this moment." Morrie dumped out the contents of the rucksack and dug through them. He pulled out two of the burner phones and turned them on. After a few taps, he handed one to me. "Take this. That way we'll be able to communicate. Don't call me – the signal isn't great up here, and if the shop is bugged they might overhear something. Texts only, and delete them after you send them. And I mean *proper* delete them. Do you know how to wipe a SIM card?"

My chest tightened as he spoke. Morrie's caution made me realize just how serious this was. I'd been so busy worrying about him shacking up with Sherlock, I'd lost sight of the fact there was a warrant out for his arrest. If we didn't solve Kate's murder, Morrie would never be able to go back to a normal life. *As normal as our lives are, living in a cursed bookshop, having a polyamorous relationship, and hunting down Dracula.*

I squeezed my eyes shut. Everything was supposed to be working out for me. I'd already been dealt more than my fair share of bollocks. My life was supposed to be a bollocks-free zone right now. Obviously, the universe had other ideas.

By Isis, I'm not letting the universe or Dracula or Sherlock-bloody-Holmes take my happiness away from me.

My eyes flickered open. *I guess we're doing this.*

I grabbed the phone. "Show me."

Morrie walked me through an app he'd installed to delete all the information on the card, then pressed the phone back into my hands. "Do that after every time you message me. We can't risk the police deciding to search you randomly and discovering you're in contact with me."

I swallowed. We'd deceived the police before, but nothing like this. *If I got caught, I'd be on the hook for all kinds of criminal charges.* "Got it."

"What else is in this bag of tricks? Oh *yes*." Morrie pulled out a small, black case.

"That's not a gun, is it?"

"It's even better." Morrie unclipped the case and flipped the lid open, revealing a checkered surface and tiny black and white magnetic figures.

"You have *travel chess* in your secret stash?"

"Laugh all you want, but I've been trapped up here for three nights with nothing to do except talk to *him*. At least now we can take up our tournament from where we left off." Morrie smirked at his naked ex. "With me thoroughly trouncing you."

Sherlock snorted. "The transition from fictional character to real-life bastard has addled your memory, Moriarty. When last we left off, I was the unbeaten champion of thirteen rounds."

"When last we left off?" Morrie sneered. "You mean when you chased me across Europe before throwing me over a waterfall?"

Sherlock leaned forward, his long body hovering dangerously close to Morrie. Tension stretched between them like strings of mozzarella cheese. Sherlock curled his lip back into a smirk that dripped with desire. "Maybe things would have ended differently if you stopped running."

Sherlock moved toward him, but I was faster. I threw myself at Morrie, knocking him back against the bed, smothering my body in his. Morrie rolled me over so that I was beneath him, and his hands moved over me with a possessiveness that was utterly sinful. The stuffy air in the cabin heated up a notch or ten.

With my lips still pressed against his, I murmured. "How are things going with Sherlock? Are you... holding up okay?"

"Sherlock who?" Morrie chuckled as his fingers reached beneath the hem of my fleece, maneuvering through my layers to press his palm against my bare skin. His fingers slid down, down, down, determined as they slipped beneath the waistband of my leggings. I gasped into his mouth as he plunged two fingers deep inside me.

Morrie murmured with appreciation as my body clenched around him.

Sherlock is right there, and he knows this and he's touching me and I don't care...

My whole face burned with heat, but I knew I wouldn't tell him to stop. I roll my hips against Morrie's hand, begging for more, pushing him deeper inside me. He gazed down at me, his eyes hooded, his mouth crooked with his signature smirk. He knew exactly what he was doing, and fuck me if I didn't love it.

He pressed his thumb against my throbbing clit, curling his finger inside me to stroke a spot that left me gasping. Morrie drummed his finger against my clit, and a tremble started in my body.

Behind us, I was dimly aware of a sharp intake of breath. *Sherlock.*

I buried my face in Morrie's chest as the orgasm swept through my body and my brain trickled out my ears. Morrie flashed me his spoiled prince look – he loved that he could undo me with just his touch.

But I knew how to undo him, too. I reached up to wrap my arms around him, bringing his head in close, pressing his lips to mine. But instead of a kiss, I spoke what he refused to acknowledge.

"Morrie, tell me what's going on. Why are the two of you naked in here?"

Morrie leaned back, studying my face in that way of his that felt like he was gazing into my soul. "If you want to ask something, gorgeous, just come out with it."

"That's not what—"

"You think I'm going back to him." The ragged edge of his voice twisted a knife through my heart.

"No. Not at all. I just…" I could feel Sherlock's seething hatred of me burning from across the room. "You never resolved things with Heathcliff after your kiss, and now you're locked in a wooden shack with your ex. Things are going to get intense. And I walk in here and you're both practically naked and—"

My protests dissolved into a moan of need as Morrie wriggled his hips, grinding his cock against my hip. "You feel that?" he whispered, his voice choked with need.

I nodded, not trusting myself to speak.

"That's hard for *you*, gorgeous. Only you. Maybe once it was hard for some other gents, but that's in the past. Do you trust me?"

When Morrie asked me that, he didn't want some brushed off answer. He demanded me to examine myself and give him the brutal truth. If there was something between us, I had to own up to it. I glanced into Morrie's eyes, and I let my mind drift to everything that had happened between us since he burst into my life and stole my breakfast and my heart. Morrie reading erotic poetry in that smooth voice of his while he touched me until I turned to mush in his hands. Morrie cradling Quoth in his arms when he thought we'd lost him. The wicked grin that tugged at his mouth every time he had a brilliant scheme. Morrie standing on the balcony at Baddesley Hall, for the first time cracking his dark heart open and revealing the vulnerable man beneath. Morrie and Heathcliff locked in that loin-melting kiss...

"I do. I trust you." I said the words, and I meant them. "I'm jealous of Sherlock because I fucking *miss you*, and because I'm scared we won't catch whoever framed you, and I'll never see you again."

"Then do what you do best." Morrie leaned back and pulled me into a sitting position. His eyes blazed. "Put that beautiful brain of yours to work and get me out of here."

"I'm trying. We've got some suspects, but since *Sherlock* refuses to work with us—" I glared across the room at the naked man in the chair, "—I don't know what you guys have uncovered."

"We don't need her help," Sherlock sounded petulant.

"The fact that I'm still stuck in this hellhole with you rather suggests that we do." Morrie's arms tightened around my body, and a little sliver of fear shot through me. "Besides, even you have sometimes found that others see what you have not seen. Their mistake, if you're to be believed, is that they cannot reason from what they see."

Sherlock frowned. "I admit, Dr. Watson's inferior intellect did sometimes provide a useful canvas for my own deductions. Some people without possessing genius have a remarkable power of stimulating it."

I folded my arms. "If that's the way you feel, you and your stimulating superior intellect can go first."

"Very well." Sherlock steepled his fingers together. It was such a typical Morrie gesture that it made my chest tighten. I did not like the idea that any part of Morrie's personality came from this guy. "My process was simple. I compiled a list of Moriarty's enemies in the criminal underworld he inhabits, and have worked tirelessly to eliminate each and every single one from suspicion. There are only three that could have been in the vicinity of the forest during the time of the murder, and only one whose particulars fit the clues left behind. All that remains is to track down this fiend, Aidan McFarlane, and bring him to justice, and that is where I have currently drawn a blank."

"This is the same fellow you showed us before. What makes you so certain it was him?"

"As you know, I purchase my shoes from an exclusive London designer," said Morrie. "A month before Kate's body was found, Aidan made an appointment with that same designer. Considering Aidan usually wears combat boots, and his sales receipt reveals he commissioned a pair of brogues, we can conclude he used these fiendish shoes to frame me."

I shook my head. "But how did this guy get the shoes into our house? I've never seen him before, and you'd have remembered if he came anywhere near the shop. Yet, the police found them in the pile at the front door, and Jo matched dirt on the soles to Barsetshire Fells. And how did he get hold of your letter opener? And does he have knowledge of poisonous mushrooms, because that's what *actually* killed Kate."

Sherlock's head jerked up. "What is this? How did you obtain this information?"

"I spoke to Jo. The forensics on Kate's body were odd. It turns out, the knife wound wasn't what killed her. She was already dead, from poisonous mushrooms. She'd also lost a lot of blood, possibly extracted from a puncture wound Jo found on her body, along with severe bruising from the murderer dragging her body through the forest from somewhere else."

Sherlock tapped his chin, another Morrie gesture that made me want to tear his arms off. "That would explain the disturbances in the dirt around the crime scene."

"It's also possible that McFarlane disposed of his brogues after the murder, and the pair the SOCOs found was one of mine. The dirt on the shoes Jo analyzed could have been from when I came to meet Kate at Wild Oats last year." Morrie said. "But nothing about Kate's death fits with what I'd expect from McFarlane. Poison mushrooms? Stabbing her post-mortem? It's all too odd, too messy, almost as if he didn't know what he was doing."

"I don't think McFarlane is the killer. We've been working a different angle – I'm not sure this is about Morrie, so much as it is about Kate and why she tried to fake her own death." I rattled off what we'd discovered so far, about Kate's financial situation and her gross boss and Tara the cosplaying glitter queen. "I don't believe her husband Dave is responsible, but he does have a financial motive. Tara wanted Kate out of the way so she could be top of the cosplay circuit. She even threatened Kate on camera. Grant Hosking sounds like an all-round terrible person, so it could be him. And then there's Sam, our Wild Oats instructor. I don't believe he did it, either, but he might have unwittingly supplied the killer with the knowledge to poison with spores.

Plus, he had reason to hate Kate for ruining his business. Although I don't see what killing her would achieve apart from nailing the lid on the coffin of Wild Oats."

Sherlock snorted. "You're twisting the facts to suit your theories, instead of theories to suit facts."

"Yeah? Well, you smell." I poked my tongue out at him. Morrie sniggered. "I'd like to visit the crime scene and see these disturbances for myself. Can you take me there?"

"I'll save you a trip through a rather nasty briar patch that ruined my favorite pair of trousers. We've already gone out there." Morrie hunted through a stack of ephemera on the table and shoved a stack of Polaroids in my direction. "Sherlock took these."

"Don't mess them up." Sherlock paced in front of the fire, the lighter clicking as he struggled to light his pipe.

I fanned out the images, remembering them from the glimpse I had the day Sherlock took me and Morrie to the cabin. Police tape wound around the trunks of five towering oaks, cordoning off a large section of forest – the primary site, where they believed the murder actually occurred. Sam said he found the body in a fallen log further down the mountain, and sure enough, there it was... several pictures of the log from all angles, with drag marks where the killer must've pulled the body into the log after stabbing her. *Of course, because they couldn't have swung the blade if Kate was already inside the log.*

I didn't bother saying that out loud. Sherlock had clearly already figured it out. I flicked through the rest of the images – most of what Sherlock shot looked like random rocks and piles of twigs and leaves to me, but I peered at each one and pretended I gleaned some important information from them.

"We also found *this*." Morrie picked up something from a petri dish and held it near the candle. It was a silver button with a distinctive crest stamped into the metal. It reminded me of the buttons on my old school uniform blazer. "The police missed it.

If you can, find out from Jo what Kate was wearing when she died. If it wasn't hers, it most likely belonged to her killer."

I took the button and slid it into my pocket. "Thanks, Morrie. Will you be able to do any hacking up here, with the bad reception?"

He held up the burner phone. "I don't have all my equipment, but I can cause some chaos. What do you need?"

"I need to know everything you can find about Kate's boss, Grant Hosking. Especially the juicy, incriminating stuff."

"Easy. I'll probably have that for you before you get off this cursed mountain."

"You mean you haven't been enjoying the peace and tranquility of nature?" I ruffled his hair, usually close-shaven and impossibly neat, but after only three days almost rivaled Heathcliff in its unkemptness. *I can't believe I was so distracted with the garrotings I didn't notice how bad things got for Morrie.*

"You know I don't do nature." Morrie patted the ereader I'd packed for him. "I appreciate this."

"I hope so. I've stocked it with all my favorite reverse harem books – J Bree, Kim Faulks, Mila Young, Steffanie Holmes."

Morrie's voice cracked. "Gorgeous, why do you do all this to me?"

"You'll thank me later. Just don't tell Heathcliff about the ereader, or he'll skin us both alive. Oh, and your algorithm came up with a new headline today. Apparently, another rare Romanian plant was stolen from Lower Loxham."

Morrie screwed his face up. "That's close."

"Yep. We'll investigate it."

"Good." Morrie looked away, his shoulders shaking.

I squeezed his leg. "What are you thinking?"

"That I hate not being able to be with you, especially with... our greater enemy closing in." Morrie couldn't speak Dracula's name, in case Sherlock overheard. He sighed. "I thought I was prepared. I thought I'd given you everything you needed for when they hauled me in. I made that algorithm, I used the last of my legitimate money – everything MI5 didn't seize – to bail out your mother. I know you have Lord Pricklybum and the birdie to look after you... but I didn't imagine it would be this hard to let go of you."

I remembered then how Morrie looked when he'd first shown me the algorithm, sick to his stomach as he handed it over. My fingers dug into his shoulder. "You knew this was coming, didn't you?"

Morrie shrugged. "I had an inkling."

"How long?" I demanded. "How long have you known?"

"I've lived on the edge of the law my entire life, gorgeous. In my last life, that got me tossed over a waterfall by the man I loved."

"Get over it," Sherlock muttered from the fire, smoke curling from his pouting lips.

"Eat me," Morrie yelled back. "I had a second chance when I came to this world, and it wasn't until I met you that I realized I might have been making the same mistakes again. There was always a chance I'd get away with my crimes forever. I even fancied myself a bit of a Robin Hood figure. But when a person who faked their death turns up dead for real, the police start digging into how they stayed hidden for so long, and all it would take was one bribed official or crooked border guard to crack and they had my name. The footprints around the body, the letter opener, my business card in her pocket – this was a calcu- lated and deliberate attempt to frame me. I've been expecting my arrest ever since they found Kate's body. I read about it in the paper the morning of Danny Sledge's murder, if you recall."

I remembered now. I'd come downstairs from Quoth's bedroom to find Morrie standing over his computer with a frown on his face. He flicked over the screen as soon as I walked in, but I'd been so distracted by Danny's death and the murder investigation his odd behavior escaped my notice.

"Why didn't you pull some criminal mastermind wankery out of your arse to save yourself? It's like you *wanted* to go down for this." And I hated the way I sounded, like a selfish cow who only cared about what I wanted and not about the poor dead girl, but I missed Morrie like crazy and the thought that he'd willingly walked into this knowing he could end up behind bars made my head spin.

"Because..." Morrie wouldn't look me in the eyes. "Because I know you struggle to reconcile being my girlfriend with that pesky conscience of yours. I wanted to do the right thing. I wanted to make you proud of me."

A hard lump rose in my throat.

Fuck.

"Morrie, I—"

Morrie stood up. "You should go, Mina. Thank you for this stuff. Sherlock and I will get to work. Keep me posted."

Tears pooled in my eyes. *We can't leave it like this.* I reached for him, but he sidestepped for me and moved to stand beside Sherlock, who shot me a gloating look.

"Don't ruin your life for me, gorgeous," Morrie whispered.

"I'm not giving up on you," I shot back.

Morrie turned away, burying his face in darkness. "Tell the birdie I love him."

Sherlock patted his shoulder, cooing something comforting in his ear, the wanker.

"He already knows." I sucked in a breath. The pain of seeing Morrie like this and knowing I had to leave him here with Sherlock in this state burned at me – a deep, physical tremor in my bones. I tore my gaze from them both and yanked the door open.

The frigid air bit my skin as soon as I stepped outside. A dark shape fluttered down from the tree and rested on my shoulder. "Croak?"

"I'll be fine," I muttered, picking up the pile of Quoth's clothing from the stoop and holding it out to him as he fluttered down to the porch and transformed back into his human form. He leaned in to wipe the tear from my eye, but I ducked under him.

"You're not getting near me, cockroach breath."

We picked our way back through the darkness in silence. My head spun with thoughts I tried to shove back. Twice, Quoth stopped me to flutter off into the undergrowth and procure himself a snack. Just when I thought we must've been about to walk off the edge of the world we'd been hiking so long, Quoth stopped.

"There's Sam." Quoth tipped his head to the side. "And is that... Heathcliff?"

Sure enough, the two men clung to each other in the middle of the clearing, naked and singing off-key. Oscar bounced between them, yipping along with their song.

I groaned. "We need to get them to bed. You get Teacher's Pet, I'll try to wrangle Sam."

As I grabbed Sam under the shoulders, he threw his arms around my neck. "Oh, Mother, Mother, I love you so much. I'm sorry I yelled at you because you didn't invest in my hemp business."

"It's..." I remembered from wrangling a drunk Heathcliff that sometimes it was best to play along. "That's fine, dear. I'll make you a mug of hot cocoa and put you right to bed—"

"No, not cocoa! The chocolate plantations are destroying the rainforests..." Sam lunged for the pot on the fire, toppling over and bringing me down with him. His head bounced on a log, and he went still.

"Sam?" *Shite.* I shook his shoulder. "Are you okay?"

Sam blinked. I breathed a sigh of relief. He sat up, his eyes swimming as he rubbed his head. "M-M-Mina? What's going on?"

I opted for a blatant lie. "You nodded off before we started building our shelters. You look a bit sick. Perhaps it was something you ate…"

"No time for building shelters now. There's an emergency tent in my rucksack. You just have to… pull the cord and it'll… pop right up." Sam winced as he touched the side of his head. "I had the wildest dreams. A giant bear attacked me and then Allan turned into a bird and fairies enticed me to sing their forest songs—"

"It's okay, they were just bad dreams."

"I feel awful. I was supposed to be teaching you about survival, and I've gone and fallen asleep." Sam rubbed his eyes. "We didn't even check the traps or—"

"Don't worry, I've learned so much already this weekend," I grinned. "For example, I now know that I should only get lost in the wilderness if Heathcliff is with me."

Speaking of Heathcliff… I turned toward the fire, only to see my boyfriend staggering around the clearing, his hands over his head as he pirouetted like a ballerina. A wreath of wildflowers circled his head, and someone – probably Sam – had woven more flowers into his beard. "Dah-dah-dah-duuuum," he cried as he attempted a graceful ballet jump and crashed into a tree. "Pardon me, madame," he stepped back and took a deep bow, before twirling off for another ecstatic dance.

Quoth stood at the edge of the clearing, his phone held up to his face as he filmed Heathcliff's mirth.

"What are you doing?"

"Capturing this moment for prosperity." Quoth hit SAVE on his video and slipped his phone back into his pocket. "Morrie will love to see this. He needs something to cheer him up."

CHAPTER FIFTEEN

"I've got three pints of house-made cider. Have you decided on your food yet?" The waitress leaned across our table at The Right Fowl – the pub where I'd waited for the bus the day Sherlock Holmes kidnapped me.

Now there's a sentence I never expected to apply to my life.

I peered up from the menu, which I had to hold so close to my face that my nose touched the paper. "I'll have the bangers and mash, please, with a side of mushy peas. Oh, and the loaded fries and also this ploughman's platter with the cheese and pork pie. And a rasher of bacon for Oscar, and a slice of cheesecake for dessert. What about you guys?"

"That's all for you, ma'am?" She sounded surprised.

I grinned. "I'm starving. We've just come from Wild Oats—"

"Oh, the wilderness foraging course." She made a face. "Did Sam make you his famous cockroach omelette for breakfast?"

I made a face. "He was a bit… off his game last night, so fortunately, all we had this morning was nettle tea. It tastes like feet."

"Say no more. I'll bring you another pint of cider, too. You'll need it for washing down the cockroach taste."

"So you're quite familiar with the wilderness center?" Heathcliff asked.

"Oh, sure. The tour groups and hippie travelers basically keep this pub in business, especially over winter." She nodded toward the mountains. "Those hills are crawling with ramblers in summer, but over the winter Sam's the only one around here who brings in business."

"So he's well-liked around here? You don't think it's a little weird, what he does?"

"Sam's a bit strange, to be sure, but mostly harmless. It's a pity about all the trouble he's had, first with that girl gone missing and then her body showing up. This place was swarming with police a couple of weeks ago. It's the most exciting thing to happen in the village since we got hooked up to mains sewage." She turned to Heathcliff and Quoth. "What'll it be for you two?"

Heathcliff peered at the menu. "I'll have the full English breakfast, with a side of chips, and absolutely *no* mushrooms."

"Porridge with berries for me," added Quoth. "And I'll have a slice of cheesecake, too."

The waitress returned a few minutes later with our ciders and cheesecakes. Heathcliff drowned his drink in one swig. Truthfully, I wasn't that far behind him. Knowing the waitress was a talkative type, I pressed for some more information. "If Sam was the one who reported the body, then who else—"

"Sam wasn't the one who reported the crime," the waitress said. "Well, now, technically he *was*, but only because he had to."

"What do you mean?"

"It was the strangest thing. A German tourist came into the pub after the police removed the body and told me the whole story over a pint. He'd been hiking in the woods on the paths that crisscross into the area Sam uses for his expeditions. He heard something odd in the trees, so he left the path and found Sam grunting as he dragged a heavy object down toward the valley. The tourist stopped to offer help and Sam *freaked out*. It was only when the tourist noticed the blood leaking from the survival blanket that he realized Sam was dragging a *body*. Sam said he was bringing the body back to hand it over to the police – it had already been badly attacked by animals, and he didn't want to leave it up there for more evidence to be lost. The German convinced Sam to drag the body into a fallen log and bring the police to it."

"That's not what he—" I stopped myself before I admitted I'd been speaking to Sam about the murder. It wouldn't do to have people in the village remembering us snooping around. "That's not what the papers said."

"Nope. The police looked at Sam as a suspect initially, but there were footprints near the original crime scene significantly larger than Sam's shoes, and they went after some other bloke for it. The coppers sure thought Sam's behavior mighty suspicious at first, but people do stupid things when they stumble onto crime scenes. Sam seemed to genuinely think he was helping by bringing the body off the mountain, and he took them right to the original crime scene further along the ridge."

She left to put our order in and I pulled out my phone and texted Morrie. He needed to know that Sam lied about how he found the crime scene, and that his moving the body probably counted for many of Kate's bruises and the drag marks around the log.

"Well, this has been a *super fun* weekend hanging out with our new friend the murderer," Heathcliff finished his second cider.

I groaned into my hands. We were trying to eliminate suspects, and now we'd just added another to our list. Sam moved the body – did he kill her in a fit of rage over his ruined business and then attempt to conceal the evidence?

Could our kind-hearted cockroach chef be the murderer?

CHAPTER SIXTEEN

*O*ur trip to return Oscar and then back to the shop was uneventful, which was just as well because I kept spinning the facts of the case over in my head. Sam moving the body. Tara's threat, Grant's sleazy behavior, Kate's financial troubles and her decision to fake her death in the first place... not to mention, the weird way she was killed. None of it made sense.

As Heathcliff pushed open the shop's front door, he sniffed the air and made a face. "Something smells fishy, and I'm not talking about your mother's lack of interest in turning our shop into a smoothie bar."

"Mum must've got fish and chips from Oliver again." I sniffed the air as I flipped the sign to CLOSED. We were a few hours early, but after all that walking I did, I was going straight upstairs to snuggle with a cup of tea.

Actually, that doesn't smell like fish and chips. It smells... fresher. I hope Mum isn't trying to make prawn cocktails again. The only dinner party she ever tried to host and she gave ten people food poisoning...

"You turned the sign?" Quoth helped me pull off my coat, and hung it in the hidden cupboard at the end of the bookcase, where we stashed all our wet weather gear. He had to kick a pile of

Morrie's shoes out of the way to get the door open. Grimalkin walked over to greet us, sniffed my boot and, upon catching the scent of dog, shot me a filthy look and trotted away.

"Yeah. I know we're home early, but I'm so shagged I don't think I can deal with customers right now. I'm looking forward to a quiet night in with some takeout food that doesn't crawl—"

I rounded the corner into the main room and stopped in my tracks. My jaw flapped open, and try as I might, I couldn't force air to make a sound.

What... is... this...?

My mother sat *on* Heathcliff's desk, her laptop set atop a teetering stack of books. She faced the screen, chattering away on camera as she held up an oyster shell and cracked it open, splattering juice and bits of oyster across the carpet. Grimalkin scampered in and gobbled up the seafood before collapsing under the desk, purring with contentment.

Beside Heathcliff's desk, soaking briny juices into the rug, were two towering mountains of oyster shells.

CHAPTER SEVENTEEN

"*M*um," I breathed. "Wha—"

This is... I can't... but what...

"Mina, boys, you're back early." Mum slammed shut her laptop and glared at the three of us. "You're interrupting my live webcast."

"Your..." I rubbed my eyes, hoping that the piles of oysters would magically disappear, like some kind of blind Mina mirage. But no, there they were – two towering peaks of stinky oysters on the rug.

"Yes." Mum frowned. "It's my latest business idea. I'm hosting a pearl party."

Heathcliff spluttered. "What in blazers is a pearl party?"

I rubbed my temple. "Mum, I thought you said you weren't involved in any more pyramid schemes."

"This isn't a scheme. It's a legitimate business opportunity." Mum folded her arms. "Just because you haven't yet embraced the value of social media to connect with your audience, Mina, doesn't mean you can shoot down my dreams. Haven't I sold a lot of books for you?"

"Well, yes, but—"

"Exactly. How can it be a pyramid scheme if I'm helping the shop? And look at this." Mum popped open the oyster in her hand, revealing a tiny, luminous blood-red pearl. "Isn't it beautiful?"

"Is it supposed to be that color?" It looked like the perfect accent for a vampire's wedding dress.

"Look, Mina, this one is perfect for you. Red is for passion, vitality, and romance, see?" Mum thrust a chart in my face. I grabbed it from her hands and peered at the tiny writing. It showed pearls in twenty different lurid colors, each one with a description that corresponded to a particular personality type.

"Mum, what *is* this?"

"It's my Jewels of the Ocean business, of course. How it works is simple – my followers can buy an oyster, and then I'll shuck it onscreen and show them the pearl inside. They can then choose any item of jewelry from our catalog, and I'll insert their pearl into the piece and then ship it off. It's like your very own person-alized heirloom."

"But how do they ensure every oyster contains a pearl, and make the pearls colored like this?" I picked up an oyster and inspected the shell. "That's not natural, or ethical. And why are you selling them *here,* in the bookshop?"

"Darling, these pearls are certified by the International Pearl Council, so I'm sure they're fine. I *was* doing my feeds from the kitchen, but doing it here at the shop sets me apart from the crowd. I'm the Pearl Bookshop Lady. My followers get beautiful pearls *and* book recommendations, and I'm able to build my busi-ness *and* support my daughter."

A headache blossomed across my temples. "Why are your pearl buyers purchasing all these books?"

"I have to try and get people to stay on my live feed as long as possible, and I don't want to use up all my pearls." Mum nodded toward the pile of stinking seafood. "That has to last me until I get my first pearl payment. So I've been hunting through the bookshelves for pearl-themed books."

"I can't believe this."

Mum pointed to a picture of a mermaid behind Heathcliff's desk. "I even sold *that*. I was going to write you a check for the three hundred pounds now, but after you've denigrated my business, I've a mind to keep it for myself—"

"Don't you dare. Quo—er, Allan painted that. He deserves the money."

"Oh, Mina. I wish you could support Jewels of the Ocean. I was inspired by all the things you've done," she explained. "You've been so creative, coming up with clever events and displays and promotions. I thought pearl parties would allow me to be creative, too..."

"But... but this is a bookshop!" Heathcliff spluttered.

"Not now Mina's in charge." Mum pointed to the noticeboard I stuck beside Heathcliff's desk with our weekly events. "Now it's a community gathering place, with book clubs and stamp collecting meets and even a Science Fiction convention. I don't see why Jewels of the Ocean can't be part of that."

My shoulders sagged. I didn't know whether to laugh or cry.

"Sure, Mum." I sighed. "You can host your pearl party."

Heathcliff's fingers dug into my arm. "What are you doing? You're letting your mother shuck oysters in our shop."

"I know, it's crazy. This is my fault. She did a half-day of good work and I thought that made her responsible. But she's really done a great job looking after Nevermore while we've been away. She hasn't called you a gypsy once. I just..." I shrugged, then lowered my voice to a whisper. "I want her to feel included. And I want to keep her close. With Dracula wandering around... and if he's really after me because I'm Homer's daughter, then he might go after Mum, too. My father's note said that Nevermore protected me. Maybe it protects her, too."

Heathcliff snorted. He wasn't angry. He was *laughing*.

I shook his shoulders. "Who are you and what have you done with Heathcliff?"

Heathcliff tried to answer, but he was too far gone. He gripped my shoulder as tears of laughter rolled down his cheeks.

～

"*Y*ou never mentioned you were a keen gardener, Mina," Edie said as Oscar and I slid out of the rideshare.

"Oh, it's a... dormant hobby." I crossed my fingers behind my back, thinking of the time my neighbor asked me to look after his cannabis plot while he visited his ma in Dublin and I accidentally sprayed the entire thing with weed killer instead of fertilizer. Edie didn't need to know about that. She certainly didn't need to know the real reason why we'd come here. "I'm particularly interested in... um, orchids and such. With spring upon us, it's a good time to start looking for new specimens."

"Excellent idea. Plus, it's a great place for you and Oscar to learn about obstacles."

Oscar trotted through the garden center, leading me through the labyrinthine rows of plants and flowers, dotted all about with bright-colored pots and strange and wonderful statues. Toward the back of the store, Oscar led me to a door with a sign that read, "RARE PLANTS: ENQUIRE AT COUNTER."

Edie beamed. "There's braille on that sign. On all their signs, actually, I'm impressed."

A friendly-looking woman appeared at my side. She spoke with an Eastern-European accent. "My mother loved to garden her whole life; even when she went blind she could do everything by feel. She especially loved walking amongst the fragrant and beautiful wildflowers of our homeland. It is because of her that I started this center, and I believe that *anyone* can take pleasure in gardening as she did." She smiled. "My name is Tatiana. Can I help you?"

"Hi, my name is Mina, and I've fallen into orchidelirium." I didn't know the modern term for being an orchid fancier, but I learned all about the Victorian fascination with the rare plants in one of Jo's books. "I'm particularly interested in wild orchids from Romania, and I heard you have a couple of specimens of *Orchis simia*. I'm interested in purchasing one."

"I'm sorry." Tatiana curled her long fingers into fists. Fury rolled off her in waves. "We *had* two perfect specimens of the rare monkey orchid, but they were recently stolen."

"Oh, no. I'm so sorry to hear that." I knew they'd been stolen, of course. It was all in the newspaper article. But I was getting quite good at acting. "I know you specialize in rare plants. Did they take everything?"

Tatiana frowned. "They did not. It was very strange. The *Orchis simia* is not our rarest and most prized orchid by any stretch, and yet the thieves bypassed every specimen in our stores to take only those two plants. Occasionally, we have these types of robberies where thieves break in with a specific 'shopping list' – they've been commissioned by a collector to acquire a specific species, which is why we don't list our orchid species on our website any longer, but..." she trailed off.

"What?"

Tatiana winced. The memory of the robbery was physically painful to her. *Of course, it's painful.* I remembered how violated and afraid I felt when the charity Christmas tree and presents were stolen from the bookshop. Tatiana leaned against the wall and wiped her hands on her apron again. "The police found a scattering of leaves under the window where the plants were extracted, from the *Orchis simia*. Why go to all the trouble of stealing the orchids only to break it in the process? It will be worth nothing to the collector if it's damaged."

That's because the flower isn't important. The thief is after the dirt – the Romanian soil.

"Sounds like incompetent thievery," I ventured.

"That was the other strange thing – the window was broken *outward*. If they got out through the window, how did they get in? All our doors were locked."

That makes perfect sense if Dracula entered the building in his bat form through a vent, then transformed into his humanly visage in order to drag the pots out through a window.

Tatiana clicked her tongue. "Listen to me, going on about my misfortune. You do not care. You only wish to see the orchids. I can tell you that we have a new shipment of Romanian specimens coming in a few weeks. If you join our mailing list I can alert you when they arrive. For now, we have a large selection of Asian and South American varieties." Tatiana produced a key from her dirt-speckled apron and unlocked the door. "Would you like to see?"

"Of course."

It was a credit to Tatiana that she didn't inquire as to whether I *could*, in fact, see the flowers, or demand my dog stay outside. She just flung open the door and ushered me in.

As Tatiana dragged me around the small space, holding up orchids and exclaiming over their peculiarities, I dared a look at the broken window patched over with cardboard. It was high on the wall; Dracula would have had to climb on the shelves to crawl back outside.

I purchased a small orchid with beautiful shell-shaped leaves for far too much money to keep up my cover story, then Edie and I caught a rideshare back to the shop. Edie and Oscar came inside to do some orientation around the shop before she took Oscar back to the guide dog center. I kissed him goodbye, feeling a tug in my chest at the idea of saying goodbye. But Edie promised the two of them would be back tomorrow.

Quoth and Heathcliff returned from their outing just as they left. "We're not with that gormless estate agent any longer, so you can stop giving me the come-to-bed eyes," Heathcliff muttered.

"I can't help it if my normal eyes make you horny." Quoth swiped a strand of shimmering black hair back from his face.

"Just because Morrie's gone, doesn't mean you have to fill the void of his annoying presence."

"If I wanted to fill his void, I'd have spent all morning calling you The Archbishop of Crankybury, instead of *my darling husband*," Quoth shot back.

"Just for that," Heathcliff yanked a ring off his finger and held it out to Quoth. "You can have your engagement ring back, *honeybunch*."

"Did the newlyweds find the perfect love nest?" I teased. While Oscar and I checked out the nursery, Quoth and Heathcliff had gone to the local real estate office with a cunning backstory to check out empty properties nearby. Nothing sold in the village in the last week would work for Dracula, so we were hoping he hadn't purchased anything yet.

"We looked at all seven properties on our list," Quoth said. "Only two fit the requirements, and one overlooks an old churchyard and cemetery, *and* there's a creepy crypt right on the boundary line."

"That's got to be the place."

Quoth nodded. "Only we didn't get to look inside. Just as the agent unlocked the door, her phone rang. It was someone who introduced himself as a friend of the developer, and he offered a large sum of money to close on the house immediately. She got quite excited and rushed us back to the office so she could finish the paperwork for her illustrious buyer."

My chest tightened. I knew it was him.

"There's something else you should know." Heathcliff slammed a glossy real estate brochure on the desk. "The property he purchased was developed by Lachlan Enterprises."

CHAPTER EIGHTEEN

"*You* mean, Grey Lachlan's company?"

Heathcliff nodded.

This information rattled around in my head. Grey Lachlan – his name kept coming up in connection to murders here in Argleton. Murders that also always seemed to involve Nevermore Bookshop. He'd tried to buy the bookshop out from under us, and *now* he seemed to be a close, personal friend of Dracula himself?

That can't be a coincidence.

"You've got that look on your face," Heathcliff growled. "The scheming look."

"Grey Lachlan's been buying up property all over Argleton," I reminded them. "He purchased Mrs. Ellis' flat, and he's been offering Oliver at the bakery an inflated sum for his building."

"*And* he threatened us if we didn't sell him the bookshop," Quoth added. Grimalkin took the opportunity to saunter in, drop a dead mouse at my feet, and slink off again, her tail in the air.

"So?" Heathcliff growled. "He's a developer. Isn't that what they do?"

"Don't forget, he knew all about Morrie's money. He was the one who told us Morrie's accounts had been frozen. That's not the sort of thing a developer should know."

Heathcliff stepped around Grimalkin's gift and slumped into his chair. "He's a scumbag, but that isn't exactly a surprise."

"He's more than that – he's involved somehow. What if he's like, Dracula's real estate agent?" I grabbed my phone from my pocket and pulled up Morrie's algorithm. The map on the screen blinked, showing all the real estate purchases near sites of the dirt robberies. I scrolled through them all, punching the different buttons to try and see the information I needed.

Quoth peered over my shoulder. "Tell us what you're thinking..."

"I'm thinking that in Bram Stoker's book, Dracula had Renfield – a man he'd pulled under his influence. What if Grey Lachlan is Dracula's new Renfield? We could find out, but there doesn't seem to be a way to see if these recent property sales are on Lachlan's books. Even without that info, if you look at the pattern..." I held up the phone, clicking off the real estate overlay to show only the robberies plotted on the map. All the recent ones clustered within a two-hour radius of Argleton. "He's closing in on us. I'll text Morrie. He'll probably be glad of a way to help us—"

I cut off as the shop's bell tinkled. A moment later, a figure appeared in the doorway.

"Well, if it isn't my favorite Scooby-Doo bookshop gang." My blood froze in my veins as I recognized the voice. Grey Lachlan.

Grey stepped into the light, brushing a fine layer of dust from the front of his suit onto our rug. Heathcliff stiffened, his hands curled into fists. Quoth moved beside me, his arm brushing mine. I sensed the tremble in his skin as he struggled to hold his human form in Grey's presence, but he set his jaw in determination and glared at the developer.

I pushed my phone into my bat-shaped purse so Grey couldn't see it. "What do you want, Grey?"

"Why the suspicious tone, Mina? What if I came in to buy a book?" He threw back his head and laughed as if this was the funniest thing anyone had ever said. Unease flickered in my chest.

Grey ran a hand through his hair, which I noticed was also covered in a fine layer of dust. In fact... now that he stood in the light of my lamps, I could see the developer was unusually unkempt, his suit rumpled, the sleeves covered in small, dark stains, his eyes ringed with circles and filled with a mania that seemed at odds with his profession.

"You're tracking dust on our rug." I folded my arms.

Grey looked down at his ghostly footprints and the circle of white, and giggled some more. "My most profound apologies. I'm currently supervising renovations to my new property, and I didn't realize they'd coated me in plaster dust. I've come to visit in my capacity as a good neighbor to inform you of the works that will be going on next door."

Grey set down his briefcase and dived inside to dig out a stack of rumpled papers, which he handed to me. I held the papers under the desk lamp and stared at the tiny words.

It was a letter informing us of construction works taking place at the building across from us, along with a photocopy of a council permit. My heart fell as I read the words.

"You're erecting a scaffold across the entire street? You can't do that. It's going to block the entrance to our store!"

"Necessary, I'm afraid." Grey folded his hands. "It's a health and safety requirement for my workers. We need to redo the pointing as a matter of urgency. The council has rubber-stamped it. You have another entrance, so it will not be a detriment to your business."

"Sure, a narrow doorway down a back alley lined with rubbish bins." Nevermore Bookshop relied on business from tourists dropped off on bus tours at the town green. We were perfectly situated to take advantage of foot traffic from those foreigners wanting their perfect slice of English village life. But even if they could get to our front door through Grey's scaffold, they'd do their best to avoid the construction noise. We were already in a precarious financial position – a couple of quiet months would do us in.

And there was something else we hadn't considered. There was an old tunnel between our basement and Mrs. Ellis' flat across the street. She'd plastered it over in January after we discovered her niece was using it to sneak over to the shop to steal the charity Christmas presents for her pet dog. It would only be a matter of time before Grey discovered it, and I didn't like the idea of that guy having an easy way into our shop, especially not since the spring that supplied the waters of Meles was down there somewhere.

"Dear, dear, that will rather cut down on foot traffic to your shop," Gary tsked. "I promise I'll be as quick as I can with the work, but I do hope you have sufficient savings to see you through this time. Of course, my offer still stands. I'll happily buy this old dump from you for six times its current worth. You'd get rid of your money woes forever and have enough money to retire in the country."

"We're not interested, so stop asking. And stop bothering Oliver," I snapped. "He's not going to sell his building to you, either. Some people care about more than money."

Grey waved his hand. "Oh, but he will. Everyone has their price, and I have an endless pool of money and power from which to draw."

"Excuse me, sir?" A boy who couldn't have been older than fifteen came to the counter, glancing between Heathcliff's glowering face and Grey's manic one.

"You need to leave," Heathcliff's voice was low, his whole body tensed as he glared at Grey. "I don't want to behead you in front of a customer."

"Very well." Grey picked up his briefcase. As he did, he noticed Grimalkin's offering at my feet. He picked up the mouse by its tail and held it up, licking his lips as if it was some tasty treat. Grey winked at me, then spun around, swinging the mouse by its tail as he headed for the door. A moment later, the bell tinkled, and he vanished from our presence.

What the fuck was that about?

"I—I—I'm sorry." The boy backed away. "I didn't mean to disturb you."

I turned to the boy and smiled. "Don't worry about it. You actually did us a favor. How can we help?"

The boy held out an ereader. "Could you fix this? The scroll function is stuck."

Heathcliff glanced from the boy's face to the device, and back at the boy. Cogs turned in his head.

Uh-oh.

"I don't think it's a good idea to give him that—" I lunged for the ereader, but Heathcliff held it out of reach.

"Not to worry, lad. I have just the thing." Heathcliff set the ereader down on his desk and drew something from the drawer. Before I could stop him, he raised the hammer behind his head and brought it down on the unsuspecting device.

SMASH.

Bits of ereader flew everywhere. Sparks flew from the device.

"There you go." Heathcliff handed it back to the stunned boy. "Good as new."

CHAPTER NINETEEN

*N*ow that we had an idea where Dracula's boxes might be, we could move forward with our plan to stop him. Luckily, Bram Stoker had left us with detailed instructions. I found a battered copy of *Dracula* on the Classics shelf and thumbed through it, refreshing my knowledge of traditional vampire slaying, and then we got to work.

Armed with the *Dracula* paperback, Quoth and I left Heathcliff with specific instructions to block up the basement tunnel and get me a meeting with Grant Hosking any way he could. We strolled across the green to the village's Catholic church. I let out a shudder as I remembered one of the last times I'd rushed into a house of worship to find Ginny Button's body crumpled at the bottom of the stone steps, and who could forget Brian Letterman garotted in the Sunday school building? Mina Wilde and churches did not mix.

Quoth's fingers slipped into mine. "You look worried."

I waved the paperback in front of my face. "Of course I am. Morrie's in trouble and we're going after a bloodthirsty, immortal vampire. That, and we're about to commit a crime inside a church. I'm surprised you're not more afraid for your immortal soul."

"I'm not sure ravens have souls." Quoth saw the horrified expression on my face and smiled. "I'm sorry, that was meant to be a joke."

I rested my head on his shoulder. "No, *I'm* sorry. You should be at school now, learning about pretentious modern art and painting landscapes upside down in your underwear. Instead, you're here with me."

"Mina, I'll always watch over you. School will wait. This is where I must be."

The church parking lot was empty of cars. One of the wooden doors stood open, and a sign listed weekly services and invited anyone to enter to enjoy contemplative prayer. I poked my head around the door, but couldn't see or hear anyone in the gloom. Not that that meant much these days.

"Father O'Sullivan?" I called out.

No answer.

"Come on." Quoth squeezed my hand, tugging me into the church.

Candles lit sconces along the walls and flickered around the altar. Quoth led me straight to the apse, dragging me up the steps to the altar covered in its pristine white cloth.

"I did some reading up on Catholic mass, and the communion is kept in this tabernacle." Quoth reached for a highly-adorned cupboard inlaid with gold, beside which burned a single candle. He reached inside and pulled out a bowl filled with communion wafers. "These must be for this evening's Eucharist. Anything inside the tabernacle has been blessed."

"Perfect." I held open my bag while Quoth upended the dish into my purse. Wafers scattered across the floor, but most of them went into my purse. I stood up and glanced around. "Now, where's the holy water—"

A sharp voice startled me. "What in the Devil's name is going on here?"

CHAPTER TWENTY

I whirled around. Father O'Sullivan stood at the door to the vestry, his arms folded and a dour expression on his face.

"Oh, hi, Father. I'm just..." I beamed up at him. "We were hoping to find you. I am currently writing a book where the main character is, er... Catholic. I've come across the term 'cilice' in my research, and I wondered if you could tell me about it."

Father beamed. "I'm glad you thought to come to me, Mina. So many people have these strange notions about Catholics and our rituals and traditions. I'd be happy to talk to you about the cilice. It's an item worn on the body to inflict pain for the sake of penance. In olden times, one might wear a 'hairshirt' garment made of rough cloth that irritated the skin, but now it's more common to don a chain around the thigh with spikes that dig into the skin—"

As the two of us nodded along with Father O'Sullivan's lecture, I pushed the sacramental wafers into the bottom of my satchel. We thanked him for the info and dashed out of there as fast as we could. Hand in hand, Quoth and I cut through a ramblers path to reach the next village over, where we entered another church. This one was empty, thank the goddesses, and I scooped all the wafers into my purse as Quoth filled a thermos with holy water.

On the way home, we stopped at the village market. They were all out of fresh garlic, so I grabbed several bottles of extra-strong garlic aioli.

Now we were ready to hunt a vampire.

We returned to find Heathcliff straightening a picture on the wall in the hallway, at the end of the row of tiny taxidermied heads of rodents Grimalkin and Quoth had killed. He turned two spotlights to point at his creation and stood back to admire his work. "What do you think?"

"What I think is that you're not downstairs blocking up the tunnel, or setting up a meeting with Grant Hosking."

"Hosking wouldn't take my call, and I've already sorted the tunnel. I nailed three huge sheets of plywood over the hole, and I called Handy Andy to come and brick it up. He says he'll be here next week, although he's a handyman so he probably means next year. While I was at the hardware store I saw this shield and got the idea. What do you think?"

I stepped forward. On a large wooden shield, Heathcliff had mounted the busted ereader as though it were a hunting trophy. The trophy faced the door, so it would be the first thing customers saw when they entered.

"And you thought Morrie was the genius." Heathcliff grinned. It was an odd sight – more terrifying than mirthful, with lots of bared teeth. I loved it – a wild smile for my wild boy.

"It's… um…" I leaned in close to peer at the shield. Behind me, Quoth burst out laughing.

"Mina?" Heathcliff jabbed me.

"I… I have no words."

Heathcliff threw his arm around my shoulders and led me

toward the main room. "I think it makes our position on electronic reading and The-Store-That-Shall-Not-Be-Named clear. Come and see what else I've done while you were out on your walk."

As we entered the room, Grimalkin tore around the corner, her paws batting a tiny blue object. Quoth lunged for it and came up with a pearl, which he dropped into my pocket. *We're going to be finding these things everywhere now.*

Heathcliff pointed to a pile of wooden stakes on the corner of the desk, beside the orchid I purchased from Tatiana that was already wilting. "I got those from the hardware store, too. They're for growing tomatoes. I've sharpened them to points. How did you get on?"

I opened my purse to show him the wafers, holy water, and aioli. Heathcliff grabbed a wafer and bit into it. "Tastes like cardboard. I can see why you wanted the aioli."

I grabbed the wafer from his hands. "You know these aren't for eating. What time should we head out for a spot of vampire slaying?"

I glanced at my phone, then cursed at myself for doing that as a wave of lime-green light bobbed in front of my vision. I had to get used to asking for the time.

"It's half six." Quoth glanced at his watch. "Dinner first, an episode of Midsomer Murders, and we can leave about 10PM for our nocturnal criminal activities."

"It's not criminal activity if we're saving the country from a psychotic vampire," Heathcliff pointed out. "The Queen would approve. In fact, she should give us all medals."

"That's exactly what Morrie would say," I smiled, but the corners of my mouth wobbled. Morrie's absence rushed in on me. I gripped the edge of the desk, overcome by the need of him – to see him, to touch him, to know he was okay.

Nothing felt right without our criminal mastermind in our

midst. We all felt it, which was why we kept quipping in his comments to fill the void of his absence.

Heathcliff came around the desk, his eyes dark and heavy-lidded. He wrapped his arms around me, pressing me against him. "Quoth and I can make you forget all about Morrie," he growled.

"I don't want to forget him."

"No, but you do want the pain to go away."

I lifted an eyebrow, catching the desire in his voice. "What about Midsomer Murders?"

"We've got more than enough murder to deal with. I don't think we'll miss it." Quoth came up behind me, laying his hands over Heathcliff's as he fluttered kisses along my neck.

I'd never been with *just* Heathcliff and Quoth before. Whenever it was more than one of my boyfriends with me, Morrie's presence loomed large, and he had a way of taking over and running things. He liked to be in control, which was part of what was so fucking attractive about him. Especially when he bashed heads with Heathcliff's wildness. No wonder those two had so much unresolved baggage.

And Quoth... Quoth was the glue that held us all together. He was the sweetness, the sunshine, that made everything better. Right now, his lips found mine, and his kiss made everything better. Quoth was like rich Belgium chocolate *and* a great haircut. He sucked my lip into his mouth, and I melted into his arms.

Heathcliff threw out his arm, and in one swing swiped everything off the desk. A cascade of books, pens, paperclips, receipts, and broken bits of oyster shell toppled to the floor. The cash register bounced across the rug, coming to a stop when it hit the table leg, the drawer popping open and spilling coins everywhere. Grimalkin yowled in fright and dashed off.

It would take us hours to sort out the mess he'd made. And I didn't give a fuck. Quoth spun me around and pushed me toward Heathcliff, whose rough hands shoved me facedown on the desk.

If it was Morrie, he'd be standing behind me now, trailing the tips of his fingers over my exposed arse, purring something filthy that would have me instantly wet.

But this was Heathcliff, and he didn't go in for teasing and tempting. He brandished his heart – and his cock – like a weapon. I had no choice but to surrender.

Heathcliff slammed into me, so huge and so hard that I gasped for breath. I tried to wriggle my hips and drive him deeper, but his body wrapped around me, pinning me in place. He dug his fingers into the flesh of my thigh, so hard it hurt in the best possible way. I threw back my head and stared up into Quoth's eyes, swimming with love and lust and need, and I came so hard I blacked out a little.

Heathcliff wasn't done with me; not even close. He somehow flipped me over while still inside me. His giant hands palmed my breasts as he stared down at me with lust hooding his eyes. His lips crushed mine, hot and savage, and his fingers fisted in my hair, arching my head back to expose my neck.

I ground my hips against Heathcliff, wanting more, more, more, not caring that the corner of the desk was probably leaving a permanent mark in my arse. Above my head I caught Quoth, watching, always watching, with the sweetest and sexiest smile playing at his lips.

I threw back my head and gave myself over to the two of them and their magic.

When Heathcliff came, he didn't let go right away. He pulled me tight against him, even though I was so high from the orgasms I was just dead weight at this point. His body shuddered against me, and he buried his head in my shoulder as he braced himself for a final thrust.

"I promise you, we'll get him back," he whispered against my ear, ragged and raw – so quiet I almost thought I imagined the words.

Heathcliff slid off me and staggered back, his eyes wide as if he wasn't quite sure what he said. His words hung between us, and instead of forgetting Morrie, they made the longing for him rise like needles in my heart. Heathcliff's eyes fluttered closed, and his breath escaped in a rasp as he clutched his fist to his chest, as if he too breathed through the pain of losing the man we both loved with a fierceness that corrupted our souls.

Quoth picked me up and carried me to the window, laying me out along the sofa and taking time to arrange my limbs and hair just so, like an artist composing a still life. His hands trailed down my body, searching, exploring. He followed his fingers with his mouth, laying trails of featherlight kisses that turned the needles in my chest into an ache that called to be sated.

The kisses deepened, and the connection between us deepened, too. Quoth pressed his lips to my breast, right where my heart stuttered out its racing, broken beat. And it felt like his lips touched something inside me, like he closed over a hollow in my chest and filled me with his light.

My tortured artist, my beautiful spirit, laying his heart bare.

I parted my legs, angling my hips upward to draw him in. Quoth entered me with a sigh that was both sad and exquisite. As he covered my body in his and became part of me, the words of his creator fell into my head...

"We loved with a love that was more than love...
  With a love that the winged seraphs of heaven
  Coveted her and me."

Later, as we three lay together in a tangle of limbs on the enormous bed the guys somehow levered up the stairs for me without killing each other in the process, the words of another author – Bram Stoker – called to me, and I felt a cold and undead thing reach through the darkness to stab at my heart, for I knew that somewhere out there a monster hungered to take from me everything that I loved.

"Even if she be not harmed, her heart may fail her in so much and so many horrors; and hereafter she may suffer – both in waking, from her nerves, and in sleep, from her dreams."

CHAPTER TWENTY-ONE

"*M*ove your feathery arse, I can't get a good view," Heathcliff grumbled.

"Croak."

"That's not a very polite thing to say in front of a lady," Heathcliff shot back, in a rather Morrie-ish tone.

Heathcliff and Morrie could hear more of Quoth's thoughts telepathically than I could, so I didn't get to hear his rude comment. (The gesture he made with his wing was pretty universal). I heard only the thoughts Quoth directed at me, but the three of them seemed to carry on whole conversations where I only heard one side. This was one of those times. However, since we were staking out Grey Lachlan's property, it was also the time for all of us to be silent.

"Why didn't you bring your dog along, Mina, to make it a whole jolly circus—ow!" Heathcliff rubbed his cheek and glared at the raven. "What was that for?"

"Croak!" Quoth hopped angrily. Heathcliff gave an exasperated sigh.

I glared at them both. "Do you think you guys could keep it down?"

"Blame the bloody great big hole in my cheek," Heathcliff grumbled.

"You deserved that. Quoth's right. In a few months, Oscar will be coming along on all our excursions, and he's probably better behaved than the two of you." I elbowed Heathcliff in the arm. "Tell me what you see."

"Absolutely sodding nothing." Heathcliff parted the hedgerow and lifted the binoculars to the row of modernist townhouses. "Do you think he's even in there?"

Taking that as his cue, Quoth fluttered across to the balcony and perched on the railing, peering into the dark windows. He made a circuit of the house before returning to the bushes.

All clear. The house is completely empty. Not a bat in sight, and no coffin in the living room.

I patted his head and shouldered my vampire kit. "Let's go."

We padded across the manicured grass and crowded under the door. Quoth kept an eye out on the street while Heathcliff fumbled with Morrie's lock-picking kit. "These bloody things weren't made for my fingers," he muttered as he dropped the tiny metal tool for the third time.

"Give it here." I held out my hand.

"You said you wanted me to pick the lock."

"Because if I don't give you a job to do, you stand there sniping and distracting the rest of us. Of course, this was when I thought you knew what you were doing." I shook my hand. Heathcliff dropped the kit into it.

"And you do?"

I knelt down at the door and shoved the pick into the lock. "When Morrie gets bored, he makes me practice lock-picking. I can't guarantee I'll get it, especially since I can't see what I'm doing, but according to Morrie it's all about feel—"

CLICK.

The door swung open. I grinned triumphantly at Heathcliff. Quoth fluttered back from the road and slipped inside first, scouting the interior before inviting us inside with a wave of his wing.

All clear.

I flicked on the light – with all the glass, it looked less suspicious than shining flashlights around – and studied the townhouse. Grey Lachlan might be many things, but he had a good design team – if you went in for minimalist cubes. The bottom floor was open-plan living, dining, and kitchen, the entire back wall floor-to-ceiling glass overlooking the river. The place was already fully furnished in crisp, modern furniture and tasteful 'non-art' on the walls, all in stark white accented with earthy, hipster tones.

My eyes searched the smooth surfaces for a box or pot where Dracula was keeping his earth, but there was nothing out of the ordinary. Heathcliff stomped around in the bedroom upstairs, while Quoth hopped along the windowsills and used his beak to open the kitchen drawers.

"Maybe he hasn't dropped it off yet?" Heathcliff thumped down the stairs.

"Or maybe he didn't want it to appear out of place, especially if he thought we were on to him. No doubt Grey has been telling him about us." I eyed the kitchen, where a row of brand-new appliances lined the bench. A cold-press coffee machine, a fancy bread-maker and... was that a craft beer brewing pail?

I lifted an eyebrow at the strange array. "Is Dracula a hipster?"

Hyuh-hyuh-hyuh. Quoth laughed his bird laugh.

"If Morrie were here, he'd be begging us to get one of these things for the shop." Heathcliff eyed the coffee machine. "All of these kitchen torture devices have containers, right?"

Of course.

Heathcliff pried the bread-maker open while I lifted the top off the craft beer. An earthy scent hit my nostrils, and when I peered down into the pail, my nose touched damp, fresh dirt.

"Found it." I held up the pail in triumph. "One box of Dracula earth, ready for neutralizing."

"Get the communion crisps and let's get out of here." Heathcliff's eyes flashed.

I held the pail under one arm as I plunged my hand into my purse. "They're called wafers, not crisps—"

Wings fluttered behind me. I thought Quoth was investigating the cupboards, but then he let out a strangled croak. Unease slithered through my chest. *He's in trouble.*

I whirled around. Quoth's wings flapped frantically as a tall man held him, pressing my raven's body to his chest as he held up a butcher's knife. The shadow of the kitchen cabinets and a black hood pulled low over his face hid most of his features from me. A smile that could only be described as maniacal spread across a pair of thin lips.

The stranger pressed the knife to Quoth's throat and held out his hand for the pail. "I think that belongs to me."

CHAPTER TWENTY-TWO

*I*t's him.

It's Dracula.

He stepped under the lights, and my body froze in terror. *He's got Quoth. He's hurting Quoth.* All I could do is stare at the figure as it advanced toward me, fingers reaching, reaching, their tips stained with dark splotches.

Blood.

Quoth reached up and gripped the edge of the man's hood with his beak, tugging it off. I reeled as I identified the face beneath. He was barely recognizable – his usually slick suit replaced with a stained black tracksuit that hung from his body in tatters, strips of flesh had been torn from his cheeks, and his eyes blazed with deranged fire.

Not Dracula.

Grey Lachlan.

Grey's hand hung in the air between us, his fingers grasping. "I'll take that dirt back, thank you."

"You mean this dirt?" Regaining my wits, I held up my hand so Grey could see the sacramental wafer in my fingers. Grey lunged forward, but he was too slow. I shoved the wafer into the dirt, scattering particles across the pristine tiles.

The developer froze, dropping Quoth. My raven hit the tiles and scrabbled to safety behind Heathcliff's legs. Grey's eyes bugged out with cartoonish terror fright as he stared at the wafer sticking out of the dirt.

"You don't know what you've done," he hissed.

"I know exactly what I've done." I upturned the pail, throwing the dirt over him, scattering it around the pristine kitchen. "Tell your boss that we're on to him. We're on to *you*. There's no way he's getting his hands on Nevermore Bookshop, and we'll stop him before he can turn England into his new hunting ground."

Grey narrowed his eyes at me. "You think you have the power to stop him, daughter of Homer? You think his plans stop at merely controlling England? You're a silly blind girl with a gypsy thug crying over his broken heart, and a useless scrap of a poem whose only power is growing feathers out his arsehole. The only one who was a real threat was the Victorian criminal, but he's been neutralized. Nothing stands in his way now."

He knows.

He knows the secrets of Nevermore Bookshop. But how?

I opened my mouth to demand answers from Grey. He could have found out about Morrie's kidnapping from the papers, but that other stuff he said...

Lightning cracked outside the window, sending a dazzling pulse across the room that blinded me. I blinked frantically, my hand clutching the stake. I lunged forward blindly, but my stake pierced only air.

Grey Lachlan had disappeared.

CHAPTER TWENTY-THREE

"Stop pacing," Heathcliff muttered.

"How does he *know?*" I dragged my fingers through my hair, slamming my Docs on the floorboards as I stomped back across the room.

We were back in the bookshop. It was well past midnight, but no way in hell could I sleep. Heathcliff had lit the fire and curled up into his chair. Grimalkin, in human form, perched on the corner of the rug at his feet. And Quoth stood in the shadows, his head hung, his pouty mouth drawn in a thin line.

"He knows about the shop because Dracula told him. If Mr. Simson—your father, I mean—has been chasing him all these years, then it's likely Dracula has watched the shop. He knows about its magic because this is where he came from, and he's probably figured out our identities through a process of elimination. It's not as if our names don't make it obvious. As for you, your father believed you were safe here. If his letters are to be believed, Dracula didn't know you existed, which—" Heathcliff coughed, cutting himself off.

"—which means something horrible's probably happened to my father," I finished for him. "I figured that out. What I don't understand is… why is all this happening now? If Dracula has been on earth for a long time, why has he waited until now to make his move?"

"Because you went to America," Quoth said quietly.

"Huh?"

"He didn't know you existed. You lived in America. Maybe it was only when you returned that he learned about you. Plus…" Quoth squeezed his eyes shut, a sure sign he was about to say something he knew I wouldn't want to hear. "If you remember, Dracula has a telepathic connection with Mina Harker. Perhaps he believes somehow that you're necessary."

"But I'm *not* Mina Harker. Sharing this same first name as her is a complete coincidence. I'm plain old normal not-from-a-fictional-story Mina Wilde. This can't all be about me." I threw up my hands. "I'm a nobody. I'm a failed fashion designer turned bookshop half-owner." *And an aspiring writer,* I thought under my breath, but still didn't have the bravery to say that out loud.

"You're Homer's daughter," Heathcliff shot back.

"And *my* granddaughter," Grimalkin reminded us, as if that was the most important thing.

"So? It's not as if that imbues me with some kind of special magic. All it's been good for is an abandonment complex and a pair of wonky eyes."

"My son was washed in the waters of Meles." Grimalkin rose up to her full height, her lithe body stretching long. She placed her hands on my shoulders, sharp nails digging into my flesh. Her eyes blazed with a fire that seemed to come from inside her, that spoke of old, ancient rites and goddesses that walked the earth. In that moment, she appeared every inch the formidable, magical nymph of legend. "That same magic runs in your veins."

I stared down at my hands. "I'm not magical. That's ridiculous."

Grimalkin smirked. "Then why does this building respond to your presence? Why is Dracula using his servant to spy on you?"

"Dracula wants the shop, not me."

"He needs both if he is to use the Spring of Meles to travel through time."

I leaped back in surprise, my leg hitting the edge of the coffee table and spilling a stack of books across the floor. "How do you know that's what he's trying to do?"

"It's obvious." Grimalkin blew on her perfect nail polish. "Why would Dracula stop at consuming all the blood of England when he could travel through time and into the worlds of books to consume every human that ever was and ever will be? He could unseat the kings and queens of history and place himself on their thrones, build whole armies of his undead slaves, and flit to a new era when he craves new blood. When one is immortal, the possibilities of possessing time travel are somewhat titillating."

I flopped onto the chair opposite Heathcliff. Green lightning danced in front of my eyes, and I rubbed my temples. "Great. Just wonderful."

"We get it. Dracula is one scary motherfucker. But we're not going to defeat him tonight," Heathcliff snapped. "And we're certainly not going to figure it out without Moriarty. We need to get back to his case."

Morrie. My arms ached to hold him. I desperately needed to hear his smooth, cocky voice, to feel his arms slip around me. I pulled out my phone and stared at the screen filled with texts from him, asking how our first foray into vampire-hunting had gone. They started off in his usual flippant style but rapidly became more concerned. *He's desperate to be here with us, too.*

I tapped out a message about destroying the dirt, meeting Grey Lachlan, and figuring out that Dracula was after the waters of Meles. *Shite. If Grey's working for him, we're really in trouble if he uncovers the tunnel. I hope Heathcliff can get Andy to show up soon. Maybe we should sprinkle holy water and put some plates of aioli around the place...*

My phone beeped with a message from Morrie. "Dracula

wanting Nevermore actually makes sense, especially if you consider that mathematical impossibility of vampires."

"Excuse me, that what?"

He typed back. "An American physicist did the math. If a vampire arrived on earth, fed only once a month, and every person he fed on eventually became a vampire, the entire population of Earth would be vampires within three years. Assuming vampires can't drink the blood of other vampires, this simply won't do if you require human blood to survive. But if Dracula could suck on the necks not just of every human in history but of every human in the pages of every book ever written... I'm glad to hear you're okay, gorgeous. I was beginning to imagine your neck perforated with vampire bites. Tell that Dracula bastard the only one allowed to bite you is me."

A smile tugged at the corner of my mouth as I dictated a reply, asking him how he fared.

"I am well enough, now I have books and chess and your occasional missives for company. Sherlock is acting strangely. The trail from Aidan has gone cold, but despite the evidence you've presented he refuses to look at Grant or Tara or even Sam the Cockroach Man as suspects. I'm concerned the time travel has addled his brain or something. What have you uncovered?"

"Not much. We haven't been able to get a meeting with Grant, and I haven't found out from Jo what Kate was wearing when she died."

"Not to worry, I hiked further up the mountain and managed to get some decent reception today. The button shows the crest of Abbythorne, an elite public school. You'd love the place, gorgeous – the buildings look like something from Hogwarts. A quick perusal of the Abbythorne alumni reveals that Grant Hosking attended the school as a boy. And look at this – he recently attended a reunion in which all the prefects wore blazers."

Morrie sent me the image of Grant Hosking with his smug

beard standing in a line of equally-smug looking middle-aged dudes. All the guys in the picture wore black jackets with shiny buttons. The same buttons as the one Sherlock found near Kate's body.

Something else about the picture looked familiar, too. Something about the blazers… it niggled at me, but I couldn't place it.

I sent my reply. "It's all connected. I know it is. Tara and Grant were seeing each other. If only we could get in to see Grant, but so far we haven't been successful."

Morrie sent me a link to a job website. Curious (and with a due sense of trepidation), I clicked on it. My phone read out the ad – a personal assistant required to work 'up close and personal' with the founder of Ticketrrr.

My lips pulled back into a wild grin. I knew exactly what Morrie was suggesting. Trust him to figure out the perfect way to get a captive audience with our number one suspect.

Quoth dropped over the arm of the chair, wrapping his arms around my neck. "What does Morrie say?" His voice hitched with concern. "Is he holding up okay as a caged bird?"

"Morrie is just fine. In fact," I held up my phone to show Quoth the text. "Now, if you'll excuse me, I must get to bed if I'm to wow my new potential employer with my wit and beauty in the morning."

CHAPTER TWENTY-FOUR

"*H*i, Mr. Hosking. My name is Mina." I batted my false eyelashes. "I'm so excited to be here. I love... um, tech."

Things move fast in the tech world, so I'd been called in for an 'informal chat' an hour after submitting my resume. Heathcliff stayed in the store to wait for Handy Andy and keep my mum from having any more oysters delivered there, while I took Oscar and Quoth up to London on the train. Quoth was handling being around Oscar so well I left them to wander around Hyde Park and get acquainted while I wowed Grant Hosking with my... assets.

I hadn't had a lot of time to prepare for my interview, so I was still pretty unsure what exactly Ticketrrr did beyond providing some kind of cloud ticketing app for large events and having three superfluous 'r's in its name. It didn't look like my lack of knowledge would be a concern. As Grant drew his eyes up my body like I was a tender brisket and he'd just got off a two-week juice fast, I knew I nailed the outfit. It was just corporate enough to get me in the door, but the skirt barely covered my arse, and adding the knee-high white socks with the bows? *Genius.*

At least, that was what Morrie told me after I texted him a selfie. He said some other things that were so filthy I blushed just recalling them.

Focus, Mina.

I'd forgotten what I'd been talking about, so I just batted my eyelashes again. Grant's Adam's apple bobbed as he struggled to formulate coherent thoughts. He placed his laptop over his crotch in such a way I knew he was thinking inappropriate things about me. I was almost proud of myself until I remembered that this guy could have killed Kate Danvers.

"We do things differently at Ticketrrr. We don't believe in hiding people away in offices and silos. We work in one large shared workspace – no assigned desks. You never know who you'll sit next to, and when a chance conversation can spark a million-dollar idea. This room is one of our shared meeting spaces." Grant glanced at the screen on the wall. "We have to leave in twenty-two minutes so the office pub quiz team can practice."

How does a pub quiz team practice? But then I noticed a beer fridge in the corner of the room, with bags of crisps and boxes of doughnuts on top, and I suspected I knew the answer.

"Fascinating. I'm so excited to be a... team player." I twirled a strand of hair around my pen. *Urgh, I'm almost criminally good at this.*

"I appreciate that, Mina. It's been difficult to find someone who can adapt to the hard and fast pace of work here. I used to have an amazing senior developer, Kate, but ever since she left, I haven't been able to find someone who'll stay for more than a few weeks."

Probably because you're a class A wanker. I beamed. "Well, I don't give up easily. Tell me, what made this Kate leave? Did she move on to a better position in the company?"

"Er, no. It's a sad story, actually. She died." Grant's gaze slid to a spot behind my head. I noticed he didn't say *how* she died.

"That's too bad."

"Yes… but we can't dwell on the negatives when we're disrupting the events ticketing space. It's an exciting time – we're a team of ninja rockstar developers, and building the plane while we're flying it. Right now we're only ramen-profitable, but our big IPO is right around the corner. Did I show you our system? We do everything in the cloud, so we're scalable and agile. I'll show you how our app works—" Grant pulled his chair so close he was practically sitting in my lap, and he brushed his arm against mine as he opened an app on his laptop.

What a wanker – I'm not even in tech and I can tell he just threw every cliche and jargon word in the book at me to make himself sound clever. I tried to act interested as Grant described the app while making circles on my thigh with his fingers. Every inch of me crawled with the desire to get out of there, but I wouldn't leave until he gave me *something*.

But how to bring up Kate and Tara in a natural way?

Grant closed the window on his laptop, and I noticed his screensaver wasn't the usual random desert island but a photo of twenty dude-bros giving the metal horns at the camera. *Gross. I bet they're all Ed Sheeran fans who've never heard a punk or metal song in their lives.*

Something caught my eye in the back row. Or rather, *someone.*

Grant turned the computer away, but I grabbed his arm. He froze in surprise. It was probably the first time a woman had ever initiated contact with him. His skin felt clammy, and I suppressed a shudder, but I kept my cool and batted my eyelashes again.

"That picture on your desktop – it looks like a fun event. Can I see closer?"

"Sure." Grant passed me back the laptop, and I peered at the image.

It's him, *I know it.*

His hair was red, and he had a hipster beard and a lumberjack shirt, and his eyes were a different color, but it was *him*. I'd recognize that face anywhere now.

Rage coursed through me, molten lava in my veins. I was so shocked and livid, I barely noticed Grant was still talking. "— picture was taken at our leadership summit two years ago. Every year we bring the best and brightest future leaders in the company on an exclusive all-expenses-paid trip. We spend the week hanging out at a luxury resort, doing leadership training and cool activities. Only exceptional performers are invited. I'm sure you'll be a shoo-in for this year's event."

Two years ago.

I swallowed. This photograph changed *everything*. "Who's that man?" I jabbed my finger at the man's face.

"Oh, Clarence? He's from our Paris office. A bit of a stick-in-the-mud, more interested in crossword puzzles than prostitutes and blow—" Grant coughed to cover what he was going to say. "Yes, well, these retreats can get pretty wild, but we do try to keep the worst stuff off social media for the reputation of the company. But this guy doesn't even use social media. I'm telling you, he's a freak. I had to threaten his job just to get him to pose in this pic."

"How long has Clarence been employed at your firm?"

"I'm not sure if he's still around. He blends into the background a bit, and we tend to turn people over quite quickly."

"This might sound weird, but can I have a copy of this? I want to put it on my vision board as something to aspire to."

Bat, bat, bat. My eyelashes had never had such a workout.

"My pleasure. Let me run one off for you." Grant tapped a couple of keys, then stood up. "The printer is in the other room. Would you like a top-up of coffee while I'm out there?"

"Sure, thanks."

Grant left, pushing the frosted glass door shut behind him. As soon as the door clicked shut I spun his computer toward me and flicked to his email client. Searching Kate's name didn't land a single result, which made no sense if she was his lead developer. Then I noticed a chat notification pop up in the corner.

Of course, a super techie office like this would be too cool for email. I clicked on the chat and found a long string of private conversations between Kate and Grant. I didn't have time to read them, so I emailed them to Morrie's secret cloud account to look at later. I closed the screen and slid the computer back just as Grant came back in with coffee and my photograph.

"Thank you so much for this." I slid the photograph into my satchel and stood up. "I'd love to stay for coffee and chat more about being, um, iterating and executing and pivoting and your truly impressive beard, but I actually forgot I have... another interview to get to, for this startup called ReWined – have you heard of it? It's an app where you can share opened bottles of wine you don't like with other people who've also opened a bottle they don't like. But you've been *so* wonderful, and I'm excited to be invited to apply for this job."

I raced out of the building before Grant could find some other excuse to touch me again. Quoth leaned against a telephone pole, his hands shoved deep in his pockets and his eyes fixed on the sky. In the greyness of London's narrow streets, Quoth stood out – radiant and luminous, his hair a shimmering waterfall of shadow. Oscar sat demurely at his feet, looking like the picture of obedience and canine perfection. No wonder a woman walking past got so distracted perving at them both that she tripped over the curb.

I threw myself into Quoth's arms. His lips touched mine, washing away Grant's disgusting touch. I shuddered against Quoth as the ghost of Grant's clammy fingers still circled my thigh.

"That man was gross." I buried my face in Quoth's shoulder, drinking in the fresh scent of him. Oscar jumped up, wanting to be part of the hug, too, so I wrapped my arm around him as well.

Quoth's eyes traveled down my body, taking in the ridiculous outfit. The edges of his dark orbs flared with orange fire. "You look amazing."

He shifted a little, so I felt his erection against my thigh. My mind flashed back to the first time I came to London with Morrie and Quoth, to investigate the fashion designer Holly Santiago who we believed killed my ex-best friend Ashley. Morrie dragged me into an alley and stuck his hand under my leggings. Quoth watched from the confines of his birdcage as Morrie drove me wild with his fingers and his filthy, vicious tongue.

A warm blush crept across my cheeks at the memory. Quoth must've been thinking about that day, too, because his fingers tangled in my hair and he pulled me into a deep, toe-curling kiss.

"I'm glad I'm not stuck in a cage this time." He pulled me against him, and I swooned a little. I wasn't usually big into PDA, but that was before I had a Quoth in my life to hug in the street. "Oscar and I enjoyed the park. He tried to chase a squirrel, but I distracted him with some treats. He seems to like me and is not at all interested in eating me alive. Was your outfit at least a success?"

"You have no idea. I managed to copy over Grant's chat history with Kate. When we get home we can go through it, or I'll send it to Morrie. I'm positive something was going on with him, but just because he's a slimy git doesn't mean he's a murderer. Especially when..."

"What is it, Mina?" Quoth asked.

I dug the photograph from my purse and handed it to him. "This is a picture taken at the Ticketrrr leadership summit from two years ago. Look at the second man on the left. I might not be seeing things right because of my eyes, but—"

"Shite," Quoth whispered, his voice tight.

"Exactly."

I glared down at the picture, knowing we had an even bigger

mystery on our hands now. Why was *Sherlock Holmes* at the Tick-etrrr leadership retreat *two years ago*, and what was he hiding?

CHAPTER TWENTY-FIVE

"*H*e lied to us," I whispered, my voice tight with rage. "That bastard *lied*. He said he'd been in our world for a couple of months, and he's been working at this company at least *two years ago*. Grant said he refused to be in any other photographs, so he was being careful to hide evidence of his presence."

Quoth frowned at the picture. "Do you think this is the real reason Sherlock didn't want your help investigating Morrie's case? He knew it would lead you to Kate's boss, and he didn't want you to find that photograph."

"Exactly. But *why?* What does it matter that he works for the same company as Kate? Why would it make Sherlock not consider Grant a suspect? If anything, it should make him more suspicious. He had to know Grant was a complete bastard—" My eyes widened. "This means Sherlock could have been at the Wild Oats retreat when Kate first disappeared. He's deeper in this than he wants us to believe."

"He's determined to pin the murder on one of Morrie's crime buddies," Quoth pointed out. "What if it's to divert attention from Grant or someone else at Ticketrrr?"

"Exactly." My blood ran cold. "Or... from himself."

"You realize what this means." Quoth's dark eyes bore into mine. "Morrie's trapped in that cabin with our main suspect."

I clung to Quoth as the horror of it washed over me, turning my blood to ice. All this time I assumed he was here to win back Morrie's love. But could Sherlock Holmes be our killer?

CHAPTER TWENTY-SIX

"*T*hat poxy bastard," Heathcliff's fingers scrunched the corners of the photograph.

After another tearful goodbye to Oscar and Edie, Quoth and I returned to the shop, where I'd thrust the photograph into Heathcliff's huge hands and spilled the whole story.

"Careful." I swiped it back. "I need that as evidence. Besides, it doesn't mean he's *definitely* the killer. I've looked through all the messages between Grant and Kate. This guy was total scum. After she rejected his advances, he brought Tara onboard as a cosplay consultant and brand ambassador even though he knew Kate had the exact contacts in the industry. When he started seeing Tara, Grant would share lewd details about their week-ends with Kate just to make her miserable. And when she made a complaint about him, he got all his dude-bros on the team to back him up, and say Kate misinterpreted his 'boyish banter' as harassment. Grant's last words to her, a couple of weeks before they all left for Wild Oats, were 'You'd better watch your back. No one wants a wet blanket on the Ticketrrr team. We've already taken care of your little events company. Make another complaint like that, and Tara and I will make sure you pay.'"

"That sounds like a threat," Heathcliff growled.

"It's *absolutely* a threat. Was it what sent Kate over the edge and convinced her to go through with the fake death? But if her death was so successful, why come back to England at all? Why not stay in the Philippines? Did she come back for Dave? I don't believe he's seen her alive – he doesn't seem like a guy who knows how to lie convincingly. Or did Kate have altruistic motives? Maybe she saw Grant was recruiting more young, hot women from the cosplay scene. She decided to come back and warn them off, and that's why Grant hasn't been able to keep a developer since. Maybe Grant figured out it was Kate scaring off all his potential creeping victims and so he decided to get revenge—"

My phone buzzed. I grabbed for it. "Morrie, are you okay—"

"Mina, I need to speak with you." Dave's voice cracked. He sounded *terrified*. "Can you meet me at my place? Please? I don't have anyone else to turn to, and I need to show you the truth about my wife's murder."

CHAPTER TWENTY-SEVEN

"*Y*ou're not going in there alone." Heathcliff grabbed my arm as I shot out of the rideshare. "This guy is still on our suspect list."

"Dave knows me. If I run in there with a hulking, angry Heathcliff, I'll scare him off. This is the biggest clue we've had yet, and I won't let you frighten him into silence."

"Fine. But Quoth's going in with you." Heathcliff flung open the door of the cage and plonked the heavy raven on my shoulder.

I'll watch out for you. Quoth's soothing voice fell into my head. I glared at Heathcliff until he retreated into the shadows of the trees lining the edge of the park, then took off toward the house.

The front garden was in an even worse state of disrepair than last time. As I approached the front door, a figure darted from the side of the house and sprinted down the lane that ran between Dave's block of flats. It might've been my wonky eyes playing tricks on me, but it *looked* like the figure wore a white angel costume that looked like it was splattered with red paint.

That was Tara Delphine, Quoth said. *Should I follow her?*

"Go." I shoved him off my shoulder. He swooped into the lane after Tara, leaving me alone on the stoop. Fear twisted in my gut. *What's she doing here, and why did she run as soon as she saw me approach?*

I raised my fist to knock, but realized the door was already open a crack. I pushed it with my foot, desperately not wanting to step inside but knowing I had no choice.

I cast a glance over my shoulder. I couldn't see across the street to Heathcliff, but knowing he was there, ready to run in, fists flying, gave me the jolt of bravery I needed to surge forward. I stepped inside. Kate peered out at me from the photographs lining the walls – the same bright green eyes and smiling face on a hundred different costumes, each one revealing a facet of her personality. I noticed a gap where one of the larger images was missing. Maybe that particular image was too much for Dave. I tried to remember which costume it was, but I drew a blank.

The house was silent. *Eerily* silent.

"Dave?" I whispered. No reply. I tried again, louder this time. "Dave. It's Mina. Where are you?"

I stepped over a pile of disarrayed shoes – mostly men's shoes but a couple of pairs of chunky pink women's boots – and a cooler bag with a bottle of wine and some cheese and crackers poking out, and peered into the living room.

A scream froze in my throat.

Dave Danvers lay on the floor, wearing a school uniform that could only come from Hogwarts, a black robe flared out beneath him like angel wings. His fingers clutched a long, gnarled wand snapped in two, and his face froze in an expression of unthinkable horror.

A long staff covered in crystals protruded from his stomach. I recognized the staff from the photograph of Kate at the FanCon cosplay awards. Someone had thrust it inside him with so much force it had pinned him to the floor and splattered his blood across the walls and ceiling.

Dave had been murdered.

CHAPTER TWENTY-EIGHT

"*E*xplain to me how you know Dave Danvers," Jo demanded as she pulled on her PPE. Behind her, Hayes and Wilson roped off the home with crime scene tape. Normally, they wouldn't be here, as this case would be under the jurisdiction of Loamshire CID, but they'd been called in because of the connection to Kate's murder.

I stood on the edge of the crime scene, my coat pulled high around my neck as my best friend glared at me like she couldn't trust a word I said. "You're not sticking your nose into Morrie's investigation, are you? I told you that won't help him, and I could get into real trouble if—"

"Don't worry, I got to Dave all on my own. I'd never dream of getting you in trouble." I tried to smile at her, but she shook her head angrily.

"If you're not careful, they're going to start looking at you as an accomplice instead of a victim." Jo narrowed her eyes. "Mina, I'm serious. I know you're smart, and you've figured things out to do with murders before, and I know you're worried about Morrie. I am, too. But the best thing you can do for him right now is to step back and let the police do their jobs. Don't go down with Morrie for this."

Her words stung. I staggered back as though she slapped me. *It sounds as though Jo's made up her mind that Morrie is guilty.* I bit back a retort. Jo shot me one final glare, pulled on a pair of gloves, and whirled around to get to work. I turned away, nearly crashing into Wilson.

"Mina Wilde." She said my name the way my mum did when I did something that disappointed her. "We need to talk."

"Yes, we do. I don't see why you're here questioning me when you should be out there chasing down Tara Delphine. She ran from the house covered in blood!"

"I'm questioning you because your boyfriend is the chief suspect in a murder inquiry, and despite being told to stay out of things, you've shown up at the scene of a second murder claiming to know both the victim and another possible suspect." Wilson fired questions at me thick and fast. This wasn't the delicate way Hayes had questioned me following Morrie's kidnapping. She had no patience. She thought I had something to do with Dave's murder. I couldn't say I blamed her.

When Wilson finally finished with me, I slunk across the road and sank into the park bench beside Heathcliff. Quoth still hadn't returned, and the police, thankfully, hadn't noticed Heathcliff sitting there or they'd be all over him, too.

"That went well," Heathcliff remarked.

"You're not funny." I could still see Dave's body in my mind – his horrified expression, the arc of blood across the walls, the staff still quivering in his chest. I shuddered.

Heathcliff turned to me. Beneath his shaggy hair, his dark eyes twinkled with dark humor. He reached across and squeezed my knee. "Go on, then. I know you're dying to theorize about what happened here. Normally you and Morrie would be shouting theories at each other, so go on – give me your best interpretation."

"Shouldn't we find Quoth first?"

"He's over there." Heathcliff pointed to a low-hanging tree on the end of the lane. "Sitting in the tree, eavesdropping on your favorite Detective Inspector over there. He circled back to the house a while ago, while you and Jo were glaring at each other. I'm guessing he lost the girl's trail."

"As long as he's safe." I cleared my throat, sitting up straighter. Heathcliff knew me too well – putting the pieces of the crime together helped me to push through the horror of what I'd seen. "We start with the facts. Dave was going to tell me the truth about his wife's death, but someone killed him before I arrived. That means three things are true. One – up until his death, Dave *hadn't* told the truth about his wife. Two – Dave was killed to keep him from revealing the murderer's identity. Three – the murderer overheard Dave's phone call to me and was known to Dave because the front door was open, and Dave let her in."

"We're assuming it's a her?" Heathcliff raised a bushy eyebrow.

"Tara Delphine ran from the scene moments before I arrived, covered in his blood, and trust me when I say that horrible act had only just been committed." Another thought occurred to me. "You could be right, though. Either Tara murdered Dave, or she saw who did. There were pink boots beside the door – women's boots. And a cooler bag with a bottle of wine and some crackers and Brie. I think Dave has a girlfriend."

"Tara?"

I grimaced. "I can't picture it, not after what she did to Kate. But that might explain why she was at his house. The whole situation is fucked up, and people do weird things, so we can't rule it out. But now that I consider it, there's another option, too. Tara might not have been running because she was the murderer. Maybe she was running to get away from the murderer, who slipped in the doorway after Dave opened it for her."

"Who else could have killed him?"

"I need to test a theory." I picked up my phone and dictated a message to Morrie. "Is Sherlock with you?"

Quoth settled on my shoulder, peering down at my phone screen. *She seemed terrified, but whether that was because she witnessed a murder, or because she didn't want to get caught is not something I could speculate on. I followed her for eight blocks until she got in a rideshare and I lost her. I have the plate number, which might help Morrie track the vehicle. The police are out searching for her now, but they're also debating holding you overnight for questioning. Wilson is for it, Hayes against.*

I lifted my finger to my lips. A few moments later, a text came back. "He's out following a lead and left me here all by my lonesome. I'm amusing myself by mismatching all his socks. When he gets back, you might see his head explode all the way from Argleton."

"Can you find out where he's gone? It's important."

Quoth peered at me with wide, orange-rimmed eyes – he immediately comprehended what I was considering.

A moment later, Morrie sent me a link, which opened a pin on my map – a pin moving along the street only three blocks from Dave Danvers' house.

"Croak!" Quoth lifted off my shoulder and swooped toward the trees. Heathcliff leaped to his feet, grabbed my arm, and dragged me around the corner. "Funnel him this way, birdie. We'll cut him off."

"Wha—" The words whipped from my mouth as I flailed to keep up with Heathcliff's frantic pace. He dragged me past rows of identical townhouses until we rounded the edge of the wood. I glanced all around, searching for any sign of Quoth. *Please let him be okay—*

"Croak, croak, crooooooak!"

A tall, dark shape burst from the trees – a man yelling at the top of his lungs as two large, black wings battered at his face. My chest burned as we sprinted toward them.

Sherlock Holmes stumbled into the road, sinking his bony hands into Quoth's neck.

"Crooooo—" Quoth's cry turned terrified. His tiny bird feet scratched and scrabbled for purchase. Sherlock cried in triumph as he pried Quoth from his face and hauled him aloft, ready to dash his brains out on the road.

CHAPTER TWENTY-NINE

*O*ith an inhuman roar, Heathcliff threw himself at the consulting detective. Sherlock crashed to the ground as literature's greatest gothic anti-hero pummeled angry fists into his face.

"Croak!" Quoth dropped to the pavement and hopped around angrily, feathers flying.

Sherlock, who'd learned a thing or two in the underground boxing rings in Victorian London, managed to pull Heathcliff into a headlock. But Heathcliff simply rolled his torso forward, flipped Sherlock over his shoulder, and slammed him against the pavement. Sherlock bounced and went slack, his head lolling to the side.

"No one hurts my birdie." Heathcliff's growl sent a shiver through me as he wrapped his hands around Sherlock's neck. He sounded like a beast of hell, so great and terrible was his vengeance. "And *no one* frames my annoying friend and gets away with it. He was an idiot for trusting you, but that won't be a problem for long."

"Heathcliff, don't kill him." I wrapped my arms around Heathcliff's neck and yanked, but it was like trying to pull an elephant from a bowl of salted peanuts. Quoth hopped on Sherlock's head and nipped the tip of Heathcliff's nose.

"Yeeeeow." Heathcliff dropped Sherlock to clamp both hands over his nose. "That bloody hurts. I was only trying to avenge you."

I nudged Sherlock with the toe of my boot, rolling him over. He winced as he slowly raised a hand to his face, wiping blood from his eyes.

"Thank you for stopping him," he mumbled, his haughty voice thick with pain.

"Don't thank me yet. I'm not done with you. I thought you were supposed to be a trained boxer." I frowned down at Sherlock.

"Yes, well." He kept his hands over his face as he rocked his body into a sitting position. "It appears I'm no match for a brutish gypsy."

"I'll kill him." Heathcliff lunged again. I managed to push myself under his arm, popping up between the two of them before Sherlock got the dismembering of a lifetime.

"First, we get answers." I pressed my palms into Heathcliff's chest. "Then you can kill him."

"Where has this hostility come from?" Sherlock sneered, spitting blood onto the pavement. "I thought we were all working toward the same end, securing our good friend's freedom."

"Morrie's *not* your friend. Especially not after we show him this." I whipped out the photograph and held it under his nose. "Care to explain what you were doing at a Ticketrrr retreat from *two years* ago?"

Sherlock's face remained perfectly still. Not a hair moved out of place. He gave away nothing as he stared at the incriminating evidence in my hand. "If you intend to turn me over to the police, I suggest you do it now. If they're as incompetent as Lestrade and his constabulary, you'll need to perform charades, paint a picture, and learn semaphore signals in order to explain who I am and my connection to Moriarty's case."

I exchanged a glance with Heathcliff. Of course, we couldn't turn Sherlock over to the police. We couldn't trust that he wouldn't reveal the truth about the bookshop. *He's seen Quoth shift. He'll turn us in, and they'd take my boyfriend to a lab to be cut open and studied.* Instinctively, my fingers flew up to hug the raven to my chest.

"This is between us." Heathcliff's hands balled into fists. "And Morrie."

Sherlock sighed. "Very well. I swear to you I did not kill the woman, and I promise to explain everything. But I should be telling this story to Moriarty first. If we return to the cabin, I will unburden myself of this secret."

"It's going to take hours to get to Barset Reach on the bus," Heathcliff growled. "Can't you just put Morrie on a conference call so I can kill you here?"

"I have a driver." Sherlock nodded to a beat-up old Skoda parked at the end of the street. Heathcliff grabbed the detective by the scruff of his shirt and dragged him to the vehicle. I followed behind with Quoth still perched on my shoulder. As I climbed in, I realized the driver was the man who owned the petrol station in Barset Reach.

We drove in absolute silence. Quoth sat in my lap, staring up at me with those wide, soulful eyes of his. I turned over every piece of information in my head, trying to make sense of the various strings. Dave Danvers. Tara Delphine. Grant Hosking's blazer button at the scene. Sherlock lying through his teeth. But what did it all mean? Who framed Morrie, and why?

The driver took us up to the same clearing Sherlock had parked the police cruiser. As I stepped out, my mind flickered back to Morrie's face the day I left him with Sherlock, when he'd lain me over the hood and shagged me senseless. My heart hammered against my chest. I was about to see Morrie again, hold him in my arms, hear his filthy words, and see those smirks that turned my brain to mush.

And I was also about to reveal to him that his ex-lover had been keeping a dangerous secret, and he might even be responsible for this mess.

If someone wanted Morrie out of the way, they could just kill him. Whoever did this hated Morrie enough that they wanted him to suffer. They wanted to take away the one thing that Morrie valued over everything else – more than money or fine wine or kinky sex.

His freedom.

Heathcliff went ahead, dragging Sherlock behind him. Quoth remained on my shoulder as I scrambled along the now-familiar path to the bothy. With every step, my rage surged and the more certain I was that Sherlock was responsible for all of this.

As we emerged over the rock face, the cabin door banged open and Morrie emerged.

"Please tell me you brought back a Bordeaux. I'm going crazy without wine, and that swill you brewed in the toilet bowl is definitely not cutting the mustard—" Morrie froze as he caught sight of Heathcliff dragging Sherlock up the slope. "What's going on?"

CHAPTER THIRTY

"$\mathcal{S}$herlock here was just about to explain to all of us why he killed Kate Danvers and her husband."

"What?" Sherlock spluttered. "Is *that* what this is about? Surely you don't believe I—"

"One more lie and I'll snap your neck." Heathcliff's eyes flashed with malice as he shook Sherlock. "I'll enjoy it."

"Hang on. I don't believe this. Sherlock's a self-centered bastard, but he's no brutal murderer." Morrie glanced from my face to Sherlock, then back to me again. "I thought we talked about this, gorgeous. Like you, Sherlock is plagued by those pesky morals. He catches murderers – he has no desire to join their ranks."

"He did it, Morrie. Dave Danvers was murdered today, and we caught Sherlock at the crime scene. *And* he's been lying to us from the beginning. Look at this." I pulled out the photograph and shoved it under Morrie's nose. "I finally got that meeting with Grant. You were right – Sherlock *was* trying to stop us seeing him – so we wouldn't discover this."

"Why am I looking at a bunch of dudebros with facial hair

vastly inferior to Heathcliff's scraggly charms?" Morrie frowned at the picture.

"That's a photograph of the team from Ticketrrr at their leadership retreat – from two years ago. Look who's in the back row." Morrie's eyes flickered across the paper. He held the photograph out to me. "Thank you, gorgeous." His voice sounded strange, far away and wooden, devoid of his usual cockiness. He turned to Sherlock.

"I suppose I shouldn't be surprised. After all, our whole relationship was a lie – a ploy to get me to trust you so you could dismantle my empire and throw me over a waterfall. But you made a vital mistake coming to this world. You messed with my friends. You upset my girlfriend. And for that, I will enjoy destroying you."

"I swear, I didn't kill the girl." Sherlock struggled against Heathcliff's grasp. "Get your giant oaf to unhand me, and I can explain."

"I'll bash his head open right now, just give me the word," Heathcliff growled. "It would be my pleasure."

Morrie's gaze fell on Heathcliff, and if I'd ever suspected there was something between them, the sparks that flew when their eyes locked blew it into Technicolor. Morrie thrust his hand into his boxers and pulled out the silver dildo. He flicked his wrist, and a thin, gleaning blade slid from the tip.

By Isis. I winced. *Where the fuck did he think he'd be sticking that thing?*

"I'll take it from here, Sir Snarkleton." Morrie advanced, and the vicious grin spreading across his face chilled my blood.

Heathcliff snarled, but he shoved Sherlock to the ground and stepped back. Morrie stared down at his former boyfriend, and the look in his eyes was so sinister it made me shudder.

For the first time, I knew I was looking at *the* James Moriarty – the man he had been before Nevermore Bookshop, before Heathcliff and Quoth. *Before me.* He was no longer my morally-corrupt boyfriend with the devilish smirk. He stood before us as the Napoleon of Crime, ruthless and unfeeling and utterly merciless – the spider with a bite that would kill.

Sherlock's betrayal had driven him back to his old ways, back to the man he swore he could never be again.

Morrie kicked Sherlock's side with the sharp tip of his brogues. "The fact that you betrayed me is inexcusable, but you put Mina in danger, and that I will never forgive."

"If you plan to make me beg, you'll be sorely disappointed." Sherlock raised pain-filled eyes to Morrie. "But if you slit my throat now, you won't get the truth."

Morrie laughed. "It's you who always cared about the truth. I'm fine embellishing a little."

"Do you really want to slit my throat here, in front of Mina?" Sherlock wheedled. "Look at her face, Moriarty. She may be angry with me, but she's not thirsty for my blood. I might lose my life, but you... you will lose so much more."

"This is just like our story!" Morrie yelled. "Only this time, I'll destroy you first, so you can never hurt me again."

"Don't you understand? You can never destroy me without also killing a piece of yourself. You don't need Reichenback to fall, James. We were always going to go over together," Sherlock shot back. "You and I, locked head to head, our final battle, and the answer to the final problem."

Morrie's smirk didn't falter. "You're even more messed up than I thought."

"You don't get it," Sherlock screamed. "You had to go. I had to rid London of your pestilence. But I couldn't live in a world where you don't exist. I joined you in the churning waters that day, just as I joined you in this hellhole. It's not my fault my author saw fit to resurrect me after."

Morrie's face contorted, his fingers closing around the knife. He raised it higher...

I threw myself across Sherlock's body, staring up at Morrie as the knife hovered above me. "Morrie, don't."

Morrie's hand froze. His smile didn't waver. "This isn't for you, gorgeous."

"I know. It's for you, and I think that's why you shouldn't do it. You can't go around stabbing people every time they break your heart." I swallowed. "That's the old James Moriarty. The criminal. But the Morrie I love isn't like that."

"Maybe I don't know how to be *Morrie.*" His voice dripped with bitterness. "Maybe I'm Moriarty, the villain, the con-man, now and forever. Maybe we can't ever escape our stories."

"That's not true. I know you don't believe that." Even though the knife hovered above my head, I kept my eyes focused on Morrie. "You've devoted your new life to protecting the people you care about. You cultivated your criminal skills in this world to help your friends – so you could get papers for Quoth, and help Lydia Bennet talk her way into the Army, and secure good employment for all the other fictional characters who came through the shop. Even this death faking business was your misguided attempt to do good in the world. You said you didn't care to ask why Kate Danvers wanted to fake her own death, but I bet that's not true. I bet you care a lot – you just don't want to admit it."

The corner of Morrie's mouth spasmed. My heart fluttered with hope.

Morrie's lips curled back and he snarled, tossing the knife at the cabin, where it plunged into the wood and stuck fast, the silver cock-shaped handle quivering in the breeze.

"What should we do with him?"

"I think we should get the truth." I knelt down beside Sherlock. "Why did you kill Kate? What information did Dave have on you? Why did you kill him? I'd remind you that I might have got rid of Morrie's knife, but Heathcliff could still snap your neck like it was a matchstick."

"I did none of these things." Sherlock hugged his legs to his chest. "I came here to speak the truth, but I can see it's pointless. I'm surrounded by lunatics and imbeciles."

"We found you fleeing Dave's house."

"I wasn't fleeing Dave's house. I was *watching* it. I had reason to suspect Dave might be a target. I saw a figure creep from the shadows to ring the bell, dressed entirely in black. Dave answered the door and invited this black-clad figure inside, and about twenty minutes later, the pink-haired one showed up and let herself in. I was moving closer to get a look when you showed up."

"Why did you think Dave was—" a rustling in the trees caught my attention, followed by a random buzzing noise. "What was that?"

"That noise? It sounded like..." Morrie's eyes swept the tree line, following the buzzing. The corner of his mouth tugged up into a spoiled grin. "It sounded like we have a spy in our midst."

Heathcliff dived into the trees. There was a *THUMP*, and someone yelped in pain. Heathcliff returned a minute later, dragging a groaning body that he dumped beside Sherlock. The figure curled into the fetal position, staring up at us with wild eyes. A mobile phone was clutched in his trembling fingers.

"Who's this?" Morrie peered at him.

"That's Sam, the owner of Wild Oats. He lied about moving Kate's body. But what I can't figure is what he's doing out here spying on us." I leaned forward. "Unless... he's the real murderer."

CHAPTER THIRTY-ONE

"*W*hat are you talking about?" Sam cried as Heathcliff dumped him beside Sherlock. "I'm not a murderer. I've never even met these two lanky gentlemen."

"Then why are you spying on us?"

"Because I was rambling nearby when I heard shouting from what's supposed to be an empty bothy. You never would have heard me if I didn't get that phone call."

"Is that true?" I narrowed my eyes. "You lied to us about finding Kate's body. You were trying to move it when a tourist stopped you. That's not the behavior of an innocent man."

"So this is all about Kate?" Sam threw up his hands. "Fine! I moved the body. I admit it. It was an awful thing to do, and it still makes me feel horrible, but I did it."

"Why?"

"Because I found it on Wild Oats territory. I was going to dump it somewhere far away, in one of the fields near the village, maybe. I thought I could make it look like she'd been hitchhiking and someone messed her up. I don't know, I wasn't thinking. Business had started to pick up again, and a murdered girl showing up would ruin us. It *has* ruined us." Sam hung his head, staring at the phone in his hands. "That was the bank calling. I've defaulted on my loans. Wild Oats is officially out of business."

"Finish the story," Heathcliff growled, advancing on him.

"Right, yes." Sam gulped. "So, I decided to move the body. But then, halfway down the mountain, I ran into a German tourist, and so I had to invent a reason why I was just carrying a body around the woods. I made up the story about bringing it to the police. But then he *wouldn't go away*, so I had to leave the body and walk back to the village with him. And that was the longest two hours of my life – not just because of the horror of Kate's death and worrying about my business, but that guy was *weird*."

Hearing Sam the cockroach chef call another person weird seemed... worth investigating. "How do you mean?"

Sam's shoulders sagged. "I don't know, just... German. Talked in a stilted voice. Seemed to know an awful lot about bodies and police procedure. And even though he was hiking in the woods, he had the strangest clothes – a fitted blazer, like the kind you'd wear at a posh boarding school, with a crest on the breast pocket and everything, and a pair of fancy shoes." He pointed to Morrie's brogues. "Exactly like those, same color and everything."

Holy shiteballs.

Of course.

How did I not see it before?

"*You.*" Heathcliff roared at Sherlock. "You're the German tourist. You spent every one of your stories showing off your mastery of disguise."

"No, it's not him." I finally clicked what had been niggling at me about the jacket. The details slid into place in my mind. There was someone else who was part of the cosplay scene, who knew a thing or two about costumes. Someone who had a motive not just for killing Kate, but for framing Morrie.

People will do crazy things for what they love. And sometimes, what they love will turn them crazy.

I thought about Sherlock and Morrie, and how they might

once have had something great – a love that could endure – if they hadn't both burned it to ash to satisfy their own egos. Morrie had learned from that mistake, and he was a different man now. Sherlock might learn it, too, in time, if Heathcliff didn't strangle him first.

Sometimes even the greatest love can turn sour.

Sometimes there wasn't a happy ending, especially not once ego got involved.

A lightbulb went off. Sparks of bright green light flashed in front of my vision. I understood what this crime was all about. Or, at least, I was starting to understand.

"What's with that expression, gorgeous?" Morrie asked. "You look like the cat who got the cream."

"That's her Morrie face," Heathcliff glowered. "She's up to something."

"Not up to something. *On* to something." I glanced around the confused and maniacal faces. "I know exactly who our murderer is."

CHAPTER THIRTY-TWO

*H*eathcliff kicked Sherlock in the side. "Of course we do. That's why we're here. To wring his scrawny neck."

"Nope." I smiled. "Sherlock's a complete wanker, but he's not our murderer. And he was right about one thing. This crime *is* all about obsession. But not in the way we suspected. And I know exactly how we're going to bring the killer to justice. It means I have to ask Heathcliff and Quoth to do something dangerous—"

"Yes," Heathcliff growled, his eyes never leaving Morrie's.

"Croak," Quoth added.

"I'll help, too, if it means Morrie goes free." Sherlock piped up.

"I don't know what you're talking about, but I'll help if it saves my business," Sam added.

"Good." I bent down and held out my hand to Sherlock Holmes. He stared at it like it might sprout tentacles, then took it and gave it a weak shake. I pulled him to his feet. "Then we're all in agreement. Let's catch a killer."

∽

"*M*ina, I can't take it any longer." Morrie's voice wavered with uncertainty – a sound so strange and foreign on his lips that it turned my insides out. "They're not going to stop hunting me. I've got to flee the country. But before I do, I need to say goodbye. Meet me in the bookshop after closing tomorrow night. 7PM on the dot. Leave the window in the Children's room unlocked. Be alone, and don't tell anyone, *especially* not the police."

Morrie clicked off his burner phone and tossed it over the mountain. It clattered on the rocks before disappearing into the shrubbery. When he turned back to me, his usual cocky mouth was set in a firm line.

"I don't like this, gorgeous." Morrie turned back toward the cabin. The sun had set now, and I could barely make out the shape of his body in the gloom, but I could tell from the tension in his shoulders that Morrie didn't approve of this plan. Which was odd, because usually he was all for a crazy scheme – and this definitely qualified as a crazy scheme.

"The only way to lure out the killer is if they believe this is their last chance to get you," I pointed out as I stepped toward him. "We know they've got eyes on the shop. Quoth, Heathcliff, and Sherlock will be waiting to pounce. And with the police trace on our phone, Inspector Hayes won't be far away. With all of that protection, nothing will happen to either of us."

"This isn't like the time we lured Ashley's killer to the shop. This person is crafty. We don't know how long they've been watching us." Morrie turned abruptly, crushing me against his body, his lips pressing into my forehead. "If something happens to you because of me—"

"I'm not worried." Okay, I was a little worried, but Morrie didn't need to know that. He already looked completely defeated by the situation. When I told him who I thought the killer was…

James Moriarty was rarely surprised, but that threw him off his axis.

"I've rubbed off on you more than I realized." That gravity he'd used on the phone was still in his voice. We walked back to the bothy, where the others had gathered around the remaining candles. Morrie threw his clothes, books, and magnetic chess game into his rucksack.

"What about all your shirts?" I pointed to the small pile of rumpled designer clothing in the corner.

"Are you kidding? They're not getting near my body ever again. They stink of *nature*." Morrie grabbed at the tailored shirt he wore. "If I didn't need this outfit to get out of here, I'd leave it behind too, but I intend to burn it as soon as I'm home."

I placed my hand over the flap of his rucksack. "Don't get so excited. You're holing up with Sam here until it's time. You're going to have to make it back to Argleton by yourself, *without* attracting any attention. Can you do that?"

"Of course." Morrie patted Sherlock's shoulder. Sherlock stiffened under the sudden touch, his eyes flicking nervously to Heathcliff. "I happen to be friends with a master of disguise."

I wrapped my arms around Morrie. He pulled me against him, stroking my hair in a tender way that wasn't like him at all. Something horrible churned in my gut.

Don't be crazy – this isn't goodbye forever. You're going to see him again tomorrow.

I knew that was true, and yet, I clung to Morrie until Heathcliff pulled me away. "Don't do anything stupid," he snapped to Morrie, who gave a mock salute.

Heathcliff, Quoth, Sherlock, and I hiked back down the mountain and poured into the old man's car. We hadn't even got the truth from Sherlock about how he'd roped this guy into helping us, but right now I didn't care.

Our driver dropped us off at the train station. I expected Sherlock to pay him, but instead, he slid long fingers into his jacket pocket and removed an envelope. "I've located your daughter. She's excited to hear from you again. Everything you need is in here."

With a silent nod, the old man accepted the envelope. As he slit it open, tears rolled down his cheeks. Whatever Sherlock had done for him, it was a beautiful thing.

I almost felt sorry about the way we'd treated him.

Almost.

We all got out of the car and caught the next train. I missed having Oscar with me to find the stairs and railing. He'd already become such a normal part of my life that I felt his absence like a punch in the gut, the same way I missed Morrie with every fiber of my being.

Mum, who agreed to watch the shop for us while we went to Crookshollow, hurried out the door in a hurry to deliver a package of smelly oyster jewelry to a client across town, leaving behind a bucket of oysters and another stack of pearl-themed books she'd sold. After scarfing a dinner of Oliver's fish and chips (they really were fantastic), Sherlock slept on the sofa downstairs while Heathcliff, Quoth, and I crowded into my bed.

The next morning we woke to the sound of banging and pounding. I peered out the window at the workers swarming over Mrs. Ellis' old flat. *Bloody Grey Lachlan. If he thinks starting construction work at 6AM is going to scare us off, he's got another thing coming.*

I pulled on a pair of skinny jeans and my Blood Lust band hoodie, and shuffled around making coffee and preparing the shop for opening. I pushed open all the windows to air out the oyster smell, but that only made dust from the construction site blow inside, so I shut them all again, except the one in the Children's room.

Instead, I tried to move Mum's oyster bucket outside, but Grimalkin pitched a fit, arching her back and hissing until I set it down in the hallway again.

"Fine, keep your smelly oysters." I watched her hit a shell across the floor with her paw, jumping on it in an attempt to free the goodies within. "Just don't choke on a bubblegum pink pearl."

Edie came by with Oscar. She stayed for an hour to watch how we worked together, then left to return to the kennels. I dropped Mum's envelopes in the mailbag, then busied myself serving customers, entering books into our catalog and shelving them. I checked my watch every ten minutes as each moment of the day crawled by like an hour. Every creaking floorboard and swearing tradesman had me whirling around, heart in my chest.

Fuck, I hope this works.

At 5:02PM, Heathcliff, Sherlock, and Quoth went out to the pub. I suspected our murderer was already watching the shop, and I wanted them to feel certain I was alone. I flipped the sign to CLOSED and double-checked the window in the Children's room was unlatched.

I peered outside into the towering ivy bushes Heathcliff promised he'd cut back but never did, but couldn't see a thing beyond the end of my nose. *Is the murderer out there?*

I flicked off the light and left the room, closing the door behind me. *Come out, come out, wherever you are.*

The shop was eerily quiet. I sat down behind Heathcliff's desk (I still thought of it as his even though I did more work there than he ever did) and tried to start on our accounts, but the numbers blurred in front of my eyes. Partly because it was too dark, partly because I couldn't focus on anything except the closed door of the Children's room. At my feet, Oscar shifted restlessly.

At 6:03PM, I took the last sip of my cold tea, made a face, and opened Heathcliff's top drawer to pillage his whisky stash.

At 6:16PM, I discovered I'd written '*murder murder murdery murd*' across two months of invoices, and tossed the entire pile in the trash.

At 6:18PM, I pulled a broken oyster shell from between the cushions on Heathcliff's chair and hurled it at the armadillo.

At 6:21PM, I poured another whisky.

At 6:24PM, Oscar's ears pricked up. The back door latch rasped and floorboards creaked as Heathcliff, Sherlock, and Quoth tiptoed through the house and got into position.

At 6:35PM. Oscar's ears pricked again. My hand flew to his lead. From behind the Children's room door, I heard the faint scrape of the window being pushed up, and the thud of a foot hitting the rug, but I ignored it and settled Oscar back down.

At 6:41PM, my stomach churned with fear and I had to cross my legs and try not to think about how much I wanted to go to the bathroom. I really, really regretted having the whisky. But not enough to stop drinking it.

At 6:45PM, I gulped down the rest of the whisky.

At 6:58PM, I heard the window shove open, and a grunt as something heavy dropped through onto the floor. A moment later, another thud, a croak of defiance from Quoth, and a strangled cry. Oscar barked with enthusiasm as we clambered out from behind the desk and burst into the Children's room.

"Gotcha!" I cried, shining a lamp into the middle of the floor.

Morrie lay on the rug, clutching his head and moaning. Behind him stood a figure dressed in a black catsuit, their arms pinned by Heathcliff as Sherlock struggled to tug off the balaclava that obscured their face. Quoth hopped along the windowsill, croaking encouragement.

"Let go of me," the killer snapped, jerking their head from Sherlock's grip.

I flicked on the largest lamp just as Sherlock wrestled off the balaclava, and all five of us got the first look at our *real* killer.

Morrie's lip curled back into a smirk. "Hello, Kate."

CHAPTER THIRTY-THREE

*O*ne formally dead cosplayer glared at each of us as she struggled against Heathcliff's grip. She didn't look afraid, only faintly amused. "How did you figure it out?"

"I'll let Mina bore you with the details later, while you're rotting in jail." Morrie staggered to his feet. I rushed to his side. That blow she'd given him must've been nasty. "For now, suffice it to say that Mina is *almost* as clever as I am."

Kate regarded me with a detached interest. "I'd be lying if I said it was a pleasure to meet you, Mina. What gave me away?"

I reached into my pocket and held out the silver button. "This. At first, I assumed it belonged to Grant because it matched his old public school uniform, but then I realized I'd seen you wearing the exact blazer in one of your costumes. You made it into a Hogwarts uniform."

"Mmmm. I wondered if anyone found that button." Kate stared down at my hand. "Grant tossed that blazer into the office rubbish bin after his reunion, and I saw it was the perfect color to go with my Harry Potter costume. I had to take the picture off the wall when I returned to see Dave, in case anyone put it together. I embroidered the house crest by hand, you know."

"I figured. You're very talented." I listened hard. *Where's Hayes? He had to have heard Morrie's phone call, and I even left the front door unlocked for him. Why hasn't he burst in here yet, guns blazing?* "I've got most of the details straight now, but I just have one question. Why did you do it? Why come back to England, pretend to be murdered, and frame Morrie? Why murder your husband?"

I didn't think Kate was going to talk, but at the mention of Dave's name her whole face tensed. "Dave was an-an-an-accident. I went to see him, to tell him I was alive, and that he could return to the Philippines with me and we could be together. But then Tara walked through the door, hanging her coat on the hook and kicking her shoes off like she owned the place, and I just saw red. I grabbed my staff from the wall and lunged at her, and Dave must have stepped in front of me, because the next thing I know he's on the floor and his blood... his blood was everywhere..." her chest heaved. "Tara ran out of there and I knew there was only a matter of time before she told the police she saw me. All I wanted to do was escape my life, and things got so out of hand. But what's another couple of bodies, right? I came here tonight to get rid of Morrie, and then I was going to deal with Tara, and then empty out Dave's bank accounts of the insurance money and head back to the Philippines."

"Why did you leave in the first place?" Morrie narrowed his eyes. "I provided you with exemplary service. You escaped your life. Why ruin it all just to come after me?"

"You don't get it," Kate screamed. "It was never about you. It was always about Dave. I did all of this for Dave, and because of you, he was worse off than he was when I was alive."

"You're talking about the insurance," I said.

Kate nodded. "Dave is everything to me. He's my whole world, and he'll do anything to see me happy. He only agreed to spend our savings on the events business because I wanted to leave Ticketrrr so badly and because he believed in me. But I let him down. I spent all our money and I couldn't make the business work. We lost everything, and the bank was coming for more, and I just couldn't take disappointing him. And then..." Kate lifted her head. "And then I remembered a guy at last year's management retreat, Clarence someone. He looked a bit like that dude—" she nodded at Sherlock, "—except his beard was more impressive. I probably got a bit drunk after Grant tried to paw me, and I was spilling all my secrets to Clarence about how depressed I was and how I wished I was brave enough to kill myself so Dave could have the life insurance money. This Clarence spent all night telling me about this guy he was in love with who'd left him to start a death-faking business, and it occurred to me that if I could find this friend, he'd make all my problems go away."

I glanced over at Sherlock, whose face had gone pale. "I thought you said *hire* him, not frame him and then try to kill him."

"And that's exactly what I wanted," Kate shot back. "Grant was getting worse. He started dating Tara, but he never stopped pursuing me. He said that if I didn't sleep with him he'd make sure I never worked as a developer again, and he got Tara to badmouth my company online until our reputation had been completely destroyed. Dave had quit his job to work on our startup, and then I was the only one bringing in money, but I couldn't work with Grant any longer. I just *couldn't*. I didn't care what he did to me, but Dave..."

"I wanted to murder him, but I'm not a killer. At least," she laughed bitterly, "I wasn't back then. So I decided to kill myself, on paper. I found Morrie and he said he could help me. A suicide note placed on my shelter on the wilderness retreat, and he'd whisk me off to a new life in the Philippines and make sure Dave collected the insurance. I wanted to tell Dave so badly, but Morrie said I couldn't. If the police or insurance investigators thought for a moment my death was fake, they'd decline his claim. Dave had to *believe* I was dead. He's not a good actor, not like me." She smiled at that, but it was a sad smile. "I hoped that in a few years, once I'd saved some money, I'd send for him and we'd run off into the sunset together. How wrong I was.

"The morning of the wilderness retreat, I loaded my things into the car, kissed Dave goodbye, like everything was normal. I drove to Wild Oats and I endured Grant's gross comments and inappropriate touches. I waited until the last night, when Sam sent us off by ourselves, and then I scribbled my suicide note and hiked to a backroad to meet Morrie, who helicoptered me to a private airport, handed me a box containing my passport, drivers license, birth certificate – a whole new identity. My picture, but not my life. Not my *name*. Not the name I'd taken when Dave and I wed."

Tears streamed down Kate's cheeks, but she kept talking. "I went to the Philippines and got a job, and did my best to forget about Dave and everything I left behind. And it worked for about a year. Then a man showed up at my apartment. He knew about Morrie's business, he knew who I was and what I'd done, and said we had a mutual interest in bringing Morrie to justice."

That bastard.

The final pieces of the puzzle clicked into place. I tugged a crumpled brochure out of my pocket and handed it to Kate. "Is that the man?"

Kate nodded at the picture. "That's him. Grey Lachlan."

Heathcliff grunted as the reality of what Kate just admitted sank in. Morrie winced, probably more pissed he hadn't figured it out than concerned about what it meant. That was okay. Plenty of time to be concerned later.

"Why did Grey come to you?" I asked.

"He said he'd been following my case in the news, and he thought I should know what happened in my absence. Morrie had drummed it into me how important it was that I didn't try to contact Dave or follow his social media, so I had no idea how much... how..." Kate struggled through her tears. "Grey showed me evidence that Dave never received the insurance money. He lost our home. He had to rent that tiny flat, and go back to work as a plumber for his dad's business, a job he hated. He lost all his friends because of our business. He lost *everything*. Meanwhile, Morrie had been living the high life while my husband suffered. Swanning around Argleton like he owned the place. Grey showed me photographs he'd taken of Morrie at this shop and down in London, and he asked all sorts of questions about the survival course and all the things I learned. He said he could help me bring Morrie down."

Isis' tits, this is worse than I thought. A chill whipped through my veins. All the pieces had been right in front of me, but I hadn't seen them. None of us had.

Grey Lachlan *said* Morrie was out of commission. He took Morrie out because he knew Morrie was onto Dracula. *This all comes back to Dracula...*

"Grey and I devised a plan. He would report Morrie to the government and have his accounts frozen, so Morrie didn't have the funds to buy his way out of trouble. I learned a lot about death fraud from Morrie – enough that I thought I could fake my own murder. Grey said he could get me a body that looked a lot like me and had died from natural causes. If we bashed her face up good enough and the DNA matched, we'd make everyone believe it was me."

That poor girl whose body you used didn't die from natural causes. She was drained by Dracula, and then Grey finished her off with the mushrooms. He was covering his tracks in case someone clever like Jo figured it out. Oh, Jo. I'm so sorry I was so horrible to you. I thought I was being selfish by thinking of Dracula, but if I'd followed up on what you said about the autopsy, I might've figured this all out sooner.

Kate continued. "Grey stole the letter opener from the shop under the pretense of trying to convince you to sell the building. All that was left was to leave footprints at the scene with Morrie's exact shoe print – easy, since I'd admired his brogues and he'd told me which exclusive London designer he used and exactly how much they cost. I simply rang them up and ordered another pair. I gave them to Grey after the fake-murder and he dropped them into the pile beside the shop door."

"This wasn't a fake murder, Kate," I said. "Grey didn't find some poor girl's body who died of natural causes. He killed that woman himself, using the poison mushrooms from Barsetshire Fells that *you* told him about."

Kate paled. "That's not true."

"It is true. You have no idea of the monster you've been working with all this time." *Why haven't the police stormed in here? Why aren't they hearing this? They could arrest Kate and Grey, and Dracula would lose his faithful servant—*

"Grey *cared* about me." Fresh tears welled in Kate's eyes. "He wanted to help me, unlike Morrie. Morrie didn't care about why I wanted to escape my life. All he cared about was the intellectual puzzle of faking my death."

I mean, that does kind of sound like Morrie. On the surface. But that's not the whole truth.

"Damn right. And there's one piece of this puzzle that still has me stumped. The DNA on the body matched yours," Morrie pointed out.

"That part was simple. I hacked into the morgue database and changed the DNA records on the corpse to match mine. Then I planted Morrie's business card in the pocket so the police knew who to look for. Grey and I carried her into the forest, then I stabbed her with your letter opener and left her to be found."

"But then Sam decided to move her."

Kate nodded. "I was watching from a safe vantage point, and I saw him drag her away. I couldn't have him hide her or destroy the body. I needed it to be discovered, and he was going to ruin everything. I had a male disguise in my rucksack, but the only clothing I had with me that could disguise my breasts was the Hogwarts blazer. I quickly changed my appearance and met Sam on the path. Now that he'd been caught, he had no choice but to report the body to the police. I stayed with him until he entered the police station, then I slipped away."

"Very clever," Morrie murmured.

"I should think so. Once I was certain the police were on the right track, I snuck into an empty property Grey offered me to wait for Morrie's arrest." Kate whirled to face Sherlock. "But I didn't count on *him* whisking Morrie away. Grey explained that you lot would sniff around, but he didn't anticipate quite how tenacious you'd be. I went to tell Dave everything, to beg him to come away with me before it was too late. But when he went into the kitchen to pour us another tea, he must've called you. He was going to tell you I was still alive." Her whole body trembled. "And now... and now..."

Her face twisted with determination. She drew her elbows together, brought her knee to her chest, and thrust back, breaking Heathcliff's grip and slamming her foot into his nuts at the same time.

CRACK. Heathcliff gasped as he collapsed to his knees, his face pale, his eyes bugging out. Sherlock lunged for Kate, but she scrambled away and pulled something from her belt, which she pointed at Morrie's head.

A gun.

Shite. My blood turned to ice. *She's got a gun. Where the fuck is Inspector Hayes?*

"Meow?" The door pushed open, and Grimalkin trotted in, her tail high and kinked like a periscope as she held one of Mum's bloody oysters in her mouth.

"Grimalkin, not now," I hissed.

I tried to relay to her through my eyebrows that she needed to run and find the inspector, but she just kept stalking toward us, staring at Heathcliff groaning on the floor and Morrie frozen and Kate with that *gun* pointed right at his head with wide eyes.

Grimalkin's whiskers twitched with mischief. *I know you're planning something, Grandmother. Now is not the time for you to decide to be a hero. Please, just get Inspector Hayes, or hell, even Earl Larson or Mrs. Ellis would do—*

"Meeeeow." Grimalkin bounded toward Kate.

Kate's eyes widened. The barrel of the gun wobbled. "What's that cat got in its mouth?"

"Meeeeow?" Grimalkin leaped onto the bookshelf and sauntered toward Kate.

"I'm allergic to shellfish," Kate yelled, taking one hand off the gun to wave in Grimalkin's face. "Go on, shoo!"

Grimalkin arched her back and leaped. She soared across the room and landed on the highest shelf, right above Kate's head. She dropped the slimy oyster from her mouth. It landed on Kate's face, sliding down her cheek before bouncing onto the rug.

"No, no, no..." Kate dropped the gun to swipe at the juice on her cheek. Morrie lunged for it, but Sherlock got there first, kicking it under the shelf. Kate spun toward the door and flung it open, but she was so disoriented that she pitched forward, sticking her foot into the oyster bucket I'd left in the hall.

"Arrrrrgh!" Kate yelled as she went down. THUD. Oysters flew everywhere, raining down on her body like, well, like stinky oyster rain. Kate made a horrible wheezing noise as she kicked and jerked, trying to free herself from the slimy mollusk pile. Grimalkin meowed happily and began to bat the shellfish across the rug.

Morrie slipped into the shadows of the Children's room just as the front door swung open, banging on the wall so hard the shelves rattled. Hayes burst into the hallway, followed by Sergeant Wilson and four officers. "Well done, Mina. We heard everything. Kate Danvers, you're under arrest for the murder of Dave Danvers. You have the right to remain—"

"I don't care!" Kate howled, twisting away as Grimalkin kicked an oyster toward her. "Just get me away from that damn cat before I... argh..."

Kate clawed at her throat. Wilson barked at one of the officers to call an ambulance, while she and Hayes tried to pull Kate free of the slimy trap.

"Morrie, where are you?" I glanced around, but so much of the room was in complete darkness to me now I could barely see the end of my nose. "Did you hear that? I think you're officially a free man. Isn't that... Morrie? Where are you?"

A lanky figure slunk out of the gloom, but it wasn't Morrie. Sherlock inclined his head, peering at me over his hawk-like nose. "He climbed out the window."

What? "Did he say where he was going?"

Sherlock shrugged. "He said he fancied a walk. Sam told him about a trail to a beautiful waterfall, and—"

A waterfall.

My heart leaped into my chest. I grabbed Heathcliff and shoved him toward the door. Hayes waved at me to stay, but I was already shoving on Oscar's coat. "No time to explain, but Morrie's in trouble. We need to get back to Barsetshire Fells. *Now.*"

CHAPTER THIRTY-FOUR

*H*eathcliff barked orders at the officer as he pulled into the Wild Oats parking lot. With the siren blaring, we made it to the Wild Oats center in record time, but we passed a black taxi heading in the opposite direction. *Morrie beat us here.*

I shoved open my door and lifted Oscar out before the car came to a complete stop.

"What the fuck do we do now?" Heathcliff held up his phone, casting a faint beam of pallid light across the ground. We'd never find Morrie in the dark if he didn't want to be found.

"Arf?" Oscar pawed at my leg.

Of course. My fingers closed around Oscar's lead.

"Oscar, find Morrie." I'd grabbed a pair of Morrie's brogues from the hallway as I ran out the door, and I held them in front of Oscar's nose. Oscar sniffed the air, and he yapped with excitement as he tugged me around the back of the lodge, where a small sign pointed to an overgrown forest trail.

I raced down the path, my boots sinking into the soft mud. Pain blossomed across my chest as I yelled, "Morrie, where are you? Morrie, it's Mina."

Spurned by my speed, Oscar took off at a trot, his nose to the ground as he followed Morrie's scent. My boots skidded over the uneven ground, but I didn't slow down. I couldn't.

Please, don't let me be too late.

The trail widened out, and the rush of water pounded in my ears. We'd reached the waterfall. Oscar led me to the edge of a river, guiding me to where a rickety wooden suspension bridge crossed to the opposite bank. My fingers grasped the railing, and I leaned over the side.

Water poured into the pool forty feet below, churning up white foam that crashed against the rocks. The water rushed in my ears, fast and hard and deadly. If a person fell into that, they'd surely be pulled under and dashed against the rocks—

"Arf, arf!" Oscar scratched at the railing, jumping against the side as if he saw something above the waterfall.

He can see something I can't.

Tears stung my eyes, but the wind whipped them away before they fell. "Morrie, where are you?"

"He's over there." Heathcliff leaned out over the railing, jabbing his finger at the rocks. The moon hung full in the sky, and in the beam of its light I could just make out the outline of a figure standing on a rock at the very edge of the waterfall.

"What the fuck are you doing?" Heathcliff cupped his hands and yelled across the chasm. Morrie's head snapped up at the noise. I was too far away to see his features, but the very fact he stood on that precarious rock—

"Don't burst a blood vessel, I'm just thinking. Get Mina away from here. It's not safe," he called back, his voice clear and decisive.

"Like hell I will. If you want to do something so tremendously stupid as throw yourself over a waterfall, you have the guts to do it to her face."

"You should do hostage negotiations," Morrie yelled back. "You have a hidden talent for it. I'm not throwing myself over. I just needed...oh, fuck off. You wouldn't understand."

The wind whipped up, sending a spray of icy water cascading over the bridge. I gritted my teeth as icy pins and needles tore at my body.

"Arf, arf!" Oscar scrabbled against the bridge. Heathcliff grabbed his paws and set them on the planks.

"You stay here," he growled at the dog. "Get Mina to safety. This bridge doesn't look strong enough for all three of us."

He shoved past me and ran to the other bank. I gripped the railings, fighting with my Docs on the slippery surface as Heathcliff's bulk threw the bridge around in the howling wind. Oscar whimpered as the bridge pitched and more icy water splashed over the side.

"What are you doing?" I yelled over the roar of the waterfall.

Heathcliff turned back. The moonlight caught the mania in his eyes, the wild set of his strong jaw. "What do you think? I'm going to save that idiot from himself."

"Heathcliff—"

He leaped off the bridge and disappeared from view. Oscar whimpered again. I gripped his leash with everything I had and commanded him to turn.

"Get back, gorgeous." Morrie's voice came back to me. "I don't want you to see me like this."

"I can't see a bloody thing," I shot back as Oscar took another shaking step toward safety. "And I'm not leaving. Don't be so bloody foolish. Why are you sitting on the edge of a waterfall in the middle of the night?"

"I told you, I'm thinking." Morrie had never sounded so certain. "I'm thinking about what Sherlock said, that there's only one way this can end. I'm a scourge on the world, Mina. Even when I try to do a good thing, it turns to shit. Innocent people get killed."

"Kate made the decision to become a murderer. That's on her, not you."

"Yes, and she teamed up with Dracula's plaything and came

after us. We got lucky this time, but how much longer before one of my nefarious dealings puts you in danger again? Or Quoth, or Heathcliff? I'd die if something were to happen to you, but the bitter truth is that *I* happened to you. I'm the biggest danger to you. I've done too many evil things in my lifetime, Mina. I don't deserve your kindness or your love. You and Heathcliff and Quoth would be better off if you'd never even known me. So I'm thinking that maybe I'll go fight Dracula on my own. Maybe one evil will triumph over another. Or perhaps it's best for all of us if I go now, in a blaze of glory. It's the way my story was always supposed to end."

"You call this a blaze of glory?" Tears streamed down my cheeks. Not even the bitter wind could stem their tide. My arms ached to hold him. "I call it a coward's way out, and I've pegged you for many things, James Moriarty – but never as a coward."

Morrie's chin dipped as he peered down at the maelstrom. "I'd do it, if it would keep you safe."

"But it won't, will it? Look, the fake death business was probably one of your less clever ideas. You messed up. We all do that. Don't go throwing yourself off a waterfall just because things didn't go your way for once. Do you know how many times I thought about ending it all after I got my diagnosis? I can't tell you how many times I pulled a bottle of painkillers out of the medicine cabinet and poured them into my hand just to feel the relief of knowing I was one step away from oblivion."

My body trembled at memories I'd locked away in a dark and secret place, of a time when I'd truly believed I was *nothing*. The futility that haunted me flooded my body, and I *hated* the idea that Morrie could possibly think that about himself...

All Morrie's strange behavior over the last couple of months rushed at me with clarity. He'd had his heart cracked open, and it made him doubt everything he knew, most especially himself.

"No, Mina." Morrie's voice strained with emotion. "That's not you."

"Damn right it was me. It was part of *my* story. And now I can't relate to the person who had those dark thoughts. She's like a stranger to me, but I must remember and acknowledge her, because if you hide from the darkness then it creeps up on you unawares. Just like you're not that person anymore. You're *good*, Morrie. You're no longer the spider devouring humanity like flies. You don't bear the weight of the world's evil on your shoulders. You could have chosen any criminal enterprise, and yet you chose this one – giving people a fresh start. That's what you did for me." I sniffed. "So don't you *dare* say I'd have been better off not knowing you. I owe you so much, you have no idea. You gave me a fresh start. You made me see myself as beautiful, and clever, and fun. You make every day an adventure, and it would be a fucking crime to deprive the world of your kissing skills. You have worth, Morrie. And I need you to remember that and get your gorgeous arse off that rock before you slip."

I was hysterical now, my whole body trembling. Oscar tugged on the leash, dragging me toward the bank as the bridge swung wildly. "Please, please, please…" I could barely speak now, I was crying so hard. "If you can't do it for yourself, then do it for us – for Heathcliff, for Quoth. For me. I c-c-can't bear it if you left me—"

"Gorgeous, please stop crying."

"I w-w-won't, until you step away from the edge." I hiccuped, the cold torture on my lungs. Oscar kept dragging me, kept trying to pull me to safety, but I couldn't move until I knew Morrie was safe.

Morrie took a step back, his hands in the air.

"You're right, Mina." His voice wavered. I couldn't see, of course, but he sounded like he was crying, too. "I've been a selfish git. Coming out here must have scared you so much. I didn't… I think seeing Sherlock has me all twisted around inside. But this was a silly indulgence and I've got a vampire to slay. I'll come back now. I'll—"

Morrie yelled as his foot went out from under him on the slippery rock. He dropped on his chest on the rocks and started to slide toward the edge. He thrust out his hands, scrambling for purchase. The waterfall had worn the rocks smooth, so he couldn't grip.

"Morrie," I screamed.

The Napoleon of Crime lifted his head, his mouth open in a silent cry, dark with pain and regret, as he plunged over the waterfall.

CHAPTER THIRTY-FIVE

*T*he wind swallowed my scream.

The world moved in slow motion. Morrie tumbled through the air, his arms flailing wildly. I leaned right out, flinging my hands toward him as if I could somehow catch his fall. Freezing water stung my face, and Oscar's whimpers barely reached my ears.

No.

Morrie.

No.

Don't go where I can't follow.

As my heart shattered and time stood still and Morrie hung in the air, inching closer to the churning waves and sharp rocks, a dark cloud barreled from the trees further down. It grabbed Morrie around the torso and slammed him against the rocks.

"Heathcliff!"

Water drenched literature's greatest gothic antihero as he struggled to pull Morrie from the torrent of the waterfall. The pair of them slipped and skidded over the rocks as Heathcliff dragged Morrie up the bank to safety.

My battered heart soared with joy, with relief. Oscar pawed at my leg, his fur drenched and his eyes wide with terror. "Sorry, boy. We can get off now." I inched my way along the bridge, stepping onto solid ground at last. Oscar trotted into the trees, barking happily at the figures emerging from the gloom.

I ran to Morrie, wrapping my arms around him, not caring that he was soaked through and shivering.

"Never, ever pull shit like that again," Heathcliff growled, his hands fisted in Morrie's shirt.

"No, I—" Morrie's words cut off as Heathcliff met him in a furious kiss.

My breath hitched in my throat as I watched the two of them explore each other's mouths, as they clutched each other like they'd been thrown from the Titanic and had found a wardrobe to cling to. Something new and free and thrilling blossomed between them. Morrie's eyes fluttered shut, and I knew he was having A Moment.

When I couldn't take it anymore, when my hunger and relief welled up inside me and burst out through my skin, I pulled them apart with my own lips and kissed them. I tasted them and they tasted each other. Laughter bubbled up inside me – a restless mirth because I thought I'd lost Morrie to the darkness, and now here he was in my arms again.

～

"*A*nother mystery solved." Morrie peered at the bucket of oysters with wry amusement before sliding into the chair opposite me beneath the window. "Thanks to your mother's latest harebrained scheme."

"Don't tell her that, or we'll never be able to get her and her oysters out of this shop. And we haven't solved everything." I glared over the chess game I'd set up between us into the shadows of the poetry shelves, where I'd seen a certain consulting detective lurking only minutes before. "The police are still trying to track Grey Lachlan down for questioning, and Sherlock *still* hasn't explained why he was lying to us about being here on earth for two years."

"Indeed." Morrie's mouth twitched into his familiar smirk. He moved his pawn across the board like he didn't have a care in the world. For a moment, he had me completely fooled – I could've been looking at the old Morrie, the one who didn't care about anyone or anything. But after seeing him hit bottom, I knew that smirk he wore was just a mask. I could sense – even if I couldn't see – the tremble in his shoulders and the uncertainty behind his eyes.

"Mina is correct. The man in the photograph was me."

I whirled around. Sherlock leaned against the doorframe. He had eyes only for Morrie.

"I didn't sneak down the stairs while you four were stupefied from sex. Although you should be careful that doesn't happen in the future. You never know who might creep out of the pages next." He said that with a glare in Heathcliff's direction. "The truth is, I've been in this world for the last three years."

"Why didn't you just tell us the truth from the beginning?" Morrie demanded, putting his queen into play. I knew I was in trouble.

"Because I knew you'd react like this. You'd wonder why I hadn't contacted you earlier. You'd suspect me, especially given the mounting evidence against you that suggested a personal grudge. I'd been watching you long enough to know Mina would leap into action in an attempt to save you, leap to the wrong conclusions about me, and hinder my investigation." Sherlock nodded in my direction, in what might've been his approximation of respect. "It turns out, I was correct on two of the three."

I poked my tongue out at him as I took Morrie's bishop with my rook. "I solved the case."

Sherlock grunted, unable to entirely concede that point.

Heathcliff slid into his chair, wincing as he pulled an oyster shell out from beneath his arse. "How come Mr. Simson never told us about you? He kept meticulous records of the fictional characters who came through the shop. I'd remember your name."

"Simson felt that he could use my unique skills to gather intel on his enemy, but I needed to operate in absolute secrecy. Should anything happen to him, he didn't want knowledge of my presence to fall into the wrong hands. I've spent the last three years hunting Dracula across the countryside, and I haven't got as close as you have in a few short months. But I hadn't drawn the connection between Kate and—"

I leaned forward. "Wait a second. *You've* been hunting Dracula. And you've seen my father? Talked to him?"

Sherlock raised an eyebrow. "I don't follow."

"Mr. Simson is Mina's father," Morrie said. "He's also Herman Strepel, famed medieval bookbinder and Homer, the ancient Greek bard who wrote the *Iliad*—"

"I know who Homer is." Sherlock ran a hand through his floppy hair. He looked defeated. "I also hadn't deduced Simson was the poet of yore. So you are his daughter?"

I nodded.

Sherlock rubbed his chin with one hand, while the other flew to his pocket. "Interesting."

Morrie nudged me. "Mina, show him the algorithm."

I pulled out my phone and touched the screen to pull up Morrie's maps, flicking through to show Sherlock how we'd figured out how to track Dracula's crimes. I pointed to the house in Lower Loxham with the red cross struck through it. "That's where we went the other night. We managed to destroy one of his boxes of earth. Only forty-nine to go."

Sherlock frowned as he jabbed at the screen with his fingers. A few moments later, he handed back the phone. I held it up to my face to peer at the screen. Eleven homes in London had bright red crosses etched through them.

"Thirty-eight to go."

"Give me that." Morrie snatched the phone from my hands. "What have you done?"

"Not half of what I'd have achieved if you were with me, lover." Sherlock shrugged. "I thought I'd start in the city, since I know it best. I'll be heading to Dartmoor next. I feel a certain pull to the place, and your device has suggested there may be a concentration of boxes in the area."

"You... you're still going to help us? Even though..." *even though Morrie picked me.*

Sherlock pulled something from his pocket and held it out to me. His face assumed his most impassive and judicious expression. "You forget, Mina. I'm stranded here now, and my mind rebels at stagnation. Give me problems, give me work... give me the most monstrous villain that has ever walked the earth, and I shall be happy to pursue him until justice is done. It would be my greatest pleasure to work alongside you. As an equal in both brains and cunning. Also, I have this for you."

I stared at the envelope in my hands. Doodles wrapped around the border and the paper had that rough, handmade look of it. My stomach plunged into my knees.

Another letter from my father.

I took the envelope, my fingers shaking. "Wh-where did you get this?"

"He gave it to me six months ago. He said that Dracula was closing in on him, and he needed to go into hiding, but I was to give this to his daughter. I asked him if I was to find his daughter, and he said she would find me." Sherlock tipped his hat. "If that's all, I'll be off. I have a train to catch. I don't want to miss my first day at my new job."

And, with a last, lingering gaze at Morrie, Sherlock slunk into the shadows once more.

"What does he mean, new job?" I glared at Morrie. "Is he hunting Dracula's dirt for us full-time?"

"Nope. He's taking that on a freelance basis." Morrie pulled me into his lap. "I used some of my contacts in the fake death business to set him up with new employment."

"You haven't sent Sherlock Holmes to the criminal underworld?"

Morrie laughed, running his hands over my hips until I squirmed in his lap, our chess game all but forgotten. "No way would I want that uptight goody-two-shoes ruining all my fun. No, he's got a job with Kate's insurance company as a fraud investigator. With Sherlock Holmes on the case, no one will be faking their death for financial gain in this country ever again."

I raised an eyebrow. "Does this mean your fake death business is shutting shop for good?"

"Not even close." Morrie reached behind me to swipe his queen across the board, taking my knight with long fingers. "A tiger cannot change his stripes, and James Moriarty will forever be a rapscallion of the highest order."

"Just the way I like him." I brushed my lips on his. Morrie's hand cupped my neck, pushing me against him to deepen the kiss.

"Now that we've dispensed with the secrets..." Morrie's fingers crept under the hem of my skirt, skittering over my skin with a touch that lit a flame inside me.

"We're not completely done with secrets yet." I rocked backward to put some distance between us. From my pocket I drew out the velvet bag. "It's time you told me about these."

Morrie opened the velvet bag and tipped the jewels onto my fingers. "I thought even when your vision deteriorates, you'd appreciate the way these sparkle in the light. I hoped... they might be your light in dark places."

"These are for me? Are they... ill-gotten?"

"I purchased these fair and square, with money I earned from my more legitimate enterprises." Morrie's smirk widened. "I didn't want a single shred of your doubting morals to tarnish them. I was going to have them made into rings by that bloke in Crookshollow who makes fantasy armor. Flynn something-or-other."

My breath hitched as I turned my hand, letting the jewels tumble through my fingers so their facets caught the light. A rare orange diamond that glistened with fire when turned in the light, just like Quoth's eyes. A sapphire as cold and clear as ice for Morrie, and something deep and black and mesmerizing that might have been onyx for Heathcliff. And for me, a brilliant emerald – the facets dancing in the light and creating rainbow prisms across my skin.

"What were you going to do with them?" My throat closed up. I hardly dared to breathe.

Morrie grinned. "Rings. One for each of us. Although I wasn't sure if the birdie wanted one that would fit on his finger or around his talon. They would be commitment rings. Puritanical marriage laws forbid us four from being married, and I didn't think a church ceremony was punk rock enough for Mina Wilde. But maybe, we could do it our own way."

"You..." My throat closed up. I swallowed and tried again. "You want to get faux married to me?"

"But of course." Morrie closed my fingers around the jewels. They felt heavy in my palm, and I knew I held more than just a few precious gems in my hand. I held Morrie's heart. "A wise woman said to me once that the four of us were written in the stars. I thought we should make things official. It was supposed to be a surprise – I had a whole thing planned, with wine and fine cuisine and some of my leather collars and whips, but I should have known you'd find out the truth, you clever woman. We shall make a dishonest woman of you yet." Morrie glanced down at my other hand, which had flown to my pocket, where my father's letter still lay nestled inside. "You'll have to open that letter sooner or later."

"I know." My finger played with the edge of the seal. I stared at the crisp paper, edged with a red border so dark and rich it made my vision pulse. "I just… it's been a rough week, you know? I don't—"

Oscar growled at the window, startling me out of my thoughts. Beside him, Grimalkin stood to attention on the windowsill, her tail fuzzed up like Basil Brush.

"What's up?" I slid in beside them, peering into the street. Grimalkin eyeballed something in the darkness and hissed.

I followed her gaze. Across the street, a streetlight gleaned outside Mrs. Ellis' upstairs window. *Not Mrs. Ellis' window now.* Signs for Lachlan Construction hung all over the scaffold that already encroached on our side of the street.

A dark shape hung in the window. My breath caught in my throat. It looked a little like a chrysalis, only huge. Or… or…

A bat.

As I watched, frozen in horror, the bat unfurled a wing and lifted its head, staring at me with beady eyes that seemed to transcend the distance between us. I saw without seeing the malice there, the demonic fury that blazed inside.

A horrible nausea swept over me. I gripped the windowsill with both hands, gasping for breath. Beside me, Oscar whimpered.

The bat opened its mouth, baring two long, sharpened fangs, dripping wet with a dark substance. Before my eyes the creature disintegrated, its wings and body transforming into a mist that curled through the window-frame and swirled in the street in front of the shop.

"Mina Wilde," a voice hissed in my ears, a voice that came from inside the mist but also from my own mind. "We meet at last."

TO BE CONTINUED

Will Mina and her men find a way to destroy literature's greatest villain, and solve their toughest mystery of all. Find out in book 6 of the Nevermore Bookshop Mysteries, *A Novel Way to Die.*

Can't get enough of Mina and her boys? Read a free alternative scene from Quoth's point-of-view along with other bonus scenes and extra stories when you sign up for the Steffanie Holmes newsletter.

FROM THE AUTHOR

Welcome back to Nevermore Bookshop. I know it's been a while since we stepped through the front door to meet a grumpy, loveable giant, a suave and cheeky criminal genius, and a beautiful and kind raven – and let us not forget the stuffed armadillo.

This book has been so much fun to write, not least of all because the research has been a real adventure. I read a book called *Playing Dead: A Journey Through the World of Death Fraud*, by Elizabeth Greenwood, and then proceeded to bore all my friends to tears with facts about the death-faking business. It's absolutely fascinating and if you're interested, I recommend picking up Elizabeth's book.

I also went on a wilderness survival course, not unlike the one Mina, Heathcliff, and Quoth took with Sam. Only with less cockroach cookery. And my husband and I spent two weeks in Romania researching vampire legends and drinking lots of *pálinka* – the results of which will appear in a future series rather than this one, because Dracula the character has very little to do with the legends of Romania.

There will be one final Nevermore Bookshop Mystery - it's called *A Novel Way to Die* and it's available for pre-order now. If the series continues to be popular, I'll extend it for four more books with a new overarching mystery – so if you want that to happen, please leave reviews on the books and tell all your friends. Heck, tell your enemies – I'm not fussy.

And if you need something to read while you wait, I've got you covered. Check out my Briarwood Witches series – it's complete at 5 books, so that's 400,000+ words about a science nerd heroine who inherits a real English castle complete with great hall, turrets, and 5 hot English/Irish tenants. She also inherits some magical powers she can't control (also, there is MM). Grab the collection with a bonus scene. Turn the page for a teaser.

And if you need something to read while you wait, I've got you covered. Check out my Briarwood Witches series – it's complete at 5 books, so that's 400,000+ words about a science nerd heroine named Maeve (you met her in this book) who inherits a real English castle complete with great hall, turrets, and 5 hot English/Irish tenants. She also inherits some magical powers she can't control (also, there is MM). Grab the collection with a bonus scene. Turn the page for a teaser.

If you're enjoying the literary references in Nevermore, check out my new reverse harem bully romance series, *Manderley Academy*. Book 1 is *Ghosted* and it's a classic gothic tale of ghosts and betrayal, creepy old houses and three beautifully haunted guys with dark secrets. Plus, a kickass curvy heroine. You will LOVE it.

If you want to hang out and talk about all things Nevermore, my readers are sharing their theories and discussing the books over in my Facebook group, Books That Bite. Come join the fun!

A portion of the proceeds from every Nevermore book sold go toward supporting Blind Low Vision NZ Guide Dogs, and I'm always sharing cute guide dog pictures and vids in my Facebook group.

I'd like to thank my amazing family of writer buddies – aka, the Professional Perverts – for keeping me sane while finishing this book before my trip. Thanks Bri, Katya, Elaina, Kit, Jamie, and Emma for all the laughs and love.

And to my husband, for putting up with all my excitement over death fraud and acquiescing to be dragged through Eastern Europe looking at old churches and eating too much cabbage.

Until next time!

Steffanie

WANT MORE REVERSE HAREM FROM STEFFANIE HOLMES

Dear Fae,

Don't even THINK about attacking my castle.

This science geek witch and her four magic-wielding men are about to get medieval on your ass.

I'm Maeve Crawford. For years I've had my future mathematically calculated down to the last detail; Leave my podunk Arizona town, graduate MIT, get into the space program, be the first woman on Mars, get a cat (not necessarily in this order).

Then fairies killed my parents and shot the whole plan to hell.

I've inherited a real, honest-to-goodness English castle – complete with turrets, ramparts, and four gorgeous male tenants, who I'm totally *not* in love with.

Not at all.

It would be crazy to fall for four guys at once, even though they're totally gorgeous and amazing and wonderful and kind.

But not as crazy as finding out I'm a witch. A week ago, I didn't even believe magic existed, and now I'm up to my ears in spells and prophetic dreams and messages from the dead.

When we're together – and I'm talking in the Biblical sense – the five of us wield a powerful magic that can banish the fae forever. They intend to stop us by killing us all.

I can't science my way out of this mess.

Forget NASA, it's going to take all my smarts just to survive Briarwood Castle.

The Castle of Earth and Embers is the first in a brand new steamy reverse harem romance by *USA Today* bestselling author, Steffanie Holmes. This full-length book glitters with love, heartache, hope, grief, dark magic, fairy trickery, steamy scenes, British slang, meat pies, second chances, and the healing powers of a good cup of tea. Read on only if you believe one just isn't enough.

Available from Amazon and in KU.

THE CASTLE OF EARTH AND EMBERS

*R*owan showed Maeve around the kitchen, pointing out the spice racks and explaining his stupidly complicated fridge-stacking system. Maeve listened attentively, and she didn't laugh or poke fun of any of Rowan's OCD tendencies. The tension slipped from his shoulders. She was affecting even him.

"What are you making here?" Maeve peered into the baskets of produce and empty preserving jars on the island.

Rowan's face reddened and his shoulders hunched back up again. I winced. That didn't last long. Maeve looked at Rowan's face as his jaw locked. He stared at his feet and twirled the end of a dreadlock around his finger.

"Rowan, is something wrong?" Maeve's voice tightened with concern. She reached out a hand to him, but he stepped back, leaving her arm hanging in the air. The awkward tension in the air ratcheted up a notch.

Time to save this situation. I stepped forward and grabbed Maeve's arm, doing my best to ignore the tingle of energy that shot through me when our skin touched. I'd have to get used to ignoring it. I dragged her across the room.

"This is really cool," I said, opening a door at the back of the kitchen to reveal a narrow staircase. "This was installed when the castle was a grand stately home so the servants could rush meals up to the bedrooms without being seen in the main part of the house. It comes up near the staircase that goes up to your bedroom, so it's a good shortcut down to the kitchen if you fancy a nightcap."

"Duly noted." Maeve sashayed across the room and peered up the narrow staircase. "Are the bedrooms upstairs? Can I see?"

At the word *bedroom* passing through her red, pursed lips, my cock tightened in protest. *Don't think about it.* But that was like telling Obelix – the pudgy castle cat – not to think about all the delicious birds sitting in the tree outside the window.

"Sure." I gestured to the staircase. "After you."

Maeve started up the narrow steps, her gorgeous arse hovering inches from my face. I made to follow her, but something heavy slammed into my side, knocking me against the wall. I cursed as my elbow scraped against the rough stone of the wall.

"Sorry mate," Flynn flashed me his devil's grin as he leapt past me and followed Maeve up the stairs. "I didn't see you there."

"I believe you," I mumbled as I followed them up. "Millions wouldn't."

At the top of the stairs, Maeve pressed her hands against the wood panel. "How do you get this open?"

Flynn tried to reach around her to unlock the clasp at the top of the door, but this time, I beat him to it. As I reached around Maeve, she turned slightly to press her back against the wall and her breasts brushed against my shirt, setting off a fire beneath my skin.

Her lips formed an O of surprise, and I couldn't help but mentally fill in that O with the shaft of my cock. I blinked, trying to stop thinking about her like that, trying to remember that it was the magic making me into this *animal*.

The air between us thinned, and an invisible force drew my

body forward, my arm brushing hers. A few inches more, and my lips would be pressed against hers—

No. You can't do this. You can't encourage her to choose you.

"Well, isn't this intimate?" Flynn shimmied his way through the gap so that he had his back against the opposite wall, his hands falling against Maeve's hips. If he wanted, he could slide her back so her arse rubbed against his cock, and even though that was totally cheating, I wouldn't even blame him. I was cheating just as bad – my face in hers, my eyes begging for her touch. All I'd have to do was lean forward, press my lips to hers, and it would all be over...

Want to find out what happens next – Start The Briarwood Witches series today.

OTHER BOOKS BY STEFFANIE HOLMES

This list is in recommended reading order, although each couple's story can be enjoyed as a standalone.

Nevermore Bookshop Mysteries

A Dead and Stormy Night

Of Mice and Murder

Pride and Premeditation

How Heathcliff Stole Christmas

Memoirs of a Garroter

Prose and Cons

A Novel Way to Die

Kings of Miskatonic Prep

Shunned

Initiated

Possessed

Ignited

Broken Muses of Manderley Academy

Ghosted

Haunted

Briarwood Reverse Harem series

The Castle of Earth and Embers

The Castle of Fire and Fable

The Castle of Water and Woe

The Castle of Wind and Whispers

The Castle of Spirit and Sorrow

Crookshollow Gothic Romance series

Art of Cunning (Alex & Ryan)

Art of the Hunt (Alex & Ryan)

Art of Temptation (Alex & Ryan)

The Man in Black (Elinor & Eric)

Watcher (Belinda & Cole)

Reaper (Belinda & Cole)

Wolves of Crookshollow series

Digging the Wolf (Anna & Luke)

Writing the Wolf (Rosa & Caleb)

Inking the Wolf (Bianca & Robbie)

Wedding the Wolf (Willow & Irvine)

Want to be informed when the next Steffanie Holmes paranormal romance story goes live? Sign up for the newsletter at www.steffanieholmes.com/newsletter to get the scoop, and score a free collection of bonus scenes and stories to enjoy!

ABOUT THE AUTHOR

Steffanie Holmes is the author of steamy historical and paranormal romance. Her books feature clever, witty heroines, wild shifters, cunning witches and alpha males who *always* get what they want.

Before becoming a writer, Steffanie worked as an archaeologist and museum curator. She loves to explore historical settings and ancient conceptions of love and possession. From Dark Age Europe to crumbling gothic estates, Steffanie is fascinated with how love can blossom between the most unlikely characters. She also writes dark fantasy / science fiction under S. C. Green.

Steffanie lives in New Zealand with her husband and a horde of cantankerous cats.

STEFFANIE HOLMES VIP LIST

Can't get enough of Mina and her boys? Read a free alternative scene from Quoth's point-of-view along with other bonus scenes and extra stories when you sign up for the Steffanie Holmes newsletter.

Come hang with Steffanie
www.steffanieholmes.com
hello@steffanieholmes.com